The Will
of the Enemy

Jody Shee

ISBN-13:978-0615874999

Purple
dreamer
Publishers

DEDICATION

This novel is in recognition of the mothers of the "milk carton kids" of a few decades ago, who, against all convention, courageously kidnapped their children as the only way to shield them from their abusive fathers, who sometimes obtained legal custody.

Many mothers sacrificed their ambitions, disguised their identities, and lived as drifters, hunted as criminals while their ex-husbands got off free.

Today, there are more laws to help protect innocent children from abuse.

INSPIRATIONAL SUSPENSE

Julie's stomach rumbled loudly. She knew Angie was famished too, as she watched the poor thing hold her stomach now and then while she played Candy Land with her new friend Brenda.

It was almost 1:15. To speed things along, Julie positioned herself in Hazel's kitchen next to anything that needed to be done. She removed the rolls from the oven into three baskets, dropped ice into the water glasses, and stirred the gravy. For her daughter's sake, she announced that everything looked done, hoping Hazel would agree and finally call everyone to the Thanksgiving table.

By 1:30 all 15 of them were gathered around either the dining room table or one of two card tables set up in the nice lady's small living room.

"Before we eat, let's all go around and say what we're thankful for," Hazel announced triumphantly.

Julie wilted, but quickly smiled and straightened her shoulders. *I was so wrong to not feed Angie this morning. I should have realized it would take this long to get such a big meal on the table. I could kick myself. We're not that low on Special K and milk.*

She didn't hear what the first three diners were thankful for as she pondered what she herself could safely say in this mixed group of casual church acquaintances who also had nowhere else to spend the holiday.

No one here really knows me. They would never believe me if I told them what I'm really thankful for.

Suddenly there was a loud knock at the front door. Hazel rose. "Who could that be? I'm not expecting anyone else."

She looked out the window and announced that a police car was sitting out front. "I wonder what this is all about," she said as she removed her apron before opening the door.

While everyone started talking, Julie instinctively jumped up and motioned for Angie to do likewise. "Please excuse us for a minute," she said quietly and ushered Angie into the bathroom with her, closed the door, and put her ear to the door.

"Hello. Sorry to interrupt your Thanksgiving dinner. I'm Officer Hellerman. I'm wondering if Julie and Angie Bradley are here."

Julie tried to catch her breath. She squeezed Angie's shoulder tightly. Right now she was thankful she had grabbed her purse and taken it into the bathroom with her. She looked around for a window.

"No, you have the wrong house. There's no one here by those names," Hazel said innocently.

Julie was also thankful that everyone in this Florida community knew them as Linda and Gabrielle.

"Well, I really don't mean to pester you, but actually, the mother and daughter I'm looking for may not go by the names Julie and Angie," the policeman said.

Julie gasped for air and examined the window. *It might be big enough.*

"The woman is 32 years old, and her daughter is eight. Are you sure there's no one here like that?"

"I don't know what makes you think the mother and daughter you are looking for are here. I know all my guests, and I can tell you for certain that your criminals aren't here," Hazel said with certain irritation and finality.

"Hey, where did Linda and Gabrielle go?" one of the guests piped up.

"They're in the bathroom," Brenda said.

Julie raised the bathroom window, yanked out the screen, and ordered Angie up on the toilet and out the window. Fortunately the air conditioner unit sat beneath the window.

Julie squeezed her petite frame out the tight window at the same time she heard a rap on the bathroom door.

She rushed Angie across three backyards and peered around the third house. Her car was parked in front of it. The police car was still at Hazel's house with no policeman in sight.

"Run to the car!" she yelled to Angie.

They both slammed their doors as Julie started the engine and threw the Chevy into gear. She looked through the rearview mirror as she laid rubber and noticed the policeman jump into his car.

"Hang on, Pookie. Stay calm!"

She tore down the street and around the corner. She knew there was an ally next to her favorite bakery. *Maybe I can lose him if I do all side streets.* She turned left at her first opportunity, then left again, then right.

She couldn't see the police car anymore. She kept speeding.

"Oh, Sweetie. That was so close!"

"I'm hungry," Angie whined.

"I know you are. I am so sorry."

Wow. That was close. Thank you God, once again.

CHAPTER 1—OCTOBER 1979

The billowy white clouds and crisp October air prevailed over Mission, Kansas. Julie and Terry's wedding day couldn't have been more perfect—less than a month before her 22nd birthday and exactly a year after their first date at Denny's.

The only thing that wasn't picture-perfect about Julie's most memorable day was that her father wasn't there to give her away—something that always darkened her wedding fantasies.

She would never forget the day she was told that he died of a heart attack. She was at recess playing dolls with her friends in the third grade when her teacher interrupted and took her to the principal's office. "I have something very difficult to tell you, Dear. Your father became very sick suddenly and he quit breathing. The doctors couldn't help him. I'm afraid we won't see him again here on earth. He has gone ahead of us to heaven."

If only he could have met this unpretentious man who shared her dreams of building a wonderful family that would travel down life's path with laughter, fun, and probably a few trials to keep them grounded. She and Terry pictured nightly walks through the neighborhood behind a baby stroller—an after-dinner ritual they promised each other they would not let go of.

She knew this would have been one of her father's proudest moments. But Julie determined the night before at the rehearsal that she wouldn't let that thought crowd out the joyous celebration of their love and pledge to one another.

Now she shifted from one foot to the other in her uncomfortable white satin pumps in the back

4

courtyard of Maple Grove Community Church, waiting for the crowd to approach the receiving line. She clung to Terry's left arm, with her mother, Rita, and sister, Melanie, to her left. The birch trees had released most of their yellow leaves, but the maple trees were flaming red and orange. Julie wanted to just soak in the day and write every detail in her diary— down to the cracks in the tiles beneath her feet.

"Here, Gretta, trade places with me," Terry's dad, Bob, told Terry's mother. "I want to stand next to Terry and introduce Julie to our family friends. I can't trust Terry to remember all their names."

Terry rolled his eyes. "Hopefully this won't last too long," he whispered. But Julie smiled. She was excited for the party of friends and family about to parade by with hugs and congratulations.

Before long, Julie's cheeks hurt from smiling so much as envious friends hugged her and told her how beautiful she looked. She was the first of her close friends to get married.

"Hey Terry, look there. See that man with the grey hair about five people away," Terry's dad said as he poked him. "That's Judge William McGraw. Be sure to say something intelligent and try to impress him. Maybe he can pull some strings to get you into the police academy."

Julie knew this was a sore subject between the men. Terry was still a security guard at the mall where they met. He couldn't decide what he should do with his life. His dad so badly wanted Terry to follow in his footsteps and become a policeman. He gave his dad a half smile rather than succumb to the loud refusal Julie imagined he felt inside.

"Hey there, William," Bob shouted as Judge McGraw approached Julie. "Meet my new daughter-in-law! They plan to live on 49th Street. Terry will be close to the police academy. We have to get him in there, you know?"

Julie felt the awkwardness of the moment. She and Terry had shared many conversations about his future and if he should just tell his dad he couldn't bear the thought of being a policeman.

"Well hello there. Congratulations young man. I haven't seen you since you were in junior high," the judge told Terry. "I'm sure someday you'll be a great policeman like your dad. I'll have to see what I can do to help."

A squalling baby suddenly drew everyone's attention. Julie looked at Melanie, who wore the beautiful, pink satin matron-of-honor dress. Someone had just handed Melanie April, her six-month-old daughter. Two-year-old Lexie now clung to Melanie's leg too.

"Sorry about that," Melanie grimaced, realizing they were now the center of attention.

"I think her diapers are in the corner of our dressing room," Julie said, guessing at the reason behind April's distress.

Melanie excused herself from the receiving line. "You want one of these?" she asked Julie, extending April in their direction.

"We want four of those," Terry said proudly. The women standing around the newlyweds murmured a collective "awww" as they saw the loving heart he had for children.

CHAPTER 2—DECEMBER 1980

"**O**h, did you just get here?" Rita asked when she turned around from putting the green bean casserole in the oven and saw her daughter. "Let's see, why don't you put that here on the table. By the way, what is it?"

Julie explained her cranberry experiment. She knew she liked pecans and celery in a Christmas cranberry salad, and had speculated that it would be great if cream cheese and orange gelatin were also mixed in. She remembered seeing such a recipe in either *Better Homes and Gardens* or *Ladies Home Journal* the year before, but hadn't saved the recipe, so she ad-libbed.

"If everyone likes it, the recipe will go in my notebook," she said. "Of course if no one likes it, I don't know what we'll do tomorrow because I'm supposed to take this dish to Terry's parents for our Christmas together."

Terry made himself comfortable in front of the television in the basement with Melanie's husband, Steve, and the two kids. Lexie had made it safely through her terrible twos—but barely. And just over a year since Julie's wedding, April, named after the month when she was born, was climbing all over her dad and the furniture.

Melanie came up behind Julie in the kitchen and poked her. "Hi there!"

Julie jumped.

"When did you guys get here and how long are you staying?" Julie asked.

She didn't get to see her sister nearly as often as she'd like since they lived in Nebraska.

"Oh, by the way, did you girls bring your empty

toilet paper rolls and paper towel rolls?" Rita asked.

"Darn! I forgot," Melanie said, winking at Julie. Their mother's face fell.

"Of course I remembered. When have I ever showed up without toilet paper rolls?"

Their mom often needed the empty cardboard tubes for her craft consignment shop. Angels, scarecrows, and princess dogs were waiting to be made from the rollers. The paper towel rollers made especially cute dachshunds with frilly collars.

"We have to head back home late tomorrow morning so we can be at Steve's parents' house by 2," Melanie said. Then she turned to Julie. "By the way, how do you get along with *your* in-laws?"

"We do okay," Julie said. "Do you have a Sprite, Mom? I'm really thirsty."

She continued, "Terry's relationship with his parents is a little strained. I guess I can see why. His dad is certainly king of the house. He keeps pushing Terry to make something of himself. What I find aggravating is that he's always telling stories of guys he arrests and how he outsmarts his partner. He really should be more sensitive. He's been through two partners since we've been married," Julie said. "He also doesn't treat Terry's mom very respectfully."

As her mother handed her a glass of Sprite on ice, she said, "What's the deal? You've never liked Sprite before."

Julie shrugged and chugged.

"Well, should we open our presents now, or wait until after dinner?" Rita asked.

"Oh, let's do it now," Melanie suggested. "Then the girls' gifts will keep them busy the rest of the time."

They called the troupe from downstairs, and soon wrapping paper, boxes, and squeals filled the room.

"Save the ribbons," Rita called over the chaos.

Rita opened a box with a pink and purple sweatshirt in it. "World's Greatest Grandmother," she read on the front of it. "Which of the kids is this from?" she asked Melanie, who was preoccupied with a new stuffed animal for April.

Melanie looked up. "That's not from us."

Rita frowned with confusion and then looked at Julie.

Julie stood, walked to Rita, and hugged her. "It's from us!"

Melanie and Rita screamed, while Julie announced, "We're going to have a baby!"

They made Julie recount every detail from the time she had found out two months earlier: the baby was due on the Fourth of July, Julie had morning sickness almost all the time, and the last thing that sounded appetizing was a wad of turkey on her plate. Mashed potatoes and green bean casserole, maybe. But that was about it.

"She hasn't craved pickles yet," Terry announced. "But I've had to go out at night and buy potato straws. I didn't even know companies still make them."

During dinner they discussed Julie's job at the mall and how long she would stay there or what she would do next. She had thought of going to college to get a journalism degree, or maybe a teaching degree. Maybe teaching junior high English would be fun, she explained. But now with the baby coming, she wasn't sure. Terry's job didn't pay enough for her to stay home.

"Why don't I watch the baby at the consignment shop for you while you work—at least until it starts walking," Rita volunteered.

"Well, I don't know . . ." Julie started to say.

"Excuse me!" Terry jumped up from the table and

abruptly left the room. He returned with a freshly full plate of food, but Julie noticed he hardly said another word.

After dinner, Melanie led Julie into their old bedroom.

"So, how is Terry doing with all this?" she asked. "I'm sure he's excited, but I know it's hard on a guy if he feels he can't fully support his family."

Julie sighed. She felt uncomfortable trying to find a way to paint a rosy picture. But the truth was, Terry was struggling.

"At first he was ecstatic about moving away from home after we got married. He loved being free from his parents, particularly his dad. But the free feeling didn't last long. He gets grumpy whenever I talk about things I'd like to have for our baby. He knows we can't afford anything. The only thing he knows he likes to do for sure is give kids swimming lessons at Fantastic Fitness Gym."

"That's admirable," Melanie offered. "How did he ever get interested in that?"

"When he was a kid, his dad forced him to take swimming lessons, and he hated it from the first day, because all he could do was the dog paddle, and other kids laughed at him. Then a teenager jumped in and showed him how to swim and coaxed him on, until he finally learned. That teenager made such a good impression, Terry later found it in his heart to do the same thing for other kids. I think it makes him feel like a man. So he's helped out at the gym for several years now. In fact, sometimes he spends more time there than at home with me."

"And what about his goal to become a policeman?" Melanie probed.

"That was really his dad's dream for him, not his," Julie explained. "He doesn't want to be like his father in any way.

"But we're really excited about the baby," Julie added. "Maybe that will make us closer. I think if we're both working on the same goal, he'll pull through this. I just think that marriage has been a harder adjustment for him than it's been for me."

Terry suddenly appeared in the doorway. He glared at Julie and told her he needed to talk to her.

Melanie jumped up from the edge of the bed. "I need to go check on the girls," she murmured as she brushed past Terry.

"What do you mean telling your sister we have a lousy marriage?" Terry demanded after closing the bedroom door.

Julie felt the bottom drop out of her stomach. "I didn't say that. I just said I was having an easier time than you are—considering your unhappiness with your job situation."

"Well, I don't want you running to your family and telling them what an awful person you think I am. I'm doing the best I can and we'll make it. I also don't want your mother taking care of our baby. I'll take on a second job if I need to so you can stay home and take care of it."

Julie hated the idea of him working two jobs. She would never see him. After he left the room, she wondered if their evenings of strolling the baby after dinner could ever possibly happen if he was never there. Tears slid down her face.

Julie and her good friend from work, Rachel, sat on the couch eating iced angel sugar cookies as Julie explained how the baby announcement went over with both sets of parents. She had long ago told Rachel she was pregnant. It was hard to hide the fact at work when she kept going to the bathroom to throw up.

"After Terry's family came down from the euphoria of becoming grandparents, his dad took him aside and had a talk about going to the police academy. Terry appears to have suddenly warmed up to the idea and quit bucking the idea of becoming a policeman. I'm not sure why, but that's a pressure off me.

"I might need you to spend the night and keep me company after the baby is born and he's at work all odd hours of the night," Julie said with sad reservation. "But at least he's thinking of the family, and that's good. I may be able to quit my job after all. He doesn't want my mom watching the baby for us."

They talked about Terry's friends Don and Greg, who used to work at the mall too.

"I don't know that it's a great idea for Terry to hang out with them, though," Rachel confessed. "You know Greg is an alcoholic, don't you?"

Julie frowned. "No. How do you know that?"

"Terry told me."

"Well, why didn't he tell *me* that?" Julie shrieked. "And he's out with him tonight, and they are going to a bar!"

Julie sighed and stared across the room. The whole conversation brought a few sore subjects to the top of her mind. She was a Christian—didn't drink and never had—and Terry hadn't been raised going to church. But he had admired her faith. He'd assured her that he realized how important it was and that he planned to develop that area of his life.

"When we were dating, I told him that what bothers me most about some drinkers is that alcohol, no matter what form, seems to consume their minds and conversations. I remember like it was yesterday.

He nodded and said drinking wasn't that important to him." She continued randomly speaking her thoughts out loud. "He has a beer now and then, but he doesn't feel he has to drink to have fun."

Julie veered from the topic of alcohol to church. In their year of marriage, Terry had only gone to church with her three or four times—mainly when she made a big deal about it. She had told her boss that she didn't want to work on Sundays because she went to church. Terry, on the other hand, often worked on Sundays and explained that it was important to him to take as many hours as possible so they could save up for a down payment on a house.

"I guess I should be grateful that he is so concerned about the future of our family. That's why I haven't pushed him any more on the topic of church," Julie finished. She got up to make some popcorn.

"Let's watch 'It's a Wonderful Life.' I have the video," Julie said.

After the movie was finished and they had sufficiently snacked their way to near sickness, Rachel decided to go home.

"Thanks for inviting me over," she said as she put her coat and boots on. Julie opened the door to the blustery breeze.

"Thanks for listening to me tonight. Sorry I was so down. Drive carefully," she called after Rachel and shut the door.

Julie picked up the plates, bowls, and cups, keeping her eye on the clock. She thought she remembered Terry telling her not to wait up for him. At the time, it was just a sentence. Now she was worried. It was 8:30 and what if he didn't come home for hours? What was he planning to do all night? What if Greg got him into trouble? Maybe Terry would keep Greg *out* of trouble.

She put on some Christmas music and started to mop the kitchen floor. But she had eaten too much junk and felt a little nauseated. She sat on the couch again with a hot cup of chamomile tea and wished she had a cat to keep her company.

At 9:30, she climbed into bed with a book. Surely Terry would be home soon.

He wasn't. She turned out the light thinking about her conversation with Rachel. Soon she was sleeping, but woke up every hour to look at the glowing clock.

She startled awake when she heard a thud, like the front door closing. Julie sat straight up in bed. It was 4:10. "Terry, is that you?"

"Yeah, go back to sleep," he yelled. "I'll sleep out here so I don't keep you awake."

Too late. She was wide awake. She went into the living room. He was already on the couch with his shoes and coat still on.

"Where have you been? I've been worried sick!" she demanded. "You could have called!"

He sat up. "I'm so sorry." He hung his head. "I had an accident. Don had to drive me home."

He told her that the roads had turned to ice, and he had run the car off the road into a ditch. He had to walk to a gas station and call Don.

Julie didn't know if she should be mad or glad that he at least was safe at home now. But then she thought she smelled alcohol on him. She could feel her blood pressure rising.

"Were you drinking?" she asked.

"Yes, but I only had a few beers," he slurred. He fell back on the couch.

Julie's stomach was upset. She suddenly felt clammy. She knew what that meant. She rushed to the bathroom where she puked, crying. "Oh Lord, please help me deal with this," she whispered.

CHAPTER 3—JUNE 1981

From the passenger seat, Julie sipped her soothing, hot tea. She felt a little crampy and somewhat deflated—more than usual these days. She stared out the window, not really caring that they were passing her favorite daisy-filled median.

Your flowers are still going strong," Terry offered cheerfully.

Silence.

He glanced around and saw a man jogging with his black lab panting alongside him. "Maybe we should get a dog," he said.

Julie closed her eyes and leaned her head back.

"Why haven't I ever heard of your Aunt Rosalind and Uncle Robert?" she finally said.

"I don't know. I guess I didn't realize I never told you about them. I can't remember what I've told you and what I haven't. Is that a crime?" he asked.

Julie felt her blood rush to her head. "If they are so important to you, and you are spending so much of your time with them, then why didn't you invite them to our wedding?" She glared at him.

"My Uncle Robert and Dad don't get along. It would have been very uncomfortable for everyone if my aunt and uncle had been at the wedding.

"Same thing with this baby shower. As long as my dad is there, it's not a good idea for Uncle Robert and Aunt Rosalind to be there too." He screeched to a stop at the light. Julie's tea sloshed onto her huge belly. She quickly opened the glove compartment for one of the napkins she kept there.

"Well, what is so special about them that you can't manage to make it home before midnight?" Lately he had been coming home late several nights a week,

15

claiming to be at their house.

Terry's pause was too long. "Uncle Robert and I play chess, and you know how long that can take. Time just slips away," he finally offered.

He had never told her about his love of chess, either. *This smells so fishy. Could he be making all this up, and he's really spending all his time somewhere else and hiding it from me?*

She decided she just needed to calm down before they got to the gym where Terry had helped rent a room for their big family and friends' shower.

"There's the happy couple," Gretta beamed as they came in the door. Yellow and purple crepe paper hung perfectly spaced in all directions from the center of the ceiling, where a beautiful angel mobile hung. Two guest-of-honor chairs waited beneath the angel.

Hmm. That mobile would be perfect for the baby's room. I'll bet Mom is responsible for that decoration, Julie thought.

She was soon enmeshed in the attention of her parents, sister, nieces, friends, and even Terry's family. She decided it had been a great idea to have both mothers in charge of refreshments and decorations. That gave them an opportunity to get to know each other better. After all, they would both lay claim to this grandbaby that was due in three weeks. It would be Gretta's first grandchild, and she was obviously looking forward to it.

Julie noticed that a long table on one side of the room was filled with presents. Two huge sheet cakes, a bowl of punch, and several dishes with nuts adorned the long table along the opposite wall.

"I hope that cake has buttercream frosting," she told Rachel, who was standing next to her, admiring the whole baby shower scene.

"I could test it for you," Rachel offered.

"That's okay. It looks store bought. They never use buttercream." Julie admired the colorful layout and hoped no one would mind if she just sat down.

"Time to play games!" Melanie announced. Groans rose from the deeper voices in the room, but the chairs were quickly arranged into two groups. The women eagerly participated while the guys hung out on the other side of the room.

The group spent 45 minutes on baby name scrambles, guessing what baby foods were in various containers, and predicting the final date, hour, and birth weight of the baby. Then it was time to cut the marble cake while Julie and Terry sat in the center chairs and opened gifts.

Since Julie and Terry didn't know if the baby was a boy or girl, they received plenty of red and yellow outfits. One of Julie's favorite gifts was a baby bouncer to hang from the door frame, courtesy of Melanie. "That will be a life saver," Melanie piped up. "Any time you want to talk on the phone or take a shower, just put the baby in that."

"She's almost put me in ours a few times," Steve chimed in. Everyone laughed.

Julie ripped into a soft package and unfolded a beautifully hand-crocheted, pastel rainbow-colored blanket with soft scalloped edges.

"Awww," everyone murmured. Julie looked through the wrapping paper shreds to see who it was from. She found a small tag that simply said "To Baby Bradley, from Aunt Rosalind and Uncle Robert."

Wow, they really do exist. What kind people, she thought. She looked at Terry.

He shrugged and smiled. "She gave it to me last week. I hid it in my locker," he said.

"It's so beautiful!" Julie exclaimed, rubbing it against her face. Her heart lifted as the cloud that had

17

hung over her dissipated. *Why do I always doubt Terry? I need to meet and thank Aunt Rosalind personally for this gift.*

Gretta wheeled the next gift over to them. It was the baby stroller Julie had seen a few months earlier at their house, but now it was filled with little packages.

"This is just the beginning," she whispered into Julie's ear. "I've been shopping, and Bob would probably think it's all too much. So what I have still at home we'll keep a little secret."

Julie knew all about the secret stash she had been collecting for months and wondered how much bigger it had become since she had last been over there. She started opening the little packages that were mostly clothes of all sizes. And bravely, some were pink and frilly while others were blue and boyish in all sizes up to age one.

"Gretta, I don't even have that many clothes. What is wrong with you?" Bob snapped. Everyone else may have thought the same thing, but probably not with the same degree of vehemence.

"It's their first baby. I couldn't help it," she responded.

"This is absurd! You must have spent hundreds of dollars on this," he continued. Julie secretly guessed that it was more like *thousands*. "You need to control your shopping obsession."

Julie and Terry looked down. Everyone else in the room stopped talking.

"Don't worry, Dear. I got much of it from garage sales over the past year." Gretta spoke quietly as she turned red.

"I'm going to have to put you on a budget, I can see . . . ."

"Dad!" Terry shouted, "Lay off of her. She's just happy for us. Give her a break!"

Julie put her hand on Terry's back.

"You see what I mean?" Terry said to her, but not caring who overheard. "I don't know how she stands him. He's always so hard on all of us. He's just obnoxious!"

"Wait a minute there," Bob said, standing up. Terry jumped up and ran out of the room. In moments Julie heard squealing tires.

Her stomach sank. In fact, she felt a sharp pain.

"What's wrong, Dear," her mother asked.

"I think I just need to rest," Julie said, trying to catch her breath.

"You *are* resting," her sister said. "Just breathe deeply."

"Actually, I need to use the bathroom," Julie said. On her way there, she felt another sharp pain and had to sit down.

"Let's get her to the hospital," Rita said as she rushed to Julie's side, with Melanie and Steve close behind her.

"We'll take her," Steve offered, as more people poured into the hall.

"Julie, who is your doctor? We need to call him," someone said.

"I need Terry," Julie cried.

But no one knew where he was; let alone how to reach him.

Julie endured a rough night. In no time, her contractions were deep, painful, and nearly overwhelming. Her mother was by her side stroking her forehead. "You're doing fine, Dear. This will all be over soon. I am so proud of you."

The two nurses were alternately concerned that her

doctor might not get there in time. "Certainly someone can deliver this baby, can't they?" Julie winced. But soon, Dr. Cannon showed up in blue scrubs, apologizing for his tardiness.

"I was in the middle of the Bee Gees' concert, and I had to arrange for my wife to get home," he said.

"Oh, the Bee Gees. I forgot they were here. I'm so sorry," Julie said sincerely; then she grabbed her mom's arm and yowled. After she recovered, she asked if Dr. Cannon had seen her husband in the waiting room when he came in.

"No, I didn't see him."

"I can't have this baby until he comes!" Julie insisted.

"Well," Dr. Cannon said as he examined her. "It looks like this baby is coming, whether you agree or not. It'll just be a little bit now."

Her mom tried to keep the conversation light between Julie's bursts of pain, yells, and rhythmic breathing.

"I remember giving you your first bath in a popcorn bowl a few days after we came home from the hospital," Rita said. "You didn't seem to mind at all."

"I know. You told me that a long time ago. I won't have to do that to my baby. Terry's mom thought of *everything*. We have a little plastic bathtub." They both looked at each other and smiled before another contraction struck.

"Okay, Julie. It looks like you're ready. The baby is just about here. When the time comes, give one big push," Dr. Cannon said.

Her mom grabbed her hand. "Squeeze as hard as you need to."

Julie pushed her head back, roared from deep within, and pushed with all her strength. The baby was soon in the doctor's hands, and then passed to the nurse. A small cry soon followed. Julie half cried and half laughed.

"You have a beautiful baby girl," Dr. Cannon announced.

They were all crying—Julie, her mom, the nurse, the doctor. Julie was soon holding her daughter wrapped tightly in a small blanket.

"Oh, look at her," Julie said, unable to take her eyes off of the baby. But she was soon crying again, only differently this time.

"What's wrong, Honey?" her mom asked.

"Where is Terry? He has to see her."

"I'll go out in the waiting room and see if anyone has heard from him," Rita said firmly.

In a moment the door opened from behind and Julie asked, "Did you find him?"

"It's me, baby," said Terry.

Once again tears poured. The doctor and nurse left the room as Julie held the baby for Terry to see.

"Oh my. Look at all her dark hair!" Terry said. The baby yawned with her eyes closed.

"Hi there little one," Terry said softly, rubbing her little head gently with his index finger. "We've been waiting for you."

"Isn't she the most beautiful baby?" Julie said smiling.

"Yes, she certainly is." Terry kissed Julie on the forehead. "I love you very much. Both of you."

Julie had never seen such love in his eyes. She was full of love, hope, and contentment.

"I wish I could climb in bed with you," he said. "I'm so sorry about what happened at the shower. I had no idea you were so close to having the baby. I shouldn't have run off like that. I just lost myself. I am just stupid. I didn't want to miss this for anything."

"I know your dad gets to you. Let's just put that behind us. You're here right now, and you didn't really miss anything. I couldn't have handled you passing out on the floor while I went through that," she said to comfort him.

"Thank you. You are always so understanding." Terry sighed. "Here, let me hold her."

Julie handed the baby over and Terry spoke sweet nothings to his new daughter. Julie saw a tender father and somehow knew he would be loving, devoted, and protective, just like she always dreamed. She experienced all the feelings she'd felt on their first date.

"She's our little angel," Julie said. "Shall we introduce Angela Claire to everyone else?"

A nurse came back in the room. "You have quite an entourage out in the waiting room. I'm going to take this little one to the nursery and let everyone see her through the window. We want to keep her away from germs. And we'll also get you cleaned up and into a room."

Terry was anxious to go to the waiting room and celebrate with everyone.

The room was filled with his mom and dad, little sister, Julie's parents, sister and brother-in-law and her nieces, as well as Rachel.

April looked at Terry. "Where's the dolly?"

He squatted to get on eye level with her. "You mean baby Angela Claire? The nurse is taking her to the baby room. Pretty soon we can go out there and see her through the glass." Then he thought a second. "You know, she's your new cousin."

All hostility between Terry and Bob was forgotten as everyone shared in the miracle of a new baby.

Nothing was ever the same again after June 15, 1981.

CHAPTER 4—JULY 1983

Tomato-watermelon sorbet. What a concept! Julie was flat on her back on the living room couch in their "new" fixer-upper house. She was catching up on one of her unread issues of *Bon Appétit* magazine while Angie napped. She kept the door to her room open with the fan blowing for a little white noise.

Since Angie was two years old now, they decided to get her a twin bed, a project Terry's mother naturally took on. Her insistence turned out to be helpful since Julie wasn't working anymore. Terry was still a security guard and was taking evening college classes to qualify for the police academy.

This sorbet would make a wonderful treat for Angie and would be a perfect way for Julie to use her abundance of garden tomatoes. As she read through the ingredients, she didn't hear footsteps. When she finally lowered the magazine, she was eyeball to eyeball with her innocent little girl, who was shirtless, holding her stuffed rabbit, and sucking her thumb.

"Well hello there my little Pookie! Have you finished your nap?" Julie scooped up Angie and blew into her belly button. Angie giggled and thrashed. "How is my precious angel?"

Terry came in from the kitchen, also without a shirt—though much dirtier than Angie. He had been working on his motorcycle in the garage. How Julie hated that dangerous thing.

"It is so hot out there, I can hardly stand it. I have an idea. After supper, why don't we go to The Purple Cow and get some ice cream?" he said.

"Wow! Ice cream! What do you think of that, Pookie?"

"Yay, ice qweem!"

The family date would be a double treat. They didn't see much of Terry these days since he was taking classes, teaching swimming lessons at the gym on Saturday mornings, and still going to his aunt and uncle's house at least one night a week to play chess until all hours of the night. Julie truly didn't know how he did it.

She also didn't know *why* he did it when he had such a precious daughter who adored him. *Daddy* was her first word, and she followed him around everywhere. Only Terry could get her to eat broccoli—by pretending it was green rabbit tails. Macaroni and cheese was both of their favorites, and they raced each other to finish it.

But supper this night wasn't so much fun. Julie planned on cheeseburgers with cheddar cheese on Angie's burger, and blue cheese with sautéed mushrooms on theirs. But Rita called while the burgers were on their indoor grill, and Julie forgot about them until they were charred. She didn't have any hamburger left to start all over again, so she tried to peel off the black crust—unsuccessfully.

Terry silently got up from the table, dumped his burger into the trash, and made a peanut butter and jelly sandwich. "I don't know how you expect *her* to eat that," he said.

"Well, why don't you make her a sandwich too, then," Julie said. So he did.

Before Julie could finish cleaning up, Terry announced it was time to go.

Julie hated to fail at anything, and she equally hated to leave the dishes undone. What might have been a welcome exit from the kitchen for anyone else wasn't good for her right then.

She strapped Angie into the backseat of the purple Mustang and plopped into the passenger seat while

Terry revved the engine. Julie rolled her eyes. "Do all of our neighbors need to know we are leaving now?"

"Yes, they do. You always tell me we don't spend enough time together as a family. I want them to know we are spending time together as a family." Then he floored it into the street.

"You didn't even look both ways!" Julie yelled.

Angie started crying.

"What's wrong?" Julie turned around and asked.

"Where's Bunny?"

"Oh, Honey. He's inside. Let's let him rest while we go eat ice cream." She hoped that would work. How could she have forgotten Bunny?

Halfway to Purple Cow, Terry told Julie, "I'm going to Uncle Robert's house while you're at church tomorrow."

"Why do you have to do that?" she demanded. "You need to go to church with us!"

"I'll tell you why. I need some space. That's why."

"Space from what?" Julie was incredulous. "You're never home as it is."

He accelerated to 65 mph.

"Slow down! The speed limit is only 35. You're going to kill us!" Julie shouted.

He drove faster, while Julie gasped. Then he slammed on the brakes. Julie instinctively put her hand in the back to make sure Angie wasn't tossed around.

They heard a siren and both looked in the rearview mirror. It was for them. Terry pulled into a nearby parking lot.

The policeman came to Terry's window and asked to see his driver's license. Then he took it back to his car.

Terry and Julie sat silently. Angie tried to look out the window. "Ice Qweem?" she asked.

"Not yet," Julie stated.

The policeman returned with Terry's license. "Are you Bob Bradley's son?"

"Yes, he's my dad. I'm sorry officer. I was just checking my brakes. I had to speed up first to test them."

"Well, I'll let you off with a warning. But that was pretty dangerous. Don't try that again."

"Please, don't tell my dad," Terry said.

The officer winked. "I won't tell him. You just be careful."

Julie glared at Terry.

"You lied to him."

Terry drove off.

"Stop the car please," Julie said.

He did. She opened the wide door, pulled her seat up, and unbuckled Angie. "Let's go for a walk, Sweetie," she said. "Go get your Purple Cow," she told Terry as she slammed the door.

He drove away.

Julie carried Angie to a gas station and called Rachel on the pay phone, praying that she was home.

Before long they were sitting in Rachel's car at an A&W, ordering ice cream from the driver's window. Julie sat in the back seat to keep Angie's mess to a minimum as she fulfilled the promise of ice cream.

Julie put on a happy face and spoke with a cheerful lilt to protect her daughter from any further effects of the fight. But the air was frosty. The ice cream didn't taste very good to either Julie or Rachel.

"Anything I should know?" Rachel finally ventured.

"Oh, it's just more of the same," Julie said, trying to sound matter-of-fact. "You can go ahead and take us home. I'm pretty sure he won't be there."

CHAPTER 5—DECEMBER 1984

Julie opened the front door to let her mother in. Rita was carrying a big box, which was open at the top with tinsel hanging over the edge.

Decorating the Christmas tree was one of Rita's favorite holiday traditions—a trait Julie wished she had inherited. The next best thing was having her mother's help. Her mom had even started a tradition of making one special decoration each year for Julie and her family to help build a collection of family Christmas memories.

"If you have the time, I thought we could string popcorn. Then I have some special paint we can spray to make it all different colors," her mom said. "Where's Angie... and Terry?"

"Terry is at the gym, training kids. Angie begged to go with him. They have childcare, so I thought it would be okay if she went along. I thought this would be good bonding time for them," Julie said.

She had made hot, spiced cider and poured some for her mother. "Let me see if I can find my Christmas tapes," Julie said. "While I'm looking, we have some Christmas photo proofs over there on the table. See which one you like best."

Julie put on the Andy Williams Christmas tape, knowing how much her mother loved the singer, and returned to find Rita looking thoughtfully at the photos.

"What do you think?" Julie asked.

Her mom looked up. "I think you look very sad in every one of these pictures."

Julie felt surprised—not that she looked sad, but that it was so obvious. "I guess I was just having a bad day," she said.

27

"Honey, I don't want to intrude, but is there anything you'd like to talk about?"

"I've just been a bit tired lately—and no, I'm not pregnant."

"Well, that's understandable, chasing after a three-and-a-half year old. But this doesn't look like tired. It looks more like depressed," Rita said.

Julie slumped down onto the couch. "Oh, I don't know. It seems Terry and I argue so much lately. He's gone so much of the time—between work, classes, the gym, and going to his uncle's. I just can't accept it. It's not right. So I'm always on him about it, and I'm sure it's driving him away from me."

"So what has changed? He's kept that schedule for a couple years. Has he been physically abusive to you?"

"Why do you ask that?"

"Honey, you can tell me anything. You know that."

"Well, our arguments are getting worse, and he has pushed me a few times. He may have even slapped me a time or two."

"How do you respond when he does that?" Rita asked.

"I certainly tell him he better stop and that he can't treat me that way. It's so disrespectful. And I don't want him treating me like his dad treats his mother."

"Hmm. Does that help?"

"Actually, it does. He doesn't want to be anything like his father."

"Please be sure to call me when things get out of hand, would you promise me?" Rita implored. "And what about some counseling? Would you be open to that? I know someone who would be very good for the two of you."

"No, no. I can't. I know things will get better. In fact, it feels wonderful to finally tell someone. Just please pray for us."

"I will do that. But let me also give you a piece of advice. You might not want to hear this, but I've watched how you respond to him sometimes, and it's like you're not on the same team. This is not tug of war. You're parents now, so you need to be united. Try to support and encourage him any way you can."

"I will. I think I needed to hear that," Julie said. Then she paused. "But there's one thing that keeps eating at me. He spends so much time at his aunt and uncle's house. It just doesn't make sense to me. It's like a part of his life I know nothing about. I didn't even know about them until more than a year after we were married.

"I met them once. Terry took me over there after Angie was born so I could thank them in person for the beautiful blanket they gave us for the shower. They were nice enough. Kind of shy, actually. But there was nothing dynamic about their relationship with Terry. I just don't get it," Julie concluded.

"Where do they live?" Rita asked. When Julie told her, Rita said, "Oh, I know exactly where that is. I get my hair done close to there."

After they'd strung some popcorn, they heard the Mustang pull into the driveway. Terry opened the door and in ran Angie, straight into her grandma's arms.

"My there, little girl. You smell like… grease."

"What happened to her?" Julie asked. "She is filthy."

"We went into a dark room," Angie said. "There was a puppy."

Terry interrupted. "We stopped off at a friend's garage to look at a car he's working on."

"I saw bright lights. I wish we had a puppy," Angie said.

"Well, I guess I'd better go to the library and study for the test I have this week," Terry said.

Remembering the need to be a team player, Julie excused Terry and turned to Angie. "Did you have a good time with Daddy?" She took a deep whiff. "I think we need to clean you up."

"I'll give her a bath," Rita volunteered.

"That would be great. I'll make us all a snack, other than popcorn."

While Julie was out in the kitchen mixing some mayonnaise, cheese, and herbs for one of her favorite cracker spreads, her mom called her into the bathroom.

In a cheerful tone, but looking deeply into Julie's eyes, Rita showed Julie some bruises high on Angie's inner thighs. "Honey, do you know how she got these?" she asked Julie. "And look at her underwear."

Julie saw blood and other fluids on her underwear and started to panic. *What is this? Oh my, what has happened to her? Where has she been? Who did this? This could never happen to my little girl.*

"Uh, I don't know, Mom. I really don't," she said.

Doing the only thing she could imagine at the moment, Julie pressed on the bruised area. "Does that hurt, Sweetie?"

"No. Not now," she answered.

"Did someone hurt you there?" Julie's mom tried.

"No. I played in the dark room. The puppy was soft."

Julie felt a combination of nauseated and furious. *What has happened to my little girl? What did Terry do to her? No, he wouldn't hurt his own daughter. Does he know about this? What kind of friends does he have?*

She ran out of the room to explode away from Angie. She went into the living room and put a pillow over her mouth and screamed. She nearly hyperventilated.

She stood there and tried to collect herself so she could go back into the bathroom. "Mom, what should we do?" she asked quietly with a shaky voice.

Very calmly, while she dried Angie off, Rita suggested that they take a little drive in her car and go visit the hospital.

"Why don't we go to the library so I can ask Terry about it?"

"Yes, we need to do that. But we certainly need to have her seen and get a report. This is a serious thing," Rita said.

It only took 10 minutes to reach the library. Rita drove around the parking lot as they looked for the Mustang. After three circles around the building, it was apparent Terry wasn't there.

"He has to be in there. Let me out. I'm going in to find him," Julie said.

What if I can't find him? Then what? He has to be in here, she thought as she raced through the library, looking around every corner and at every table. *Where could he possibly be?*

"Let's not worry about that right now," Rita said, taking control of the situation after Julie returned to the car frantic. "Let's just go ahead to the hospital."

"I forgot to bring her stained undies!" Julie exclaimed.

"Don't worry. I put them in a plastic bag. They're in my purse," Rita consoled.

"Um, I'm here to talk to someone about my daughter," she whispered to the hospital receptionist, not wanting Angie to overhear, though Rita was doing a good job of keeping her distracted. "I'm pretty sure she's been molested, and I need to have her checked out."

"Please have a seat," the receptionist said. "We'll get her in as soon as possible."

Julie explained to Angie that they were going to visit a nice doctor who would give her a checkup since she hadn't had one recently.

"Will he poke me?" Angie asked with fear in her eyes.

"No, Honey. They won't give you any shots today. They'll just look you over."

Finally Julie was called to follow a nurse. Her heart was pounding. *Oh Lord, I hope I'm just over-reacting. Let this turn out to be nothing*, she breathed as she, Angie, and her mom paraded down the hallway into the exam room.

Julie stood while her mom sat in a chair and Angie was seated up on the exam table.

Before the nurse left the room, she advised Julie to undress Angie.

"This is so the doctor can check and make sure you are in perfect shape," she told Angie.

Soon an older, silver-haired doctor with reading glasses in a white coat knocked on the door and entered with a clipboard. "Um hmm," he said as he read the reason for the visit. "We're going to check you out, and if you're really good, I'll give you a sucker before you leave."

Angie recoiled and started crying, not wanting the doctor to touch her.

"I'm sorry doctor; she's not usually like this," Julie said patting her daughter. "Angie it will be okay," she told the cowering girl.

"Why don't I have Dr. Melissa Taylor come in and take a look."

Julie was apologetic, but relieved. "Thank you."

Dr. Taylor came in cheerfully and without a doctor's jacket over her dress.

"How are you Angie?" she asked. "I have a little girl about your age. Do you like puppies?"

"Yeah!" Angie exclaimed.

"So does my little girl. When you leave, I have something special to give you."

"A puppy?"

"It might be. You'll have to wait and see."

The doctor did preliminary checking—checking Angie's ears and her heart with the stethoscope—which Julie guessed was to get Angie used to the doctor touching her.

Dr. Taylor looked at Angie's bruises on the insides of her upper thighs and gently did some tests with wooden sticks and cotton swabs a little higher up.

Angie pointed to her belly button. "Mommy and Daddy blow on me here!" she said.

"Does it tickle when they do that?" Dr. Taylor asked with a smile.

"Yes. And a big man too," Angie said.

Without missing a beat the doctor asked, "What big man is that?"

"I don't know."

Julie gasped. "When did that happen?" she demanded, startling Angie.

"I don't know," Angie whispered.

"You can put your clothes back on now, Angie." The doctor said. "You look very healthy, Angie."

"Mom, let me have the plastic bag," Julie said to Rita.

"This goes along with the exam. She came home today with this soiled underwear. Can you test it?"

"Yes, I was going to ask you if you had anything like this," Dr. Taylor said as she accepted the bag with its contents. "We will have results in a few days and we'll give you a call." She lowered her voice as she added, "I think you're probably right about what you suspect."

Julie's heart thumped in her chest. *Where could Terry possibly be? He surely has the answers to all of this.*

As promised, Dr. Taylor had a surprise—a small puppy finger puppet.

Angie jumped up and down. "Look Mommy!" she exclaimed. "Look! Look!"

"Yes, Sweetie. Now don't forget to say 'thank you.'"

Julie couldn't hide her emotions, as tears streamed down her face.

"You crying?" Angie asked sweetly. "You want my puppy?"

Julie was glad she didn't have to drive. She slumped in the front passenger seat reeling with chaotic thoughts while Angie sat in the back seat playing with her new toy and singing her ABCs. *Who molested my baby? It happened today when she was with Terry. Maybe we're all wrong and she just played in something. Oh, who am I kidding? I've just got to talk to Terry. Has this happened before and I'm just noticing it? Now, where all did he take her today? He mentioned a friend's garage. Is he the big man Angie was talking about? She was in daycare at the gym. But there's something about a dark room. It must be the guy's garage.*

They were almost home. Julie looked over at her mom, who appeared lost in her own thoughts.

"Pookie, when we get home, would you like to go

make a tent in your room and have a tea party with your dolls?" Julie asked.

"Yea! Let's have a tea party!"

She knew that would occupy Angie. A tea party was a very special occasion. It meant that she could have little cups of lemonade, or apple cider in this case, and Cheerios in her room, something that would normally have been forbidden.

After Angie was set up with her tea party, Julie and her mom went to the kitchen to pool their thoughts.

"Okay, let's try to figure out Angie's schedule today," Rita started.

"No, let's try to figure out where Terry is. I'm tempted to go to the library again."

"Wait a minute," Rita said. "Before we do that, you need to level with me. Is there any chance that Terry could have done this to her?"

Julie sighed. "I don't know. But I think I should tell you what I know *has* been going on. Terry has pushed me a few times, and he definitely has slapped me. I didn't tell you that one time he threatened to shoot me if I didn't shut up. So, I've become afraid of him. But I don't think he would molest his own daughter. He doesn't get mad at her as much as me."

"I wish I knew more about what makes a man molest children," Rita said. "Does Terry have any habits that might lead him to do this? Does he drink or use drugs or anything?"

"He does drink, I'm afraid. I've never told you, because I knew you wouldn't approve. But he's not an alcoholic. I just can't believe Terry has anything to do with this," Julie said defensively.

"You mentioned he threatened to shoot you," Rita continued. "He has a gun?"

"Well, naturally. He's a security guard. He has two of them. In fact, one of our fights was about guns.

After he threatened me, I hid the guns. When he couldn't find them, he confronted me. I told him the place I hid them was much safer than where he kept them. He got so mad, he pushed me down." Julie hung her head, then quietly continued. "Then he kicked me and told me to never do that again."

Julie wanted to change the subject. Fortunately, so did her mother.

"We have to find Terry and see what he knows," Rita said.

Before Julie could respond, she heard little footsteps. Angie's tiny tea-party pitcher of apple cider was empty.

"Here, my little Pookie, let's get you some more. And more Cheerios?" Julie asked. Angie didn't want any more of the cereal. Come to think of it, Julie had mindlessly given her a whole bowl full of them to start with.

"I think what I really need to do is clear my mind here and prepare myself for when Terry does eventually come home. My head is spinning, and I need to unwind and sort out my thoughts. Would you mind if I just handle this from here… at least for today?" Julie pleaded.

"Yes, of course. I'll try to calm down too. My mother instincts are as strong as yours. How about if I call you tomorrow?"

After her mom left, Julie felt guilty about how little playtime she spent with Angie. She sat down in her room with her and made up stories about the dolls.

It was 5:30 p.m. and mostly dark by the time Terry got home. Julie had been so lost in her mental stew that she forgot to plan dinner.

She refrained from bombarding him with angry questions and startling information. She had to be sensitive to Angie. "I'm sorry, I don't have dinner ready," she said. "Can we just order pizza?"

"Pizza!" Angie shouted, jumping around the room.

Terry agreed.

I better handle this right or it could get ugly around here, Julie thought.

"Sweetie, while we wait for our pizza to be delivered, wouldn't you like to play in your room?" Julie asked Angie.

Fortunately, she agreed.

"After you left for the library, we took a little trip to the hospital," Julie said, trying not to inject the hysteria that was just under the surface.

"Why? What happened?" he asked with seeming genuine surprise.

"Oh, but first, were you at the library?"

"Yes, of course, but why did you go to the hospital?"

She explained about the bath, suspicious bruises, soiled underwear, and emergency room visit.

"The test results will be back in a few days," she said, now folding her arms across her chest and raising an eyebrow. "So, where all did you take her today? And I don't want vague answers."

Terry just looked bewildered with his jaw dropped and a far-away look in his eyes, as if he was thinking.

"Okay, let me get this started," Julie said. "Did you take her to the gym with you this morning?"

"Yes, and I left her in the little green room with a few kids who were younger and two babysitters, probably in their 20s. They were girls."

"How long was she in there, and were there any guys in there?"

"It was probably an hour and a half. I didn't see any guys go in there, but I wasn't watching."

"How was she acting when you picked her up?"

"Perfectly normal. She was happy."

Julie paused before her next question. *I just know this is going to lead nowhere. He could be lying, and I wouldn't know. He lied about being at the library, he'll probably lie about where else they went.*

"Where did you go after that?" she asked.

"My friend Brett's house. He's working on a '61 Corvair in his garage. So we stopped and sat around for a few minutes."

"I don't think I know anyone named Brett. What does he look like?" Julie remembered that Angie had said the man in the garage who blew on her belly button was a big man.

"He's just an average looking guy. About my size."

"So, he's about five feet ten and skinny?"

"Yeah, something like that."

Just like I thought. We're getting nowhere.

"What else can you tell me, Terry? We're missing something. Did you ever let her out of your sight when you were at Brett's?"

"No, honest, I didn't. We didn't stay long because Angie was starting to get into things."

"Did Brett happen to blow into Angie's belly button?"

"No, of course not! And I'm just as puzzled by this as you are."

The doorbell rang. It was the pizza delivery guy.

As all three of them ate their hamburger and cheese pizza at the kitchen table, Julie asked him if he went straight to the library after he dropped Angie off at home.

"Yes, and I was there all afternoon."

"We saw the libwawy," Angie spoke up.

Terry raised his eyebrows.

"Yes, we went looking for you, and you were not there," Julie said, with anger rising in her voice. *That jerk wasn't there.*

"Well, you didn't look hard enough, because I was there."

"Why wasn't your car there?" Julie asked.

"It was there, on the west side of the building."

I give up, Julie thought. *He is such a liar. How come I never saw this side of him before we were married?*

Terry simply was not helpful and didn't appear to be nearly as concerned as she was. *I'm not going to get much sleep tonight,* she thought.

The next morning at church, Rita greeted Julie at the front door.

"What did you find out?" she asked Julie after they dropped Angie off at Sunday school and went straight to the restroom.

"I got nothing out of him," Julie spouted. "I am so mad. He also said he was at the library yesterday. We know *that's* not true!"

"Well, I really prayed about this last night," Rita said. "I think we need to get some other answers too. When does he usually go to his uncle's house?"

"Right about now. And on Wednesday nights."

"Well, you said that's the most puzzling thing about him. How about after he leaves home Wednesday night to go visit them, you call me, and I'll go over there and see if he actually makes it there?" Rita suggested.

"You can't do that. He'll see you!"

"No, I'll make sure he doesn't see me. I'll park somewhere else and walk down the street. Please. I can do this and not raise any suspicions."

"I don't know," Julie said. "What if someone recognizes you?"

"I'll wear an old coat and a scarf over my head. Now I've thought this through."

"Why don't I do it instead?" Julie asked.

"No, you stay home with Angie. I know where the house is. It's by my hairdresser. I can even picture where I'll hide my car."

"Oh, okay. It would be good to know if he really does go over there," Julie conceded.

###

Julie decided it was time to catch up with her former work pal Rachel and called her to have lunch on Monday.

Over chicken salad sandwiches made crunchy with celery and roasted pecans, Julie caught up on former co-worker gossip.

"So, how are you and Terry doing," Rachel asked.

What should I tell her? Oh, she already knows we're struggling since the day we went for ice cream.

"All I have to say is, just be thankful you're single. And if you ever tell me you're interested in someone, let me check him out first."

"You will be the first to know if anyone ever looks at me twice," Rachel promised. "So, what's going on?"

Julie poured out her heart, first about Angie and the trip to the emergency room. "I'm supposed to get the results back from the hospital tomorrow or Wednesday. My stomach is in knots waiting." She noticed the startled look on Rachel's face.

After pondering who could have abused Angie, they started talking about Terry's denial or indifference to the situation.

Rachel sat back in her chair, looked at nothing in particular and said, "Very interesting," several times.

Julie told Rachel about their fights, giving details she hadn't even told her mom—like the time Terry missed the trashcan when he was throwing a chicken bone into it. He angrily picked up the trashcan and threw it, hitting her.

"I was so love-struck when we got married, I never saw these things coming," Julie said. "Do you see anything unexpected in Terry's life at work?"

"Well, I don't see him a lot at work since he covers such a large area," Rachel began carefully.

Julie noticed her hesitation. "Don't hide anything from me."

"Okay," Rachel ventured. "Remember the conversation we had about Terry's buddies who drink? I'm not sure if you know, but he actually drinks a lot himself, and more than beer. In fact, I think he has a drinking problem."

"What in the world makes you think that!" Julie demanded, a bit defensively.

"I've seen inside his locker at work. He has vodka. It's pretty well known that he drinks."

Julie's jaw dropped. "Why didn't I know that? And why didn't you say something before?"

"I wasn't sure if I should. At first I thought you already knew, but when I realized you didn't, I couldn't decide if it was my place to tell you. Now I know I should have told you."

"Yes, you should have told me. I'm so mad. Not at you, but that I didn't figure it out. I want to believe the best about him, and I guess I just can't anymore."

"There's something else I should tell you," Rachel said. "This week one of the guys told me he saw some terrible pictures drop out of Terry's locker. They were of men touching small children without any clothes on. I didn't want to hear the whole description. But the guy who told me said Terry picked up the pictures quickly and slammed them in his locker."

"You're kidding!" Julie screamed. She jumped up

and started pacing around the kitchen, her mind in turmoil. *Why would he look at pictures like that? And now his own daughter has been molested. What is this guy capable of? But he wouldn't do it to his own daughter, surely. He loves her. What kind of a freak looks at pictures like that?*

She sat back down. "You don't suppose he's the one who molested Angie, do you?" Julie pleaded with Rachel. "Someone who looks at pictures like that is sick. Is it an addiction like alcohol that when you look at dirty pictures you feel compelled to act it out yourself?

"Oh, what am I going to do?" she continued, now with her head buried in her hands.

Rachel put her hand gently on Julie's shoulder.

"I know it's horrible, but the bad pictures don't mean Terry abused Angie," Rachel said.

She paused while Julie calmed down a bit before she spoke again.

"Look, my Aunt Elizabeth works as a counselor at a women's shelter. I think you should go see her," Rachel said.

"I'm not going to a women's shelter." Julie stated.

"No, what I'm saying is my aunt has talked to hundreds of women in all kinds of situations, and she's helped many of them figure out what to do next. She has heard everything. And I mean everything. I think she is fascinating, and she's told me that she specializes in abused women. I can give you her phone number."

Julie tried to insist that she didn't need that kind of help, but as the idea sunk in, she felt a little less resistant.

Rachel wrote down the name of the shelter and her aunt's name and phone number.

###

Julie blew her nose and picked up the phone to call her mom. "The hospital just called with the results of the tests they did on Angie and on her underwear. The lady told me she was likely molested."

"*Likely* molested? Don't they know for sure?"

"That's what I asked. The woman told me Angie probably was molested, but they just don't like to state it in absolute terms in their written reports in order to avoid lawsuits."

"Oh, that is so awful."

"She said *likely molested* is good enough and should indicate to anyone that it really did happen."

"But they won't officially confirm it," Rita stated with disgust.

"No. But they aren't denying it, either. I asked them to mail me a copy of the report. Anyway, I have something else to tell you. I had lunch with Rachel. Remember, she works with Terry? She told me he keeps vodka in his locker at work. Everyone knows he has a drinking problem. And, get this, he keeps child pornography in his locker too!"

Julie could hear her mother let out a gasp. "I don't even know what to say. But I'll tell you what. I'm going to find some answers tonight. Isn't this when he goes to his uncle's house to play chess?" Rita asked. She explained her plan to Julie once again. This time, Julie was all for it.

"Please call me as soon as you get home, will you?" Julie asked.

The second stunning phone call of the day came about 7:45.

"Are you sitting down?" Rita asked. She explained how she put on her wool scarf and her brown winter coat that she hardly ever wears, so no one could recognize it. She left home at 6:40 to drive to the uncle's neighborhood. "I really prayed that this trip would provide some answers or insight into what's going on. God certainly answered my prayer."

"So what happened already?" Julie urged her. She sat on the edge of the couch.

"Well, there weren't any cars in the driveway. I figured his uncle keeps his car in the garage. At about 7:20, I decided to park on the next street. I found a spot where I could see his uncle's driveway from between two houses. At 7:25, I saw some car lights on his street, and I saw what could have been a purple Mustang pass the driveway. I figured maybe he was going to turn around and park on the street in front of the house. But I waited and didn't see the lights anymore.

"So, I got out of the car and walked to the street, and I saw the Mustang in his uncle's neighbor's driveway. I wondered if I wrote the wrong address down. Why would Terry park in the neighbor's driveway?

"I didn't know what to think, so I started walking back to my car to figure it out. Then I heard a front door close. I turned and saw Terry and a girl with long, dark permed hair, blue jeans, a leather jacket, and high heels walk down the driveway and get into his Mustang with him."

"You are kidding!" Julie shouted.

"No, I'm not kidding. I turned so he wouldn't see my face. I pulled my scarf over my head. He revved his engine and took off quickly. He zoomed past me, stopped at the stop sign and turned left. And he was gone, just like that."

Oh no. Who is this guy and what is going on? This is not the person I married. How could he do these things? He's a complete stranger.

"Mom, are you sure it was him? How could he do something like that?"

"It was him. I know this is awful. But be thankful that pieces of the truth are finally coming out so you can have a complete picture of who he really is," Rita said with unusual strength in her voice.

"Mom, I can't stay with him. You know what this means don't you?"

"Yes, Honey. I know. I don't ever condone divorce, but with everything that's happened, I've come to grips with it, and I don't expect you to stay with him."

That's a relief, Julie thought. *But I can't leave him just yet. I need some answers.*

CHAPTER 6—DECEMBER 1984

The dining room table was set with their best dishes, which Julie had only used twice in their five-year marriage. It probably didn't make sense to use them now, but she decided this was an important evening, and she would give it every advantage she could. At the very least, the formal setting would throw Terry off when he walked in the door from work and saw a nice candlelight roast-and-potatoes dinner on the table. Maybe it would jolt his deteriorating resolve to be a respectable husband, father, and human being.

Julie shook her head to snap herself out of her bitter mental spiral. As much as anything, the serene setting might help her to keep her own composure.

She was wearing her favorite navy blue, linen slacks and a long-sleeved blue and pink stripped knit turtleneck. She felt her pocket for the list of everything she wanted to bring up at dinner. She was thankful that Angie was spending the night with Rita, away from the confrontation Julie was afraid could get rough.

It was 6:30, about time for Terry to pull up. Julie put dinner rolls in the oven.

By 7:15, the rolls were done—and cold. Julie paced between the kitchen and hallway.

Where is he? Probably at his girlfriend's house doing who knows what. Or maybe he's at the gym.

She stopped pacing as the thought struck her: *How do I even know he goes to the gym when he tells me that's where he's going? Maybe he goes to a bar drinking with his buddies. Which of them got him into child pornography? Or has he always been this way and he's just managed to hide it from me for all these years?*

Again, she had to catch herself. If she let herself go in front of Terry, she may never get answers, and she *needed* to know the truth.

By 7:45 her imagination had exhausted all possibilities of his whereabouts and what he must be doing and she prayed he *wouldn't* come home, because she was ready to kill him.

At 8:10, she decided to give up and went to their room to change into her pajamas. But she heard a familiar rumbling outside. She ran to the living room window, and there he was, shutting off the engine in the driveway.

She ran to the dining room table to light the cinnamon candle. She had to pull herself together once again.

Please calm down. Don't snap at him, she advised herself.

Hearing his footsteps on the porch, she opened the door.

And there he stood with a little fluffy puppy. A real one.

Julie was speechless. He kissed her on the cheek.

"Where's Pookie?" he asked as he came in and looked around. "I bought her a puppy for Christmas."

"Uhh. She's spending the night at my mom's house tonight. Where did you get that?"

"It's a bichon, and it won't get much bigger than this," Terry proudly said as he held the wiggly white ball of fluff up for Julie to see better. "I had to cover for Phil at work tonight, and as soon as he came, I ran to the pet store to buy him. I've been looking at him for a few days now. What do you think?"

"It's very cute," she said honestly. "I can't hold him right now, I'm getting food on the table."

Terry put the puppy down and took off his coat,

throwing it on the couch.

"Oops, I left the dog food in the trunk," he exclaimed as he dashed out the door.

Julie watched the dog sniff and jump up and down. *Oh my gosh. A dog. Now what do I do?*

Terry brought in the food and a dog kennel and got the puppy settled inside it.

"I'm starved!" he exclaimed. "Mmm. Roast and potatoes! My favorite!"

"What's wrong with our other dishes? Are they all dirty?" he asked as he dug into his dinner.

Julie shook her head. *I better get on task here.*

She tried to remember the order of topics she wrote on the paper in her pocket. She got up and grabbed a piece of paper from the corner of the kitchen counter and brought it to the table.

"We got this today," she said, handing him the lab results from the hospital. She showed him where it said "likely molested."

He put down his fork and looked carefully at the paper. "Hmm, with all their money and equipment, they don't even know anything for sure," he said. Then he put the paper down and continued eating.

What a strange response, Julie thought.

"Our daughter was molested, and that's all you can say? Come on, Terry. Tell me what happened!" she shouted.

He pushed back his chair. "How should I know what happened to her? Are you accusing me of something? Probably nothing happened to her!"

Julie gained control of herself, remembering that she needed plenty of other answers. She couldn't afford to hit a brick wall this early in the conversation.

"No, I'm not accusing you of anything. I'm just upset. We need to figure out who did this to her and make sure she never sees him again."

She mentally rearranged the topics she wanted to bring up. It might not be safe to mention the child pornography right then, though she certainly wanted to.

"Terry, I've been wondering lately. You know with the holidays, do you think you struggle at all with perhaps drinking too much?" She thought she had handled that tactfully.

"Why do you ask?"

"Well, you get out of sorts so quickly lately, I just wonder if drinking might have something to do with it."

"No, I do not have a drinking problem!" he announced angrily. "Why are you on my case? Can't I just have a peaceful dinner for once?"

Amazingly, Julie was not afraid of what might come next. Instead she decided she badly needed another answer before he completely lost control.

"Terry, who is the girl you've been seeing?"

He turned red and jumped up from the table. Then he kicked the dog kennel, springing the latch. The puppy spilled out and yelped as if it was in pain. Julie stood.

"I don't know where you're getting these crazy ideas, but I want you to shut up right now!" Terry shouted. He slapped her, then pushed her into the kitchen and shoved her against the stove.

Julie wasn't sure exactly what happened next. When she came to, she was alone, except for the puppy laying next to her, head between its paws and with sad eyes looking at her. When their eyes met, the puppy jumped up and danced.

CHAPTER 7—MAY 1985

At exactly 4 p.m. Julie was still driving around on E. 32nd Street looking for the building. She hated to be late and was getting knots in her stomach, although these days, she always had knots in her stomach. She finally saw the sign on the front of the three-story brick building, "Hope House," and couldn't believe she didn't see it the first time she drove by. She parked her mother's car on the side of the street and rang the buzzer next to the door.

"May I help you?" a woman's voice crackled over the intercom.

"Yes, I'm here to see Elizabeth Karty. She is expecting me."

She heard the door click and took that as her cue that she could get in. She had to wait for the door to close behind her to enter a second door, only after she heard another click. *They must really take safety seriously here,* she thought.

"Would you please sign in here?" a woman sitting behind a counter asked. "Then please be seated."

Soon a thin, middle-aged woman with glasses and her brown hair tied in a ponytail entered the waiting room and invited Julie into her office. Besides a desk, cushioned chairs faced each other with a coffee table in between. Julie noticed beautiful photos of mountains on the wall. "Did you take those?" she asked.

"My husband took them on vacation a few years ago. It's Breckinridge. Have you ever been there?"

"No, but it's sure beautiful."

"Would you like a Coke or a Sprite?" Elizabeth offered.

They chatted about Rachel as they sat in the chairs.

Finally Julie asked, "Did Rachel tell you anything about my situation."

"She said a little. But why don't you tell me. And I can assure you that nothing you say will leave this room," Elizabeth said.

Julie paused, wondering where to start.

"My ribs have finally healed. My husband beat me. I don't know if Rachel told you about that." She didn't often verbalize what had happened. It felt strange coming from her lips.

"And where are you living?" Elizabeth asked with penetrating eyes.

"I've been living with my mom since it happened. Fortunately Angie—my little girl—wasn't around to see it happen.

"But I don't really care so much about what he did to me. I'm worried about my little girl." Julie produced the hospital report and showed it to Elizabeth. "I know she was molested. She mentioned something about a big man, but we haven't gotten anything else out of her."

"Is this the only episode of sexual abuse?" Elizabeth asked, not even questioning the nebulous conclusion on the report.

"As far as I know. I've been checking her incessantly for bruises and any other signs, but I haven't seen any more. I've asked Angie many times if anyone touched her, but she always quickly says no.

"But I'm so afraid of Terry. I have nightmares that he is standing beside my bed with a bat raised over his head, about to hit me. But I'm even more afraid for Angie. He's been looking at pictures of children being molested. Someone at work saw them."

Leaning forward, Elizabeth said "Oh really? Tell me more about that."

"The pictures fell out of his locker. I didn't get

many details of the pictures. All I know is that men were touching little children in the genital area.

"Right now, I feel so out of control. When Angie spends time with him, I have even less of an idea of where they go and what they do than I did when we were together. I know they spend a little time at his parent's house. I think she's safe there. And I don't want to prevent her from being with her dad. She is crazy about him. Plus, the two of them share a puppy they love."

She finally got to the heart of her reason for coming to see Elizabeth. "Rachel told me that you've seen everything. I need to know your impressions of what I'm seeing in Angie."

"I was just going to ask you about her behavior," Elizabeth said.

"She used to be so carefree most of the time. Now she comes home from her visits with Terry like a zombie."

"What do you mean by that?" Elizabeth asked.

"Well, she's like a robot. She doesn't seem to have any emotion, other than extreme tiredness. I don't know. It's like she has no life in her." Julie thought some more. "And this is going to sound strange, but she tells me I need to die."

"*You* need to *die*?" Elizabeth clarified.

"Yes, she has said that several times, and always after she has been with Terry.

"Another odd thing is that Angie doesn't like to go to Sunday school any more. She doesn't like the man teacher. A young couple works in her class, plus two female helpers. It makes me wonder if any abuse is going on in there, but I just don't see how that could be possible. At any rate, now I keep her with me during Sunday school."

Elizabeth frowned. "I am hearing some things that

I often hear when abusers coach their victims—the fact that Angie so quickly denies that anyone ever touched her bothers me. And those strange words about your dying. But Terry's involvement in child pornography is the biggest red flag."

"Should I get a restraining order against Terry so he can't see Angie any more? I really feel I need to keep Angie with me." Julie sighed, knowing the problems it would cause with Terry and his family—especially his mother, who adored Angie as much as her own mother did.

"You won't be able to get a restraining order to keep him from seeing Angie," Elizabeth explained. "If I were you, I would file for divorce and legal custody of Angie as soon as possible. It's to your benefit that you have that report," she said, pointing to the hospital report. "I wish it was worded more conclusively, but it's a good start. If you see any more signs of sexual abuse, get her to the hospital and get another report on file. Meanwhile, do everything you can to prevent him from getting her.

"If you need to hide from him, you can stay here at the shelter. Or, I have a network of people who take in abuse victims," Elizabeth said.

"A network?" Julie asked.

"Yes, things like this happen more than you can imagine. There is a well-organized underground network of women who help each other." She explained how professional, discreet, and effective they were. She also gave Julie more signs to watch out for in Angie's life, especially a fear of men, bed wetting, and a detachment from everything going on around her.

Their discussion made Julie feel empowered and scared at the same time.

As she got up to leave, Julie agreed that filing for

divorce and legal custody would be her next step.

"Please, keep my number handy. In fact, let me give you my home phone number," Elizabeth said as she wrote it on the back of her business card. "If you need any other advice or have any other questions, please call me. I want you and Angie to be safe. Please, keep me posted."

Julie thanked her and drove back to Rita's house.

Why didn't I ask her for the name of a lawyer? Julie asked herself. Perhaps her mother would know of one.

###

Julie sighed deeply with her mom sitting across from her at the kitchen table. "I know we talked about this briefly before, but I need to file for divorce and custody of Angie. I can't get a restraining order to keep him from seeing Angie," she said.

"And just so you know, I don't plan to live with you forever. I want to get back on my feet and become independent."

"First things first, Honey. And I don't mind having the two of you here at all. In fact, I cherish every minute I get to spend with my granddaughter. I wish my other granddaughters lived closer. And about the divorce, you do what you need to do. I'm behind you every step of the way.

"Wait here for a minute," Rita said as she stood and walked out of the room. In a few moments she was back with a white department store box.

"What is this?" Julie asked with surprise. Her birthday wasn't until November.

"I was going to wait and give it to you next weekend for Mother's Day, but I think this is a good time for you to have it."

Julie guessed it must be a blouse, until she held the box, which was heavier than clothing. Tissue paper covered whatever it was. She pushed the paper aside and saw the large decoupaged loose-leaf notebook. It was covered with purple and pink stripped paper, with black and yellow fabric flowers and gold foil. The black-lettered words *Thoughts & Prayers* boldly emblazoned the front. Julie was in awe of its beauty, and that it was a notebook—her very favorite thing.

"This looks so professional!" Julie commented. "Did you make it?"

Turns out she didn't. A box of the notebooks had arrived at the consignment shop that week, and Rita had immediately thought of her daughter. "I know how much you like to write, so I liked the fact that you can add more paper to it. There's more in there," her mom urged.

Julie felt around the tissue paper and found a pen. It was also decoupaged in purple and pink with a small pink feather extending from the top.

"This is beautiful, I love it!" Julie exclaimed, hugging her mom.

"Open the notebook. I want you to read something."

A Bible passage was permanently embedded on the inside cover.

"Go ahead and read it," her mom coaxed.

Julie read out loud: "*The Lord is my light and my salvation; whom shall I fear? The Lord is the strength of my life; of whom shall I be afraid? When the wicked, even mine enemies and my foes came upon me to eat up my flesh, they stumbled and fell. Though an host should encamp against me, my heart shall not fear: though war should rise against me, in this will I be confident. One thing have I desired of the Lord, that will I seek after; that I may dwell in the house of the Lord all the days of my life, to behold the beauty of the Lord, and to enquire in his Temple. For in the time of trouble he shall hide me in his pavilion: in the secret of his tabernacle shall he hide me; he shall set me up upon a rock.*"

Tears filled Julie's eyes. "This is so beautiful . . . and perfect for what I'm going through."

"Keep reading," her mother encouraged.

"*And now shall mine head be lifted up above mine enemies round about me: therefore will I offer in his tabernacle sacrifices of joy; I will sing, yea, I will sing praises unto the Lord. Here, O Lord, when I cry with my voice: have mercy also upon me and answer me. When thou saidist, Seek ye my face; my heart said unto thee, Thy face, Lord, will I seek. Hide not thy face far from me; put not thy servant away in anger: thou hast been my help. Leave me not, neither forsake me O God of my salvation. When my father and my mother forsake me, then the Lord will take me up. Teach me thy way, O Lord, and lead me in a plain path, because of mine enemies. Deliver me not over unto the will of mine enemies: for false witnesses are risen up against me, and such as breathe out cruelty. I had fainted, unless I had believed to see the goodness of the Lord in the land of the living. Wait on the Lord: be of good courage, and he shall strengthen thine heart: wait, I say, on the Lord.*" Psalms 27:1-14.

"Oh my gosh, what a breath of fresh air that is!" Julie said. "I'm going to treasure this."

"I hope it will always be a breath of fresh air. Sometimes it helps to write your prayers to God. When you do, write the date—and go back and write the date when it's answered. Not only will it build your faith, but also, maybe someday when Angie is older, she will read it and understand how real and near God is. You will both need this book. And the other thing you can do is read those verses over and over and pray those words to God."

"That won't be hard. I already feel many of the thoughts expressed in those verses," Julie said. She thanked her mother again for everything.

"Oh, by the way, do you know a good lawyer?"

Her mother didn't, so Julie decided she would consult the Yellow Pages. As she got up, the phone rang.

"I'll get it," Julie said.

It was Terry. "Hi Julie. Hey, don't hang up. I'm just calling to tell you I miss you." He paused, but Julie remained quiet. "And I'm sorry about everything that has happened. I'm not really sure what has gotten into me."

This is a first, Julie thought. "So what happened? Did you break up with your girlfriend?"

He quietly answered no, then paused. "I just accidently backed over the dog."

Julie gasped. "You're kidding! Is he okay?"

"No. he's dead. I just put him in a box and put him in the trash."

He began to cry and a flood of conflicting emotions rushed through Julie. Part of her wanted to comfort him, while part of her grieved for Angie. Angie constantly talked about the puppy and always wanted to go see it.

It was so sad to Julie. *I just hate this. I can't encourage him. But I'd be a rat to not show concern, and a wimp to give in to his emotions. Ahhh! This feels so manipulating.*

"I'm so sorry, Terry," she ended up saying. "Try to get some sleep." She softly hung up the phone.

Oh Lord. What a stupid thing for me to say. She held her new journal to her chest and went into her room, closed the door and read the passage again.

###

Julie stood at the door of the house she and Terry had shared. She felt a sense of freedom since she and her mom had just bought a 1981 Chevrolet Caprice for her. It was yellow with a little rust here and there, but she loved it for the independence it gave her. Plus, it was sturdy, which gave her a little assurance for Angie's safety.

She knocked, waiting for Terry to answer the door. She knew he was home because his car was in the driveway. It was just past 5 p.m. on Tuesday. It wasn't one of his days to go "visit his uncle." She still hadn't gotten any information from him about his girlfriend.

Just as she was getting ready to knock again, he opened the door—shirtless. He looked thinner than he used to. His eyes were red around the edges, and his hair was a mess.

"Yeah, what do you want?" he asked.

"Can I come in? I have something I want to talk to you about."

He opened the door wider and went in the house. She followed him. The place was a mess with dishes on the kitchen and dining room table and in the sink. Julie imagined he must surely be harboring roaches.

"I went ahead and told Angie about the puppy," she started.

"You didn't need to. I could have done that. And why didn't you bring her with you?" he asked.

"I told her about the puppy because I thought I could soften the blow. I didn't tell her you backed over Rascal. I just said he was hit by a car, but he's okay now. He's just in heaven."

Angie had whimpered and said she wanted to see Rascal. Julie had held her and told her everyone would miss him and that after some time, maybe they could get another puppy.

Angie had eventually found her dog finger puppet she had gotten from the hospital doctor and pretended that it talked to Rascal in heaven.

Julie took a deep breath as they stood in the living room.

"I didn't bring her with me because I wanted to tell you something. I contacted a lawyer and I'm filing for divorce. I wanted to tell you in person rather than have you be surprised when someone shows up at the door with divorce papers."

He looked down and rubbed both sides of his head with his hands. "How does Angie fit into this?" he finally asked, looking up.

This part was going to be hard, Julie knew. "I'm filing for legal custody."

"What! What makes you think you can have custody of her? She's not just your daughter you know. I have just as much right to her as you do!"

Walking on eggshells wasn't Julie's strength, but she had to finish her thought. "Given the things that have happened and the way you have become, I feel Angie would be safer with me."

"Oh come on. Don't get holier than thou. Do you actually think I would hurt Angie? You act like you think I'm some kind of animal, and you always have," his voice escalated as he continued. "You need to erase this monster picture of me from your mind, because I don't want you poisoning my little girl with it."

Julie stiffened. "You need to look in the mirror. You have absolutely no self control. You don't even know yourself what you'll do when you get mad. You knocked me unconscious and broke my ribs. What if Angie makes you mad? What will you do to her? Besides that, you have a drinking problem that you don't want to admit. And what kind of freak looks at pictures of naked children and adults doing who knows what?"

She was talking so quickly and yelling so hard that she barely took a breath. "As bad as all that is, you won't acknowledge that someone has molested your daughter. You choose to bury your head in the sand. I don't want her with you because I don't know what other horrible things you are capable of doing or denying."

"Where are you getting these crazy ideas?" he yelled back. Why are you accusing me? Just so you can get custody of Angie?"

He grabbed her by the arm and shook her. "You will not get away with this. I'll kill you and her if you try to keep her away from me, I swear I will."

Julie suddenly realized that she'd better settle down or he might *really* kill her and Angie. He was a maniac.

She quieted down. "This doesn't mean you'll never see her again. I realize you are her father. We will work something out with the judge so you, and your parents, will have plenty of opportunity to see her." Then she paused. "On a controlled basis."

He frowned at her. She could tell he was deciding something. "All this better work out fairly. You know who my father is, and he knows people in important positions. So don't be so cocky thinking you'll get custody."

Julie wondered if she could get out of there unscathed if she changed the subject.

"Okay, well, we will see. By the way, I still have some clothes in the closet I'd like to get. Can I go in the bedroom and get them?"

He sighed and told her to go ahead.

"I'm just so mad!" he said. "I'm not the horrible

monster you think I am."

You just threatened to kill me and Angie, and you aren't a monster? She thought. But in her sweetest voice, Julie told him she was sure he wasn't a monster and that she never would have married him in the first place if she'd thought that.

As she left, she wondered, *why did I marry him in the first place?* But one thing she knew, they had a beautiful angel together whom she was going to protect—no matter what.

CHAPTER 8—AUGUST 1985

"Julie, settle down. I can hardly understand you," Melanie said. Julie had instinctively called her sister as soon as she got home from the divorce and custody hearing. Their mom had driven Julie to court—even though Julie had been sure it would be an open-and-close case leading to legal custody of Angie.

"What exactly did the judge say?" Melanie asked.

"Well, first of all, it was Judge McGraw. Remember him from our wedding? He's practically best friends with Terry's dad. I knew I was doomed as soon as I saw him. He told me it was presumptuous of me to expect custody when there was obviously no reason to think that Terry wasn't a good father. He said that just because we had our differences, there was no justifiable reason to deny Angie her father." She paused with a deflated sigh. "What am I going to do? I went through this whole exercise so I could keep Angie safe. Now I'm required to give her up half of the time until the judge makes his final ruling."

"I'm so sorry, sis. You are in such a tough position. But I don't understand why the judge didn't think that the issues of drinking, child pornography, breaking your ribs . . . . What am I missing?"

"And having a girlfriend on the side," Julie inserted.

"Yeah, when you add all those up, isn't it obvious what the ruling should be?"

"You should have been there. I've certainly gotten an education. I've made so many mistakes in this." Julie's voice choked up. "I'm so stupid."

She composed herself and blew her nose.

"When we got in that fight and he broke my ribs, I didn't tell the doctor that my husband did it. I was too ashamed. Why wasn't I thinking? So my lawyer told me there was no point in even bringing that up, because there was no supporting proof. I'd told the doctor I was walking our big dog on a leash and that it took off running and pulled me with it and I fell headlong on the sidewalk."

"What big dog is that?" Melanie asked.

"I made it up!" Julie sobbed.

Melanie reminded her again of the child pornography and how that should certainly be a red flag to the judge.

But Julie said it wasn't even mentioned because she had no proof, and again, her lawyer had told her it was pointless to bring that up without proof.

"What about the hospital report?" Melanie asked.

Julie had brought that up to the judge, who only showed slight interest when he heard the words *likely molested*. "It was like the information was interesting, but not entirely relevant. He decided not to assume that Terry did it after Terry insisted that he had no idea how something like that could have happened.

"Then his lawyer worked in how Terry was an upstanding man who worked well with children. He reminded the judge that Terry was a security guard, studying to enter the police academy, and that he volunteers at the gym every week to teach kids how to swim.

"What made me think this was going to be easy?" Julie said.

"Who was in the courtroom?" Melanie asked.

"Just Terry and me—and our lawyers. No one else was allowed in, fortunately. Terry's parents were waiting outside the building, and Mom was in the cafeteria praying."

"So, what happens next?"Melanie asked.

"This was just a preliminary hearing. The judge

will weigh the case and get back with us, but he's definitely not leaning toward giving me sole custody, that's for sure. I'm so upset I can hardly see straight."

Though it was 3:30, she hadn't even eaten all day. She just didn't feel like it.

"We're going to pick up Angie from the babysitter at Mom's shop," Julie said before hanging up.

"Wait, before you go," Melanie said. "I'm going to come visit you with the girls. I already asked Steve if we could come and stay awhile. The girls have three weeks left of summer vacation. I think we'll stay most of that time. But let me talk to Mom a little later to see if it's okay with her."

"You're kidding! I would love that so much! Mom would too. She talks about not getting to see you guys enough."

Julie felt her stomach ease a little after the call.

Of course in the few minutes on the phone, she hadn't covered everything that had happened at the courthouse. On their way out of the building, Terry's parents had approached her and her mom. Gretta said how sorry she was for this fiasco and that no matter how things turned out between Julie and Terry, they wanted to have a place in Angie's life.

Julie felt numb, so the words had barely registered with her. But the look in Terry's dad's eyes would stick with her. Bob had scowled, and the fire in his eyes was a mirror of what she'd seen in Terry's eyes during their worst fights.

"I don't know what you are thinking," Bob had said. "But I'm warning you. Don't you ever try anything stupid to keep Angie away from any of us. We know where you live."

Somewhere from deep within, Julie found it in herself to ask him, "Are you threatening us? Because if you are, let's just go back inside and have a little discussion with the judge."

In the car Julie's mom had commented, "Wow, Julie. You really put him in his place."

"Where's your camera?" Julie asked Melanie. "I have to get a picture of Angie with that clown."

"Oh my gosh, I forgot the camera!" Melanie groaned. "I think I left it on the table in the hall."

They moaned. After all, how often were their three girls together?

This would be a perfect Monday at the zoo before Melanie, Lexie, and April headed back to Nebraska. Fall was beginning to wrestle with summer, and the temperature, for once, was pleasant.

Normally the Omaha zoo was better than the Kansas City zoo. But not today. They were having a special end-of-summer Kids' Day for Charity.

"I don't like that clown," Angie announced and folded her arms across her chest.

"I do!" six-year-old April said. The clown, making balloon animals, was surrounded by kids and parents. April darted over to watch.

"I want to see some *real* animals," eight-year-old Lexie whined. They had only just gotten to the zoo, and she had already made it clear that she wanted to see the elephants.

"Be patient, Lexie. We'll see all the animals before we leave," Melanie said as they followed April to the clown.

As he finished making a mother swan and swan babies, the clown asked, "Who wants these?"

All the kids screamed at once, jumping up and down to get his attention. All the kids except Angie. She just watched and hung on to Julie. The clown noticed her and went around the other children to hand the swans to her.

"No. No. Leave me alone!" Angie screamed. She hid her face against Julie's leg, hanging on to her mother for dear life. Julie was embarrassed and surprised.

"Honey, he won't hurt you. He just wants to give you something!" She apologized to the clown.

Julie hadn't had a chance to get her bearings with Angie since Terry had returned her, just as they were packing lunches to take to the zoo.

Julie and Terry had agreed that while they were waiting on a final ruling, Terry could have Angie Thursday night through Monday morning and Julie would take her the rest of the time. Julie hated her new part-time Mom assignment, and hadn't figured out how to come to terms with the idea of Terry getting *any* custody of Angie, but she was trying to stay reserved and positive for the final ruling.

After the attention was off them, Julie stooped and asked Angie why she was so afraid of the clown. "You've seen clowns before. They are very nice."

"No. They make me take my clothes off. It's cold."

Trying to stay calm, Julie gently led Angie to a nearby bench and breathed a quick prayer that she might ask the right questions of her almost four-year-old. "Were some clowns mean to you?"

Angie told her no. But they were scary and she was afraid of them.

Julie asked her where she saw the clowns and how many there were.

She held up two fingers and said they were in a dark house. But sometimes she saw bright lights, and then she saw their faces.

Julie remembered that Angie had mentioned bright lights before. She tried to remember the context.

"Did you know anyone in the dark house?" Julie asked, grasping for straws.

"No. But I went with Daddy."

Julie asked her when this was, but Angie didn't have an answer.

"Did the clowns touch you?"

"They wanted to play doctor with me."

Julie could hardly breathe. She held both of Angie's arms as she talked to her.

"Come here, Angie," they both said. "We're getting ice cream!"

"Just a minute, Lexie," Julie shouted. She turned back to Angie, who clearly liked the idea of ice cream. She asked her again about the clowns wanting to play doctor, but Angie said she didn't want to talk about that any more.

On a whim, Julie told Angie she needed to use the restroom and wanted her to go with her.

Melanie was just walking up and heard that Julie needed to use the restroom. "I can watch her for you," she said.

"No, I *need* her to go with me," Julie said and took off on a mission to find a restroom.

When they found one, Julie asked Angie if she needed to go. When she answered no, Julie told her to come on in with her and try any way. She pulled down her pants and saw how soiled her underwear was. *Oh, it's happened again! This looks just like the last time.*

While trying to decide what to do next, Julie instinctively put toilet paper on the seat and told Angie to go. "I don't want to," Angie said. "It hurts."

"Oh Lord, no," Julie said out loud.

When they came out of the restroom, Melanie was there with the girls.

"We have to go," Julie said. Everyone complained.

"We haven't seen the elephants!" Lexie said.

With her eyebrows raised, Melanie asked Julie if everything was okay.

"Umm, I think we should go to the hospital." Julie tried to sound casual, but was about to burst.

Melanie took over. "Okay girls, we are going to leave right now. We forgot about an appointment we have to see a doctor. But I promise, we will come back tomorrow."

The girls all moaned and Melanie said that the person who was the most cheerful would get a cupcake when they got home.

Julie picked up Angie and carried her to the car, explaining that they really did need to go see a doctor. "Remember the one who gave you the puppy finger puppet? Maybe we can see her again," she said.

"Can I get a cat this time?" Angie asked.

"Maybe."

Julie saw the comprehension dawn in Melanie's eyes—Julie had told her about the finger puppet from that first traumatic episode.

CHAPTER 9—FEBRUARY 1987

Julie slumped on a swing at Roosevelt Park near the house. The air was freezing, and she only had on a jacket over her t-shirt and jeans—but she felt nothing. She was wasted from crying and had no energy to do anything but sit and drift on the squeaky swing.

The sun had already set over the trees, and lights started to glow from the windows in surrounding houses.

"Julie." She looked up to see a vaguely familiar stranger.

"I'm Elizabeth. You might not recognize me with a coat and hat on," she said.

Julie just looked at her, recalling the visit she had paid her nearly two years earlier at the women's shelter.

Elizabeth sat on the swing next to Julie and looked into the sky with her.

"Rachel told me she was worried about you and asked if I'd come to your house and check on you. Then your mom told me how worried she is and said that you walked over here."

"Hmm," Julie uttered mindlessly.

"I hope you don't mind, but I'd like to talk this through with you," Elizabeth said. "Rachel told me that Terry got legal custody of Angie at a new hearing today."

"Yes, he did." Julie looked numbly at Elizabeth. "And do you know why?"

"I do. You're mom told me. I'm sure you're probably very angry with me, but you did the right thing."

"It doesn't matter anymore, does it? Because he gets her now. He got just what he wanted, and his dad

69

was probably behind it," Julie said.

"I don't think I have to tell you that it does matter," Elizabeth said. "You took your daughter to the hospital each time you knew she had been abused because that's what a mother does. Plus, as I told you before, it's completely necessary legally."

Julie sighed heavily. "Yeah, and look what it got me." Shaking her head, she started sobbing again. "I just don't understand. I don't get it. Why?"

Elizabeth placed her hand on Julie's shoulder.

"I'm just guessing. Tell me if I'm wrong, but did each hospital report have a vague conclusion?" Elizabeth asked.

Julie confirmed that all four had said either *possible molestation* or *likely molested*, which wasn't convincing enough for the judge.

"He told me I was abusing my daughter by constantly subjecting her to invasive hospital tests. Then he told me ..." She got choked up again. "He told me I'm a horrible mother to do that to my daughter, and I was deluded to think I should have full custody of her. He said he was giving legal and physical custody to Terry effective immediately."

Elizabeth shivered. "Here, let's go sit in my car." She got up and lifted Julie's elbow to guide her out of the cold swing.

When they were in the car with the engine running and the heater on, Elizabeth continued the conversation. "This is a true injustice. But it happens more than you can imagine, and I'm so sorry it's happening to you. From what I've seen in other cases, there's not a lot you can do unless you can catch Terry engaged in something egregious. Others have hired investigators, and some have gotten results. So that's something to consider," she said. "Do you get visitation rights?"

"No, not unless Terry agrees to supervised visitation time, which I doubt he will." Julie answered. She started crying. "This is my worst nightmare.

"I know now Terry has everything to do with Angie's abuse. If he isn't abusing her himself, he is certainly letting his friends at her. I finally figured out from what Angie told me that he takes pictures of her without any clothes on. I can't even imagine what else they do to her. And there's nothing I can do about it. Why is the judge so blind? Why does he side with Terry?" But she knew the answer. It had everything to do with Terry's dad's influences, and the fact that she felt like her attorney was incompetent. She wondered whose side he was on sometimes.

"Some mothers in your situation find that they have no alternative but to run away with their children. I don't know if you have ever contemplated that. Have you?" Elizabeth asked.

Julie looked her in the eyes. "No, I've never considered that."

"If you ever think that might be your only solution, be smart about it," Elizabeth said. "It could be done successfully, but it involves changing your identities, and it's permanent. To everyone else, it would be considered kidnapping, and it's illegal. You would be hounded by the law your whole life. Basically, you would be a fugitive."

Julie shook her head. She'd find some legal way to turn this around. There surely must be something she hadn't thought of. She'd have to begin by finding a new lawyer.

"Okay," Elizabeth said. "I just wanted to throw that out there. If you ever change your mind and decide to run, please contact me. I can tell you how to do it successfully and put you in touch with people who can help you."

"Are you talking about that underground network?" Julie asked.

"You remembered. Yes, I am. If you choose to run, there are people who can guide you, and I have some suggestions I can give you."

Elizabeth put her car in gear and drove Julie home.

"I'm pulling for you. Please keep in touch," Elizabeth said before driving away.

Julie stepped inside the front door and was met by her mom. Julie couldn't help noticing the concern in Rita's eyes.

"Can we talk tomorrow?" Julie asked. "I just think I'll go to my room now."

She sat on her bed and thought, partly about the things Elizabeth had said. Then it struck her. *I can not afford the luxury of moping around and being a victim. I have a daughter who desperately needs me to rise to the occasion and figure something out.*

She pulled out her *Thoughts & Prayers* notebook, which didn't have much written in it. She opened it to read inside the front cover again.

The whole passage was a breath of fresh air to her, just like it was the first time she read it, but her spirits lifted when she read, *Teach me thy way, O Lord, and lead me in a plain path, because of mine enemies. Deliver me not over unto the will of mine enemies: for false witnesses are risen up against me, and such as breathe out cruelty. I had fainted, unless I had believed to see the goodness of the Lord in the land of the living. Wait on the Lord: be of good courage, and he shall strengthen thine heart: wait, I say, on the Lord.*

She took out the fancy matching pen and wrote in her notebook: "I can not, will not give up on my little girl. I will never again let hopelessness control me, causing me to lose sight of the goal to raise my bright, healthy angel, safe from evil."

Then she looked at the passage again and wrote, "Lord, teach me how to go forward. Please make the path clear to me and lead me out of this darkness. Don't let the enemy win the battle. Unless you help me, I will be in danger of fainting and failing my little girl. While she's in the presence of the enemy, keep her safe, and help her to know that her mommy loves her very much and is fighting for her."

Julie put her pen down, came out of her room, and went to the kitchen to make a sandwich. She was lost in her thoughts when her mom suddenly appeared.

"I thought I heard you out here. How are you doing?" she asked timidly.

"I am going to be okay because I have to be okay."

They sat down at the kitchen table.

"I just got an idea," Julie announced. "Do you have a typewriter around here somewhere?"

Just as she had done each morning for the previous week, Julie ran to the end of the driveway to get the newspaper. She sat down with it on the living room floor and opened it to the opinion page.

She scanned the names at the bottom of each of the letters to the editor, and there it was. "Mom, they finally printed my letter," she called out.

She hadn't let her mom read it before she sent it. Now she read it aloud to her.

"Someone needs to hold our judges responsible for injustices done to our children. I am referring to Judge McGraw who listened to me describe in his court the sexual abuse my five-and-a-half year old daughter has faced over the past several years while she was in the care of her father, my ex-husband, and

rather than give me custody of her, he scolded me for subjecting her to hospital tests and gave legal and physical custody to my ex-husband.

"Now there is no one to look out for the safety of my daughter because rather than think for a second that I was telling the truth, Judge McGraw caved in to pressure from outside influences that were no doubt behind this reprehensible decision.

"I am not making up stories in order to get custody of my daughter. I have hospital reports to back up the sexual abuse claims. Why did he disregard the reports?

"It is apparent that Judge McGraw doesn't have a daughter, because if he did, he would do everything in his power to get to the bottom of the situation and do his moral part in protecting an innocent child from a sexual predator.

"The buck needs to stop with him, but he has failed. He's failed as a judge, and he's failed as a human being. I dare someone, anyone, to check into his qualifications to be a judge."

She put the paper down and looked at her mother. "Can you believe they printed it?" she asked.

"I can't believe you had the courage to *say* that, is what I can't believe. But anyway, you did say it very well. You are an articulate writer," Rita conceded. "You know, I'm going to take this with me to my Bible study later today and read it, and we are going to pray that something will become of this."

"Thanks, mom," Julie beamed. "Now I better get ready to go to work."

Julie's mom had put up signs at church and at her shop for anyone needing a house cleaner. It was something Julie thought she could easily do to earn some money, and now she already had three clients.

But first she stopped in Angie's empty room and

looked around at the bright pink and green wall paper adorned with flowers and ladybugs. A matching blanket and pillow case were on the bed with her stuffed animals and dolls neatly lined up, waiting for her to come home.

Julie's heart ached to tuck Angie in bed at night and read to her and tickle her when she woke up. She missed the tea parties and giggles and wiggles.

"You hang on tight," Julie said into the air. "We will get you away from him and back home where you belong."

She felt a sense of victory in seeing her letter in the newspaper. People would read it and hopefully rally on her side to do something about that horrible judge.

Then she had another thought. What if she photocopied the letter to the editor and handed it out to people—near the courthouse? She laughed out loud. That's exactly what she would do.

Soon she was off to clean her first house. She only had one other house that day, at 3 o'clock, so she came home for a few hours at lunchtime.

While she was spreading tuna salad on her crackers, the phone rang.

To her surprise, it was local television news reporter Theresa Scott. "I was reading the opinion page of the newspaper, and your letter caught my eye," she said. "I was really moved by your situation. It seems like there really is an injustice there, and I asked my producer if perhaps we could do a story on this. Would it be okay with you if I came over for a visit and taped a segment for the news?"

Julie's heart fluttered. *Wow. The media.* "Of course I'll do it." What an opportunity to shake things up. However, she did have that house to clean at 3 o'clock and it would take the rest of the afternoon. Theresa offered to come to the house the next morning at 9 o'clock with a cameraman.

Julie called her mom at the shop, and they both agreed that this could open doors for her to possibly get Angie back.

Elated at the idea of telling her story to the world, Julie wrote down notes of everything she wanted to remember to say in the interview. Before she knew it, it was nearly 3 o'clock. She quickly put on her coat and scarf and went to her car.

She noticed an envelope under the windshield wiper. It wasn't sealed and there was no writing on the envelope. She opened it and pulled out a slip of paper.

"You had better think before you say anything like that again."

She blinked and read it again. Then her mind raced. *Who wrote this? I don't recognize the writing. It's not from Terry. Whoever it is knows where I live. Terry's father has my address.* Actually, many others had her address too. She had to fill out forms for the court, so obviously the nasty judge had her address too.

What would this person do if she did speak up again? Then a thought occurred to her for the first time: *Judge McGraw. I just offended him. He has the power, and now probably a stronger will, to make sure I never see Angie again.* Her heart started to race. *I bet I just shot myself in the foot.*

But just as quickly, she had another thought. This note would make her television news story that much more interesting and enraging to those who could see her side. She vaguely recalled a few words from the passage inside her notebook. Didn't it say something like *Deliver me not over to the will of my enemies?* She felt like she needed to write in her notebook. But it would have to wait until after she returned from her house cleaning.

As she drove, Julie recommitted her resolve to do anything to get Angie back. *It might get hard, but I know it's hard on Angie too, and I'm going to be strong for her and not shrink back in fear.*

Julie and her mom walked the reporter back to the news van. The interview and video session had lasted about 45 minutes. Julie told her story and answered questions about the abuse, and the hospital visits, and pondered the mystery of why she was denied access to her sweet little girl when she wasn't the one who had abused her. At that point, she had broken down and asked to be excused, hoping the cameraman would turn off the camera. Theresa had turned to him and nodded to turn it off.

Julie finally continued with her disgust at the justice system that would turn a blind eye to child sexual abuse, allowing it to continue.

She felt like she got her point across well. When the interview was done the cameraman asked to see Angie's room and taped Julie looking at the room, wishing her child was there.

In the driveway, Theresa offered her sympathy. "I like doing stories like this because it gives me a sense of purpose," she added. She agreed that something should be done, and that maybe this segment could play a part in a resolution.

"When will this be on the air?" Julie asked.

"I'm hoping they have room for it tonight on the 6 o'clock news. It depends on what breaking news happens today. If it's not on tonight, then hopefully tomorrow night."

Julie and her mom made dinner early so they could be sitting and eating when the news came on. They could hardly wait for 6 o'clock. Sure enough, at the beginning of the news, a short promotional piece about what was coming up later showed Julie's face. The announcer said a local mother was doing whatever she could to get justice for her daughter who was being abused.

Finally, about 6:15, the piece came on. Much of what Julie had said was not aired. They only devoted about three minutes to it. But she felt like the gist was conveyed adequately, and the video of her looking around Angie's room gave an impression of her little Angie that hopefully would move someone or some group to some kind of action.

Julie wondered if Angie saw the news. She wasn't allowed to talk to her daughter, though she had tried many times. Either no one answered the phone or Terry would not put Angie on the phone. Visits were out of the question. That's what gave Julie the drive to do as much as she could.

She also wondered if Judge McGraw happened to watch the news. If not, she was sure others would tell him about it. She could only hope.

The rest of the evening the phone rang as friends called to say they saw the news. Elizabeth, Rachel's aunt, was one of them.

"Julie, I'm so proud of you! You did an excellent job. And it was so smart of you to wear a dress for the interview. It made you look like a wholesome mother," she said.

"You noticed! That's exactly why I wore a dress. I'm so glad the mommy image came across."

Before she went to bed, Julie pulled out her *Thoughts & Prayers* notebook. *The Lord is my light and my salvation; whom shall I fear? The Lord is the strength of my life; of whom shall I be afraid?*

She needed that perspective, because she was a

little afraid of the results of that newscast. "Dear Lord," she wrote, "Let something good come out of this. Please let me see my little girl again. And please, as always, keep her safe tonight and let her know her mommy loves her." Then she added. "And let her know that you love her."

She dozed off, and the next thing she knew, the phone was ringing. Julie looked at the clock. It was 9:15 a.m. She grabbed the phone and tried not to sound like she had just awakened.

"Hello, Mrs. Bradley? My name is Debbie Graves and I'm from the welfare office. We were just contacted about a case involving a child, your child, who needs assistance."

Julie sat straight up in bed and ran her free hand through her hair. "Yes?"

"It has come to our attention that abuse might be involved. We would like to assign a case worker to check into the situation and see if we need to step in to protect the child."

Julie didn't know what to say. "That sounds great, but I don't really know what to say or what exactly this means."

The woman explained that Terry was also being contacted and that separate meetings would be set up with all parties involved, and statements would be taken, including statements from Angie. Finally, a court hearing would decide what should be done for Angie. There would be another round of investigation, this time by the government.

Is this a positive thing? She could only hope.

"Okay." Julie was caught completely off guard. Then she thought to ask, "How did you know about this?"

"Your attorney turned in a report this morning," the woman said. "And your attorney is petitioning the judge to appoint a guardian ad litem for Angie.

I thought he was so lame. He must have seen the news, Julie thought.

"In fact, you will probably want to call your attorney," Debbie said. "A caseworker will contact you within the next week to set up a time to take your statement. I'm just calling to get the process in motion."

Julie thanked her, got up, and quickly put herself together. First she called her mom at work. Rita was as shocked and speechless as Julie had been. But they agreed, this was certainly a step in the right direction.

Then Julie called her lawyer's office. She got his secretary, Beverly.

"Yes, Mr. Samuelson saw you on the news last night and felt there was more he could do to turn this around, so he just filed the report. I didn't expect them to contact you so quickly. Mr. Samuelson was going to call you later this morning. He's with someone right now or I would put him on."

"That's okay. But what all does this mean?" Julie asked, hoping that Beverly wouldn't make her wait to talk to her lawyer.

"Your case worker will act as a fact gatherer, taking statements from everyone about your daughter's welfare."

"Angie. Her name is Angie," Julie said.

"Right. Well, the caseworker will talk to Angie as well and see what she will say about how she has been treated by her father and anyone else. After everyone's statements have been gathered, there will be a welfare hearing."

"With a different judge than Judge McGraw?" Julie interrupted.

"Correct. This will be a judge specializing in child welfare cases," Beverly said.

"Is it possible I'll get Angie back . . . quickly?" Julie asked.

"It is possible. But I have to warn you of another possibility. I only say this because you need to know. It is possible that the judge would determine she needs to be put into foster care."

"What! How much worse can this get?"

"I'm only telling you it's possible. Hopefully that won't happen in your case," she said.

When the call was over, Julie had to concede that involving welfare was probably the best she could hope for. But now she worried about Angie being interrogated by another stranger and the possibility of losing her entirely. She sat down in a heap on the couch. "Oh, Lord, please help."

Then she had that feeling again—the realization that if she didn't fight for her daughter, no one would. This situation was progress, and she'd better rise to this occasion too. So she got up, fixed breakfast, and called her mom again.

Julie met the case worker at the door. Sandra Redding was a short, pudgy woman with dark curly hair. She almost seemed masculine in her brown polyester leisure suit. She certainly seemed confident.

Sandra explained that she had been a case worker for 11 years. "Just to put you at ease, there's nothing to worry about. I am here to get to the truth of what is going on. I'll just let you tell me your story and occasionally I'll ask you some questions. Just so that I won't have to sit here and write notes fast and furiously, I plan to tape our conversation. That way I won't miss anything, and we'll have proof of what you said."

"Okay, well, let's sit at the kitchen table. Let me get you a drink," Julie offered.

"First, I want to tell you that in cases involving young children the best way to get their statements is by using a psychologist. So I have assigned one to go visit Angie. It will be a woman, and she will have a taped conversation with her somewhere where Angie feels comfortable. "

"Oh, she is the most comfortable here with me," Julie blurted.

"No, we can't do that. Neither you nor your ex-husband will be present when the psychologist meets with her."

"Does this psychologist have experience working with young children?" Julie asked. She was far more concerned with the discomfort Angie might experience than with her own interview.

"Working with children is what she does. Most parents are shocked at what she can learn from their children that they themselves can't get," Sandra said. "Any more questions?"

Julie shook her head.

"First, let's start with any documents you have indicating abuse," Sandra suggested.

Julie went to a drawer in her room and pulled out the four hospital reports.

"My goodness. You have certainly been vigilant," Sandra said.

"Yes, I have, and now can I tell you my story?" Julie asked.

"Please, go ahead."

Julie explained their rocky marriage and how Terry had started off as a loving man, but soon morphed into something she didn't recognize and that it was likely a result of drinking too much, which she didn't realize was happening.

"He's a closet drinker for sure," Julie added.

They both wanted children badly and were thrilled when Angie arrived. "Although interestingly enough, Terry left in a fit of rage at the baby shower, and minutes later I went into labor. He got to the hospital just as I was delivering Angie."

She talked about the day her mother gave Angie a bath and how they saw bruises and soiled underwear and took her to the hospital.

From there, Julie went over the other rough encounters she'd had with Terry and the other times it was obvious Angie had been molested and how she'd taken her to the hospital.

Sandra was at Julie's house for three hours listening and asking questions and making notes while she taped the conversation.

Julie realized she had probably said far more than Sandra wanted to hear, including her opinion of Terry's father and the influence he probably had on the judge's decision. Maybe it was more therapeutic than anything, for Sandra did not take sides nor encourage Julie's suspicions.

"Well, thank you for coming," Julie said as she walked Sandra to the door. "What will happen next?"

"I'll be in touch with Terry to get his side this week. The psychologist will meet with Angie this week too. Then we'll set up a hearing date. If you don't hear anything in about a week, you might call your attorney," she said. "However, I've also heard that a guardian ad litem is being appointed on Angie's behalf, so it will take a little more time than usual."

Julie felt fidgety with all kinds of thoughts flashing in her mind. She felt as if she'd just rehearsed her whole life. She had to do something, so she got out her recipe notebook and found the perfect recipe. She would make a Texas sheet cake. It called for three sticks of butter, sour cream, cocoa, and a pound of confectioner's sugar. Nothing sounded better. Off to the store she went with her grocery list.

As she rounded the dairy aisle with her cart, standing right in front of the ice cream case was Angie with Terry's mom Gretta.

"Pookie!" Julie yelled.

"Mommy!" The two ran toward each other and ended up in hugs and kisses on the floor.

"Ohhhh, it's so good to see you!" Julie swooned. "I love you sooo much!"

"How come you never come see me?" Angie asked.

"You can't see her," Gretta announced.

Julie glared at her, then turned her attention to Angie.

"Honey, I want to come see you so bad. And I'd love for you to come home and sleep in your room. And you could play with your stuffed animals and dolls and we would have tea parties. I hope that someday soon we can do that. What fun things have you been doing?"

"Grandma took me to the circus. We saw elephants and bears!" Angie said. "But Mommy, take me," she said, hugging Julie. "Daddy is mean."

Julie looked up at Gretta.

"We have to go now," Gretta said, taking Angie's hand.

"But you haven't gotten her ice cream yet," Julie said. She looked in the case with Angie. "Here, why don't you get vanilla ice cream and some root beer for a root beer float," Julie suggested. Angie grabbed Julie's neck and hugged her hard again.

"I love root beer floats!"

"The root beer would just go bad before we could use it all," Gretta said.

84

"Well, why don't I buy it for you," Julie stated.

"I saw you on TV," Angie announced. "But Daddy took me away."

CHAPTER 10—APRIL 1987

What more needed to be said? Julie was squirming in her seat with a box of Kleenex sitting on the table in front her in the court room. Terry was seated at the table next to her. Their lawyers sat on the inside near the aisle, so at least Julie didn't have to look at him.

Sandra, the caseworker, was standing to the side at a podium, and Judge Brecken was seated behind a big desk facing everyone. Sandra had just finished reading the notes from the psychologist's visit with Angie, as well as recommendations from the guardian ad litem. Angie's report was as bad as Julie had imagined, and she grieved for her daughter, wondering how she could ever bounce back and live a normal life after all that abuse.

Julie noticed that the judge was very interested in what he was hearing. That was good, because she had feared he might be like Judge McGraw, who hated Julie and disregarded all the facts.

Both she and Terry had told their sides of the story, and of course, he denied any wrong-doing. It was brought up again that he was studying to be a cop and that he was upstanding in community service. But Angie had described some horrific circumstances that were very painful, and certainly humiliating, had she been old enough to understand that part. The description was awful. As the findings were revealed, Julie had sobbed and yelled "Why? Why does she have to go through this?"

Her outburst was stifled by the judge.

"I think I've heard enough," Judge Brecken said. "I'll call for a recess. We will reconvene in two hours at 4:15."

Everyone relaxed. Julie's lawyer ushered her into the hall to a bench with a vending machine nearby. "This is where I usually wait," he said. "Would you like a Coke?"

"Yes, please." She sat quietly for a minute unable to fathom the horrible things that had happened to Angie. She so badly wanted to find her and take her away from Terry.

"So, how do you think it went? I mean, how do you think the judge took it?" she asked.

"I think it went very well for us. You did a terrific job of keeping to the facts. Emotional tirades tend to turn judges off," he said. "I don't think you gave him any concerns. I don't think Terry was convincing in his defense. He just didn't come across like a concerned innocent father. And Angie's story was very compelling. I think it looks very positive for you. You may have Angie back today, with any luck."

That was something Julie tried not to dream of too seriously, because she'd been let down hard before.

"My sister is here from Omaha waiting with my mom at our house. Can I call her now?" Julie asked.

"I don't see why not. In fact, they might as well come wait with us."

She found a pay phone and called home.

"In consideration of everything that was said here today, I will tell you that it didn't take two hours to come to the conclusion that Angie has been severely abused. At age five-and-a-half she has already had a lifetime of experiences that most of us could never imagine," said Judge Brecken.

"I am convinced that Julie had nothing to do with the abuse. I see her as a loving parent living the hell her daughter has gone through.

"It seems quite evident from Angie's statements that Terry has behaved despicably as a father, and at best, has observed the molestation.

"Terry, I'm not sure how you could stoop to this level. I would like to give you the benefit of the doubt, considering your career ambitions and your community service. But I could not live with myself if I did give you the benefit. It sounds as though one judge gave you more than enough chance to prove yourself, and you haven't. You endangered—and I'm inclined to conclude that you have harmed—your own child. Shame on you."

Julie leaned forward in her chair and barely breathed, as did her lawyer.

"So, I believe the choice here is clear. Angie would be better off in the sole custody of her mother."

Julie gasped and uttered a loud "*Thank* you!" She put her head down on the table and cried, releasing all the pent-up anticipation of this moment.

"Angie should be released to her mother today. I expect her to be sleeping soundly in her room at her mother's tonight. Can we make that happen?" he asked, directing his attention to Terry.

"Yes, your honor," Terry said quietly.

"And we would like to petition for visitation rights," Terry's lawyer said.

"Has he not had enough opportunity to abuse her?" Julie's lawyer asked.

"I was about to come to that," Judge Brecken said.

"I am generally not inclined to deny visitation rights as I believe it is important to maintain healthy bonds. If I felt the bonds between this child and her father were healthy, I would grant more liberal visitation rights. But as it is, I will only allow supervised visits once a month for two hours. I will let

Ms. Redding work out those arrangements, as well as assure that Angie is transferred to her mother today."

Julie was beyond thrilled at the prospect of getting Angie back and away from abuse.

When they were finished, Julie went up to the judge. "I could hug you. Thank you so much. You will never know how much this means to me."

"Good luck to you," he said. "I hope we got it right today."

Then Julie approached Terry, who was looking down at the table. He hadn't moved yet.

"Terry, I don't even know what to say to you." Then she looked around. No one was listening. "But I know what you've done to her, and I don't want you to ever have a chance to do anything to her again. I just hope she can grow up to live a normal life."

Terry smirked. She turned and walked away, thanking God that the worst was over.

She walked out of the courtroom to the hall where her mother, sister, and two nieces waited. They hugged and cheered, and Julie beamed with gratitude. The black cloud that hung over every thought for the past several months was gone.

Sandra, the caseworker, congratulated Julie and expressed her pleasure that the hearing had turned out in Julie's favor.

"I will get Angie and bring her to your house as soon as I can get over there and collect her things," she said.

"Thank you for all you did," Julie said, hugging her. She saw Terry's parents talking to him. They all looked angry, and especially Terry's dad. He looked at Julie just as she looked at him. He scowled and shook his head. Julie just hoped there was nothing he could do to sabotage this justice.

Julie and her family walked to the car, talking

about how they would celebrate that night. Julie felt a tap on her shoulder. She turned around and was startled to face Terry's dad. "Don't you try to keep her away from us. It wouldn't be to your advantage."

His harshness made her stomach flip in the same way the note on her car several weeks earlier had, and she asked, "Were you the one who left a note on my car a few weeks ago?"

His face turned red. "I don't know what you're talking about." He turned and strode away.

"Can we stop by the store on the way home?" Julie asked. "I want to buy a cake mix and some ice cream and root beer."

At home, Julie recruited Angie's cousins to help make the cake. They also helped Melanie and her mom make *Welcome Home* signs—one for the front door and one for Angie's room.

"Maybe we can go to the Kansas City zoo this weekend and see elephants," Julie told Lexie.

A few hours later, there was a knock at the door. Everyone ran to the door and found Sandra and Angie.

"Mommy!" Angie shouted as she was scooped up and hugged and kissed. Everyone took turns to personally welcome Angie home.

"We made cupcakes," April announced. The girls squealed with delight.

"You all enjoy each other," Sandra said before departing. "I'll be in touch later with the arrangements of when Angie can begin having visits with her dad."

Angie suddenly became quiet and withdrawn. Julie picked her up and kissed her and asked her if she felt okay.

"Mommy, please don't make me go back to Daddy. He hurts me."

Julie wanted to promise her she wouldn't have to see him ever again. Instead, she made the best promise she could. "I promise that you won't have to see him again alone. There will always be someone else there with you."

Angie started to cry. "I don't want to see him anymore." She became almost like a rag doll with no energy.

"Would you like to sleep with me tonight?" Julie asked.

"Yes!"

Julie's heart ached. She couldn't imagine what hurts and confusion Angie must be holding inside her little innocent body.

CHAPTER 11—JUNE 1987

"No! Don't make me go see him!" Angie screamed. A welfare supervisor had just arrived to pick up Angie to take her to the courthouse for her two-hour visit with her father. They would meet in the courtyard with a representative near at all times.

Angie ran to the bathroom and locked herself in, crying and refusing to come out. Julie didn't want her to have to go, but she had no choice. So she calmly asked Angie to please open the door for Mommy. She eventually did.

"Can you be a big girl for Mommy and go with this nice lady? Daddy won't hurt you. He is going to play with you at a playground with others around."

"But he always plays with me at a playground, and I don't like it," she cried.

"Well, it's only for a few hours, then you can come home and we'll make something you enjoy. How about a pizza?"

"Can we finger paint?" Angie asked.

"We certainly can."

Soon she was off, and Julie collapsed on the couch. *What kind of sick world is this that I am forced into coaxing my daughter to spend time with her abusive father? Is this what life is going to be like forever? I want to protect her from him, not make her go see him*, she thought. Every time Angie came back from spending time with her dad, she was an emotional wreck. She would wet the bed, lose all her energy for a few days, and be a sassy little brat, the exact signs Elizabeth had told her she could expect.

As she contemplated this new lot in life, the phone rang. Julie thought about letting it go to the answering machine, but decided she better not.

"Hello, Julie? This is Terry's father."

Julie sat up, her heart in her throat. "Yes?" she said.

"I'm calling you while Terry has Angie so I can talk to you privately. Terry's mother and I feel this arrangement with Angie is not in everyone's best interest. There is no reason why we as grandparents should suffer in the crossfire between you and Terry, so we are petitioning for visitation rights. I want to prepare you for this so you won't be caught off guard. This has been difficult for everyone, but I think we can come to some sort of balance that won't necessitate one person having complete control of Angie."

"She is not a pawn," Julie stated. "She is my daughter."

"And she's our only grandchild," he interrupted.

Julie thought she should get a complete understanding. "Just what kind of visitation rights are you looking to get?"

"Well, unsupervised rights. After all, we haven't been accused of anything," he said. "And I know the people to talk to and the forms to fill out in order to get visitation rights, so I'm certain we can accomplish this. That's why I'm calling you. I want you to get used to the idea so it will be less traumatic when we have her for a day or a weekend."

Julie dared to ask, "And if you get visitation rights, will Terry be there too?"

He paused. "I don't see why he couldn't be there."

"Okay, thank you very much," she said and hung up.

That does it! Julie stood, took deep breaths, and paced around the living room. She felt like Angie was slipping through her fingers once again. Angie wasn't free of Terry after all. This was her worst nightmare coming true—again.

"It's just not possible to avoid the abuse, is it?" she asked aloud to the thinning air in the room.

She sat down again. "I know what I'll do."

She looked up a number in her address book and dialed.

"Elizabeth? This is Julie. Are you doing anything right now?"

"Why? What's going on?" Elizabeth asked.

"I think I need some advice. Can you come over here?"

Elizabeth agreed, and with Rita at work and Angie away for a few hours, Julie felt she could have some quality time.

In 15 minutes, Elizabeth was at the door, ushered in, and given a glass of orange juice.

"How great is it to have Angie back?" Elizabeth asked with a smile.

Julie explained that it was wonderful, but mentioned the behavior issues, which she concluded must surely be normal, given the circumstances.

"Probably," Elizabeth said, "Though I'm not a psychologist."

"I know. Let's sit down in the living room," Julie said. "I need to ask you something. It's about what you said, about your network."

"Oh, that. Why do you bring that up?"

Julie explained the visitation arrangements and the phone call she had received from Terry's father. "I don't see any way to keep Angie away from Terry and out of danger. He can easily go see her and do who knows what at his parents' house. Who's to say they would be at the house the whole time watching Terry? I'm sure they will be more lenient with him than a welfare representative."

"You could be right," Elizabeth said. "So, tell me, are you seriously thinking about running with her?"

"I don't know," Julie admitted. "I haven't had time to think about anything, but I need to talk this through with someone, and I think I need to hear what you know."

"Okay," Elizabeth said. "But as I mentioned before, if you run with Angie, this will be a permanent decision. You will be hounded by local authorities, and if they find out that you have left the state, you will be hunted by federal officials, and they have policemen and the FBI and private investigators at their disposal."

Julie began to wonder. Maybe she shouldn't have had Elizabeth come over. She wasn't sure she had whatever it would take to launch that much upheaval.

"What I'm worried about," Elizabeth continued, "is that the moment you think that Angie is really in danger of being abused again, you might snap and run with her without thinking first—and that would really be a bad thing. She could be taken away from you permanently if you are caught. So, I'll tell you what you need to know so you will be completely prepared. Do you have something to write on?"

"Wait a minute." Julie ran into her room to get her *Thoughts & Prayers* journal. Then she listened as Elizabeth laid out the stark realities of life on the run and how she could survive.

"Write down my phone number, first of all. You'll need that so I can direct you to the right people who will take you and Angie in. There are families all over the country who will be sympathetic to your cause. They have taken people like you in before."

That was reassuring to Julie.

Elizabeth discussed school, and it turned out that it was good that Angie had not started kindergarten yet and therefore didn't have school documents that would need to be transferred. She was supposed to start kindergarten in just a few months.

"Be sure to always enroll Angie in private schools. If she's in a public school and you guys are found out, the principal will automatically turn you in to the police. Private school administrators are more likely to first ask what's going on and give you the benefit of the doubt. This is very important."

Elizabeth told her to keep copies of school records as well as identification in one place, and preferably not at the same location where she was staying, if at all possible.

She explained how someone would help her and Angie create a new identification, which was sometimes the hardest part of the whole process.

"Another thing, don't carry suitcases. They are too obvious. Always have big plastic bags. When you move from one place to another, no one will be suspicious if you carry plastic bags."

Her next point really jolted Julie. "You will not be able to call or write to any family members—the police will likely stake them out, perhaps tapping their phone lines. Your family can't know where you are. It's in your best interest as well as theirs for them to not know where you are."

Julie quit taking notes. She didn't think she could go to this extreme. *Not tell my mom?*

"If you run," Elizabeth said, "you need to take this paper you've written with you. You can't have these notes sitting around for the police to find."

"Oh, if I run, this journal is the first thing that will go with me," she said. "It's like a body part."

Elizabeth told her to start a list of the things she would take with her so if the time came, she could gather everything quickly. She also told her to take whatever money she had in the bank and keep it in the house. It would do her no good in the bank after she ran. She should also take her car title with her. "And be sure to buy a pager. That will become incredibly important."

As she got up to leave, Elizabeth wished her luck. "If you run, just know that you are not the first mother to do this. It can be done successfully, and while it will be a nomadic life, if you are smart about it, Angie can have a normal life, free from abuse."

After Elizabeth left, Julie sat again and thought hard. She opened her journal to the front cover to see if there was any guidance there.

Teach me thy way, O Lord, and lead me in a plain path, because of mine enemies. Deliver me not over unto the will of mine enemies: for false witnesses are risen up against me, and such as breathe out cruelty. I had fainted, unless I had believed to see the goodness of the Lord in the land of the living. Wait on the Lord: be of good courage, and he shall strengthen thine heart: wait, I say, on the Lord.

She wrote in her journal. "I need to trust God to lead me. But I also need to make myself ready for whatever I need to do next. I will not let the enemy have my daughter, and I will do whatever I have to do to protect her, even if it's uncomfortable. I am responsible to God for her. I'm not even sure God would forgive me if I forced my daughter to go see her father for him only to abuse her again. I will not put her through that. Dear Lord, hear my prayer. Teach me your way. Make your path plain to me and give me strength to do whatever I have to do."

When she finished writing in her journal, Julie felt assured that time would tell what she was supposed to do. She flipped the page and made a list of things she would take—if it ever came to that.

When she finished her list, Julie looked at the clock and saw that she had time to go to the bank down the street and close out her lockbox and account. She would not tell her mother what she was up to.

CHAPTER 12—AUGUST 1987

"Here, let's buy these four dresses," Julie told Angie after spending 20 minutes in the dressing room and amassing a pile of clothes as Rita kept a steady supply of options coming their way. Julie and her mom were cheerfully devoting their Saturday to buying school clothes and supplies for her. It was only a few weeks until the first day of school.

They finally emerged from the dressing room and faced a line of women and little girls standing at the cash register with the same agenda.

"What does that sign say?" Angie asked.

Julie followed her finger. "It says 'cashier.'"

"Pretty soon, I'll be able to read signs. They teach you how to read in kindergarten, you know," she said.

"Yes, but I don't want you to get your hopes up that they will teach you how to read the first day of school," Julie warned. She remembered that she thought she would be able to read the newspaper when she came home from her first day of kindergarten.

"Are we hungry yet?" Rita asked. They all agreed it was time to go home and make lunch.

As soon as they walked into the kitchen from the garage with all their bags, Rita saw the light blinking on the answering machine. She pushed the button to listen to the message.

"Julie, this is Sandra Redding with the welfare office. I'm wondering if you could please call me back as soon as you can."

As Julie listened, the bottom dropped out of her stomach. "Mom, I feel like this is going to be bad news." She had told her mother about the call she had received from Terry's dad. "I'll call her from your bedroom, if it's okay."

Sitting on the edge of her mom's bed, Julie dialed Sandra's number.

"Hello, Julie, thanks for calling me back. I know it's Saturday, but I've just heard from my supervisor that Terry's parents have been approved for visitation rights with Angie. It looks like the arrangements will be that they get her from Friday night to Saturday night every other week."

Julie fell back on her mother's bed. "Oh no. Why? Can't you stop it?" she asked.

"I understand how you feel, believe me. I think it's odd myself."

"Do I need to call my lawyer?" Julie asked.

"Well, to be honest, I don't think that would help. Terry's dad hired a high-powered attorney to help get visitation rights, and the judge told him that there should be no problem."

"What judge was that?" she asked.

It turned out that a new judge was consulted, whom Sandra didn't know much about. "To be honest," Sandra said, "Your father-in-law is a shrewd and well-connected man in this city, and I'm sure that he used whatever powers he has."

Julie groaned. Sandra certainly grasped her father-in-law predicament. Any argument with Sandra would probably be pointless. But she had to try. "I do not want to give Angie over to them. What if I just refuse?" she asked.

"That would be the wrong move," Sandra advised. "They could get their lawyer on it and file contempt of court charges. Then your situation would be even worse. And I don't have to tell you what that means, do I?"

This time Julie sighed and felt the blood rush to her

face. "Ug! I could just scream! When is this supposed to go into effect?"

"Starting next Friday night."

Julie hung up with a moment of certain clarity. *I am not going to let Angie be in Terry's parents' house. I know what Terry will do. It's too dangerous.* She knew what she had to do, and she had exactly one week to pull it off.

Julie went out to the kitchen to help her mom fix lunch.

"So, what was the phone call about?" Rita asked.

"Sandra said that Terry's parents get visitation rights from Friday night to Saturday night every other week, beginning this Friday night."

Rita asked Julie what was to keep Terry from going to his parent's house when Angie was there.

"Surely they wouldn't allow that," Julie said dismissively. She actually knew nothing could be done about that as long as Angie's visits with her grandparents were unsupervised.

"Well, you're handling this remarkably well," her mom said. "I'm not so sure I trust his parents."

"I'm just going to trust God to take care of my little girl when I can't be there," Julie lied.

Her words sounded hollow to even herself. There may be a time to be passive and sit back and trust, but not now. This was a time to gather her strength and do what she knew she needed to do, but her mother couldn't know.

That night before she went to bed, Julie opened her journal. She drew a line down the center of a page to write a "pros and cons" list of running away with Angie. The cons came to her mind easily. Running with Angie would make them vagabonds, a very uncomfortable prospect. Angie would be ripped away from her comfort zone and into a life of uncertainty.

She may never see her grandmother or aunt or cousins again. If they were caught, Angie might be taken away from her permanently.

Next Julie listed the pros of running away with Angie. She could prevent her daughter from ever being abused again by her father. And that was all she needed to write.

"This is the only way to settle it," she wrote. Then she wrote a prayer. "Dear God, I just can't sit back and trust you that Terry will never get hold of Angie again. I'm going to do what I have to do. Can I please trust you that you will protect us and provide for us and guide us to safety? I can't do this without you. I am just going to abandon myself and my daughter to you."

She stopped writing, for she couldn't see through her tears. After a few minutes, she read her prayer and added, "and if I die, I die." She dated it August 10, 1987.

Rita told Julie she'd like to take Angie with her to the shop, as she frequently did on Mondays. Julie knew her mom had already realized she wouldn't have those Monday opportunities much longer since Angie would soon start school.

Julie was more than happy to let her mom have Angie. For one, Julie had some things to accomplish. For another, she knew her mom's visits with Angie were numbered.

As soon as Angie and her mom were well on their way to work, Julie called Elizabeth.

"Hi Elizabeth, this is Julie, and I'm really nervous." She explained Terry's parents' new official visitation rights. "What should I do?" Julie asked.

"I can't tell you what to do. What do you think you should do?" she asked.

"I was hoping you would tell me everything is going to be okay and that Terry's parents can't have visitation rights. But you can't tell me that, can you?"

"No. I can't tell you that."

"Well, then. I do know what I'm going to do. I'm going to have to leave with her."

"How does it feel to say that?" Elizabeth asked.

"I feel pretty solid about my decision, Elizabeth. I need your help."

"Okay. I don't have to tell you how serious this is. Let me make some phone calls and get back with you," Elizabeth said. "You aren't telling your mother are you? I would strongly advise you not to."

"I'm not telling her. I'm not telling Angie either. I'll just tell her we are going for a long drive when we leave."

"Good. Now you hang in there and I'll get back with you as soon as I can with some contact information."

Julie hung up quietly. *I can't believe I'm really doing this. It feels so... permanent.* She felt confident she did the right thing, but sick at the same time.

About an hour and a half later Elizabeth called back. "There's a woman in Oklahoma City who is happy to take the two of you in. She's very sympathetic to women in your situation and likes to be a first responder. Her daughter was in the same situation and had to run with her son."

Elizabeth gave her the woman's name, phone number, and address with instructions to call her from the road after she was long gone from Kansas City.

"Do you have enough money?" Elizabeth asked.

"Yes, I've already taken out my savings. I have $3,000."

"Okay. But be assured, there is financial help available if you need it."

Wednesday morning, Julie had two houses to clean, so her mom took Angie to work with her. It was important to Julie that she clean the houses so everyone would see that life was going on normally. Plus, the money would come in handy. She also decided that when she got home from house cleaning, she would call Terry's mom and make arrangements for them to pick Angie up for their first visit on Friday night. Julie put on a cheerful voice when she called her.

"Hi there," she said to Gretta. "I was told that you have visitation rights with Angie beginning Friday night. What time would you like to come get her?"

"Yes, we are so looking forward to having her. We have a room all decorated for her so she'll feel right at home. Can we come get her at 5 o'clock? We'd like to take her out to dinner."

"Sure, 5 o'clock sounds great. I'll make sure she has her pajamas and toothbrush packed."

Next she wrote a list of everything she needed to take with her and made a trip to the store to buy a plastic, sealable folder to hold all their valuable papers, including her car title, social security card, and their birth certificates.

When she returned, she unrolled four plastic bags and packed as much as she could without raising suspicion if her mom happened to look around.

What she needed to do next was hard to think about, and Julie kept putting it off. But now it was time. She took out a piece of her favorite pink and purple flowered stationery and a matching purple envelope from her top desk drawer. She had thought about what she would write to her mother the whole day.

As she wrote, Julie couldn't decide if she should tell her mom when she would call her. She wanted to tell her, because she knew her mom would be devastated and would need some hope a promised phone call would bring. But her better judgment warned her not to give a time.

By the time Rita and Angie came home from the shop, Julie had everything under control. She had even started making tuna noodle casserole. She knew this would be their last dinner as a family.

CHAPTER 13—AUGUST 1987

R ita came home from work tired as usual on Thursday at about 5:15. She was surprised that Julie's car wasn't in the driveway. *I don't remember her saying she had somewhere to go. They must have gone to the store,* she thought.

Rita flipped on the television to listen to the news and went to her room to change clothes. She took her earrings off and attached them to the earring tree on top of her dresser. In her dresser mirror, she saw something purple on her pillow. She turned.

It was an envelope, and immediately a foreboding feeling overwhelmed her.

She read it once, not sure she understood the point. She read it again.

Dear Mom. I don't often tell you that I love you. But I want you to know that you're the best Mom I could ever imagine. I don't know when you went from being my mom to becoming my best friend, but you are. We share so many things in common. We have kindred hearts, though I think you are closer to God than I am.

Please do not worry about me or Angie as we are away. I promise you that we are not in harm's way. We are taking good care of ourselves, and we are going to remain the lovely young ladies that you have always told us we are.

You remain in our thoughts and in our prayers. Please keep us in your thoughts and prayers too.

Love, hugs and kisses, Julie and Angie

Rita was stunned. She rushed to Julie's room. Her bed was neatly made as usual, and her perfume and jewelry box were still on top of the dresser. A few books and a box of Kleenex still sat on her nightstand.

Rita was relieved that everything looked normal, until she opened the closet. Many of Julie's clothes were gone. Panic set in.

She ran to Angie's room, and her heart sank. Most of her stuffed animals and dolls were gone.

Questions flooded her mind. *Where are they? Why did they leave? When are they coming home? Who knows about this? Why didn't she say anything before about going somewhere?*

"Melanie!" Rita said aloud. *Maybe she knows something about this.* She called her.

"Have you talked to Julie today?" Rita asked.

"No. Why?"

Rita read her the note and explained that some of their things were gone.

"Wow," was all Melanie could say at first. She said it several times.

"Apparently she has run away from home. Why would she do that?" Melanie asked.

"You know, starting tomorrow night, Terry's parents are supposed to have visitation rights with Angie every other weekend. But Julie didn't act like that particularly bothered her," Rita said. But now it dawned on her *why* it didn't bother Julie.

"That must be it," Melanie said. "When I talked to her on the phone earlier this week, she seemed apprehensive about that. She was especially concerned that Terry would have greater access to Angie."

"Oh Julie, Julie, Julie. What have you done?" Rita questioned aloud. "What has been going through her head? She could be anywhere. Why didn't she talk to me about this? She has gone off half-cocked without thinking this through. She'd better come to her senses quickly before certain people find out and the consequences are irreversible."

"I don't know. It sounds to me like she has thought

this through. She probably has no intention of ever giving Terry access to Angie again. I hate to say it, but she could be gone for. . . " She paused. "A very long time."

"Well, if that's the case, she is certainly naïve. Running away with a child is beyond irresponsible," Rita stated.

"It's not irresponsible if you think your daughter is in danger, Mom. Can't you see how Julie must be thinking?"

"She just wasn't thinking straight. She's putting both of them in danger. Where do you suppose she could have gone?"

"I'm sure she'll call. She's not as irresponsible as you think," Melanie concluded. "I have to hand it to her. She sure has guts."

"What am I supposed to say when Terry's parents come to pick up Angie tomorrow night?" Rita asked.

They agreed that would set the authorities off. After all, Terry's dad *was* one of the authorities.

"Oh Lord, please bring Julie home before tomorrow night," Rita prayed.

Julie and Angie were hours into their trip headed south on I-35. They had already stopped for lunch at McDonald's in Wichita, and Julie led Angie in the fun songs they liked to sing together like "The Grand Old Duke of York" and "I'll Fly Away."

"Let's sing 'It's a Happy Day,'" Julie suggested as cars whizzed past them. She refused to drive even two miles over the speed limit, because she surely didn't want to be stopped by the police.

It was sunny and steamy hot. Julie knew she could save gas money if they turned off the air conditioner and rolled down the windows. But she opted for comfort, thankful that her air conditioner worked. It had been repaired earlier in the summer.

"When are we going home?" Angie asked.

Julie had only told her that they were going on a little trip, planning to tell her what was really going on only when she felt the time was right. She decided this was it.

"Honey, we won't be going home for some time. We are going to stay with a lady in Oklahoma City."

"But I want to go home to Grandma's," Angie whined.

"I know you do, Pookie. But remember how I promised you that you wouldn't have to be alone with Daddy again? Well, I am keeping that promise, and if we were at home, you would have to see him very soon and possibly be alone with him."

Julie held her breath, hoping that explanation was good enough.

Angie seemed to think about it for a minute. "Okay Mommy. Can I play with Chatty Cathy?"

Julie released her breath. "You certainly can. We'll pull in to a gas station soon and I'll get her out of the trunk." Chatty Cathy had been Julie's doll when she was younger, and she had passed it on to Angie, who liked to play with it only when she wanted to pretend she was an adult. Listening to Angie's conversations with Chatty Cathy were often entertaining and revealing.

Rita barely slept Thursday night. Acid churned in her stomach as she worried about Julie and Angie. When she got up Friday morning, she decided she needed to call someone in her Bible study group to get the prayer chain going.

The worst that could happen would be for someone to say something to the wrong person that would get the authorities unnecessarily involved, but she knew that was likely to happen anyway in the next 12 hours, when Terry's dad showed up at the door to find his granddaughter missing.

Rita felt like she needed prayers as much as Julie and Angie did. She, after all, was the one who would face the fallout of Julie's decision.

She couldn't skip work like she felt like doing. She had no one else to watch the shop with no advance notice. It was just as well. What would she do at home, besides worry? She could do that at the shop.

One of her Bible study friends, Diane, called her at work.

"Yes, Julie is gone with Angie," Rita told her. "Please pray for their safety. But also, pray for me tonight. I will face Terry's dad, who is a policeman. He just got visitation rights and is coming to the house to pick up Angie tonight. I can't even imagine what this will lead to."

"Have you thought about calling him ahead of time and telling him not to come over, that Angie is not there?" Diane asked. "That way you won't have to face him in person."

"No. I guess I don't want to stir the hornet's nest any sooner than I need to. Plus, since Julie is running to get away from this very situation, I want to give her as much time as possible to get as far away as possible. And I'm just assuming that's what she is doing."

After the call, Rita pondered how she should handle the situation that night. She decided she wouldn't mention the note. In fact, she would act like the absence was nothing unusual.

Rita closed the shop at 4:30, arriving home by 4:50. She quickly changed into jeans and a t-shirt and made a cup of tea.

At 5 o'clock, the doorbell rang.

In Oklahoma City, the doorbell rang. Julie hardly slept Thursday night. She looked at the bedside clock. It was 7:30 a.m., and fear gripped her stomach. She sat straight up, positive it was the police. She listened and heard Mrs. Croft speak to a man. She got out of bed and inched toward the bedroom door, trying not to awaken Angie, who was still asleep in the other twin bed. She listened closer and heard the front door close. Soon a lawnmower was roaring outside the window.

Julie would have put on her bathrobe, but she realized she hadn't packed it. So she quickly threw on some jeans and a t-shirt and went out to the kitchen where Mrs. Croft was washing a few dishes. She wore a flowered housedress and had pink sponge curlers in her hair. Julie instinctively picked up the dish towel to dry the dishes.

"I heard the doorbell ring." Julie tried to sound casual and hoped Mrs. Croft would assure her it was nothing.

"Oh, that was Adam next door. He cuts our grass. He's trying to get in as many more jobs as he can before he goes off to college next week," Mrs. Croft said. She stopped washing and looked long at Julie.

"You must be frightened. It's been so long since I took anyone in, I've almost forgot what it's like for you girls. Why don't we sit at the kitchen table? I have some cinnamon and raisin English muffins I can toast for us. Here. Let me get you some juice."

Julie sat at the beat up white wooden table. She

couldn't help but notice old, mismatched plastic cushioned chairs. The off-white wallpaper covered with small, gold triangles was yellowed. The white appliances all had brown stains and nicks. The house had certainly been well-used. Somehow, Julie felt like a young girl living in a much earlier era, or else this was a dream.

"Did Elizabeth say much about us when she asked if you would take us in?" Julie asked.

"No, but that's okay. In these situations, I like to respect privacy."

"Well, I knew it was a big decision. But now that I've made it . . . " Julie didn't finish her sentence. She didn't really know how to. She wasn't sure how she felt.

Mrs. Croft buttered the English muffins and sat down. She gazed into the distance as she bit into her muffin.

"I probably took in five other girls like you. As far as I know, only one was caught. She kept calling home, and her momma kept calling her here. Turns out the calls were traced. The police showed up at the door, and that girl put up a mighty fight, she did."

"I sure hope nothing like that happens to us. I didn't even tell my mother I was leaving. I didn't want to put her in an uncomfortable position to have to lie about where I went."

Julie ate one of her muffin halves. "But somehow, some time I will want to call her and let her know we are okay. She's probably very worried about us."

Julie looked up to see Angie in her pajamas quietly shuffle into the kitchen carrying her bunny. "Well hello there, Pookie," Julie said, holding out her arms. Angie quietly came over and sat in her lap.

"You're a shy little thing," Mrs. Croft told Angie, who just looked at her. "Do you know where you are?"

Angie shook her head. "I saw ants in the bathroom."

"There were just a few, weren't there? Here, let me give you the other half of my muffin," Julie told Angie, changing the subject.

"Why don't you girls explore around the area today. It's not too hot. And tonight, we're having a game night at church, if you'd like to come along for something to do," Mrs. Croft offered.

Hmm. That might me kind of fun. I bet people around here are pretty nice.

"Do you need any cleaning done around here? I'd be very happy to help out," she said.

"No, I cleaned up before you two came."

Mrs. Croft wasn't a big talker, Julie decided. It was probably just as well. She excused herself and Angie to get dressed. "But we'd like to go to the church game night tonight," she said before heading back into their room.

With the door closed, Julie asked Angie if she'd like to explore the neighborhood.

"Can I take Chatty Cathy?" she asked.

"Of course you can."

Angie took her doll from the black plastic garbage bag and told her to get ready. "Don't cry Chatty Cathy. This will be your new home. No one will hurt you here. I'm your mommy and I will take care of you."

Julie took the conversation as a positive sign that Angie was working through the change. She just hoped Angie would keep believing this was for her best.

After taking a walk and discovering several neighborhood dogs and visiting a few garage sales, Julie was happy to settle into Mrs. Croft's backyard where there was an old swing set. Two old wooden chairs had a weathered wooden table between them where Angie played with her Barbie dolls.

"You want to go to church tonight and play games?" Julie asked.

"Yes, I like church," Angie said.

Later, as they were in the car with Mrs. Croft, Julie asked her the name of the church.

"Word of Faith. It's a Pentecostal church."

Julie didn't think she'd ever been to a Pentecostal church before.

Before long they were inside the church basement meeting all kinds of people. Mrs. Croft introduced them as new in town.

"We are so glad to have you," one grandmotherly woman said with a friendly smile. "What is your little girl's name?"

The woman led Angie to the corner where children were playing. Julie scanned the area for any teenage or older boys who might play with the kids. She hoped there weren't any or she would have to be extra vigilant. Angie had developed a fear of older boys, and Julie couldn't blame her. She hoped Angie would eventually get over that or she would have to get a counselor for her.

Soon Julie found herself in a small group of men and women playing the card game, Spades. Other games were going on at other tables throughout the church basement. She'd never been that fond of Spades, but under the circumstances, she was just happy to blend in with some nice people.

"So, where are you from?" a 30ish looking man named Bill asked. He had dark, neatly combed hair and a mustache. Julie hadn't even considered that she would be quizzed. But of course that would happen to a new person in a group of people who all knew each other.

"Oh, I'm from the Kansas City area," she said, desperate to avoid revealing much about herself.

"She's staying with Flo," the redhead sitting next to her said.

"I'm sorry, I don't know Flo. I guess I haven't been coming here long enough to have met her," Bill said.

Flo? Julie thought. So that was Mrs. Croft's first name.

"So, what brings you to the area?" Bill pursued.

"Umm. I'm here looking to find a job." She felt her face turn red. But she was pleased that something reasonable had come out of her mouth, because she certainly hadn't thought this through.

The redhead pointed to the cards and told her it was her turn. Julie decided it was time to get the attention off of herself.

"So, Bill, what about you? What do you do?"

The older woman across the table answered before Bill had a chance to speak. "He's the church's new security man. He's an FBI agent," she said proudly. And he's single!" She winked at Julie.

The FBI? No way! Julie could hardly breathe. *Surely the woman was kidding. What are the chances that the first person I would talk to in Oklahoma City besides Mrs. Croft would be an FBI agent?* Her instinct was to go grab Angie and get out of there. Her next concern was why Mrs. Croft hadn't warned her or prevented her from this meeting with the law. But her mind instructed her to be cool and try to act like a normal person.

"You know, after this game, I think I'll go over there and play Bingo," Julie said.

She soon managed to get away from the card table, though she noticed that Bill looked at her now and then. Her new red-headed friend got up and grabbed a cookie at the same time as Julie.

"You certainly made an impression on Bill. I think he's interested in you," she said, lightly jabbing Julie with her elbow.

Julie forced a smile and said "Oh great," perhaps a little too sarcastically. She looked for Mrs. Croft, who was in a corner with some other women crocheting.

"Hi there," Julie said, interrupting their conversation. "Can I talk to you for a second?" she asked, looking into Mrs. Croft's eyes.

When they were alone, Julie told her she needed to go back to the house. "You didn't tell me about Bill."

"Bill who?"

"FBI Bill."

"I don't know who you mean," Mrs. Croft said.

"Don't you go to this church?"

"Yes, but I don't know any man named Bill."

"Well, I was just playing cards with him, and he's an FBI agent, and he's been staring at me all night! Can we please quietly leave?"

"Of course," Mrs. Croft said. "You go get Angie and I'll slip out and start the car."

Angie was coloring a picture of a horse on a mountain when Julie interrupted her and announced it was time for them to go. She picked up Angie and found her way back to the staircase. Bill came around the corner from the bathroom.

"Oh!" Julie said, stunned. "You scared me."

"I'm sorry," Bill said. "I see you're leaving. Don't be in such a hurry."

"Umm, I have to go," Julie said, walking away from him.

"Can I call on you?"

"No, thank you. Bye!"

When Julie and Angie made it to the parking lot,

Mrs. Croft already had the car waiting for them at the edge of the sidewalk. They jumped in.

"Whew, I'm glad we're out of there," Julie said.

"I had fun. I made a new friend called Laura," Angie said.

"That's nice, Sweetie," Julie assured her.

"Did you tell him where you live?" Mrs. Croft asked.

"No. I tried not to say much." Then Julie thought about the conversation at the table. "Wait, the lady with the red hair said I was staying with you. But he doesn't know who you are."

"Does he have my name?" Mrs. Croft asked.

"I suppose he does. How many ladies named Flo can a person know?"

"What else did he find out?" she asked.

Julie supposed nothing, other than that she was looking for a job.

"I see. When we get home, we'll want to have a little talk," Mrs. Croft said. This was the most emotion Julie had seen in her.

As Julie put Angie to bed, she still had a knot in her stomach, an uneasy feeling. She read a book to Angie that they had picked up at a garage sale earlier, but before she was finished with the story, Angie was asleep. Julie kissed her and told her to sleep tight. Then she went to the kitchen where Mrs. Croft was heating some water for tea.

"I didn't want to say anything with Angie listening," Mrs. Croft said. "But I think you are in danger of being caught now. You can't stay here."

CHAPTER 14—SEPTEMBER 1987

"Thanks again for buying the girls' clothes," Melanie told her mom as they all came in the house after several hours of Labor Day shopping in Omaha. I know you need to get back to Kansas City, but why don't you . . . " the phone rang. "Just a second," she said as she answered the phone.

"Julie!" she shouted.

"Julie?" Rita said. "Give me the phone." Melanie handed it over and ran to get on the extension in her bedroom.

"Julie, where *are* you?" her mother asked. "How are you? And how's Angie? Is everything okay?"

"Mom, it's so good to hear your voice! Oh, you have no idea how good it is. Is there any chance the phone is tapped?" She had to ask.

"Well, no, I don't suppose it is," Rita said.

Melanie chimed in. "Hi Sis. Boy did you stir up the hornet's nest. The FBI was here after you left, but everything is back to normal."

"It's a good thing you called here," Rita said. "My house is ground zero of suspicion."

"I figured that. That's why I haven't called until now. I remember you said you wanted to visit Melanie on Labor Day weekend. I'm calling from a pay phone. I have so much to tell you."

"So do I!" Rita said.

Melanie interrupted. "Julie, tell us what's going on."

"First, I'm sorry for leaving so abruptly. I know I caused you a lot of grief. But I did what I had to. I hope you understand. I just refused to put Angie at risk for another incident. Mom, I don't know if anyone will ever understand, but I'm the one who has to live with these . . . nomadic consequences. And I'd do it again and again. I don't care how uncomfortable it gets."

Rita stopped her. "At first I was very upset, and sometimes I still get anxious, but after what happened here the weekend you left, I see that since you got the ball rolling, there is no other path for you now unless you want to lose Angie forever. I'm just sorry you felt you had to do it."

"What happened when Terry's parents came to pick her up?" Julie asked.

"When Bob came to the door, I told him in my sweetest voice that neither one of you were there, and I wasn't sure where you were. I just tried to act like it was nothing out of the ordinary."

"And how did he take that?"

"He's certainly not good at hiding his emotions. He raised his eyebrows and asked why you and Angie weren't there. Then he yelled at me and told me that Angie better be there in the next half hour or he was getting his department on it. Then he said that as soon as I closed the door, I better be on the phone with you getting Angie home if I knew what was good for me."

"I'm so sorry to make you have to incur Bob's wrath."

"Well, that part is over, and I'm glad. He came back a half hour later. His face turned beet red when neither of you were there. He said he would forget the police and call his lawyer. I hoped it would blow over, but for the next few days, I heard from his attorney and others in law enforcement."

Rita explained all the questions she answered and forms that were filled out and ultimatums that were made. "I thought that was bad. Then the FBI was knocking on my door. I answered the same questions over and over."

Melanie jumped in. "And then I received calls and a visit from the FBI. I also saw police cars around here off and on, just kind of keeping an eye on things here for the next few days."

"Julie, it was quite the event around here. And that was just the beginning," Rita said. "Then I got a few calls from TV reporters. I refused to talk to them, but they made news stories out of it anyway, interviewing Terry's dad and some FBI guys. They are calling it kidnapping. They feel certain that you left Kansas with her, and that's why the FBI has become involved."

"Wow, that's just what Elizabeth told me," Julie interrupted.

"Elizabeth. Isn't she the one who came over to the house looking for you that one day?" Rita asked. "Who is she?"

Oops. I probably shouldn't get Elizabeth mixed in with this, and I shouldn't give Mom and Melanie information for the police to drag out of them.

"She's just a friend. But I guess I've put everyone through it, haven't I?" Julie asked.

"So how is Angie, and where are you?" Melanie asked.

"Oh, Angie is doing amazingly well. I've realized that she is so young that to her, wherever I am is where home is, so most of the time, she's content to play with her dolls and do whatever activity I suggest. She's been a real angel. She's keeping me sane. And that's kind of strange, because I'm doing this for her."

Melanie continued to press for an answer as to where Julie was. She thought about it for a moment and at least felt comfortable to discuss the first few days.

"I drove to Oklahoma City and stayed with a woman for exactly two days. She was going to keep us until we got our feet on the ground and some paperwork could be done changing our names. But I met an FBI agent by accident at a church event, and he kind of latched on to me. I don't know if he was on to me or if he was just *in* to me, but either way, he found out my name and where I was staying, so it was too dangerous to stay around there. So I left."

"Have you changed your name?" Melanie asked.

Julie explained how they were both given new birth certificates. Her name was now Brenda Mathews. Angie was now Heather. "I didn't really like *Heather* at first, but I looked it up, and it means *flower*. I think that's okay," Julie said. "Once Angie found out what her new name means, she was okay with it."

"And I'm sorry, but I can't tell you where we are right now. I can only say we're safe. Angie starts school tomorrow. Mom, you'll be glad to know she will be going to a good Christian school."

"When can you call again?" Rita asked.

"I don't know. I don't trust that your phone isn't bugged" Julie said.

"That's a disturbing thought," Rita said. "The FBI and police have been to the house several times. I didn't have my eye on all of them all the time. I hope I'm not being bugged. I frequently see police cars and other mysterious cars in the neighborhood. I'm sure they are casing the house for clues or some big break."

That answered the question for Julie. She couldn't call her mom at the house.

"And what about the shop?"

It turned out they had visited Rita there as well. So that was out.

"I just can't say when I can call again for sure. I'll have to figure something out," Julie said. "I miss talking to you so much, and Pookie misses you tremendously."

Rita asked her if she had money.

"I do. And I have some odd jobs. Hopefully I'll pick up a few more," Julie said. "Oh, who is this? I can't believe it. Someone actually wants to use this phone. I have to go."

"Heather seems to be a happy little girl," Mrs. Hutchins said. "She seems to easily get lost in her own pretend world, but that's normal for some children at this age, and especially those who are an only child."

"I think she gets along with all the others pretty well, doesn't she?" Julie asked the teacher. "I mean, it's only been a week, but you must have a feel for her."

She was assured that Heather was doing fine and adjusting well. It helped that this was kindergarten and the whole experience was new to everyone, although many of the children already knew each other from church there in Jackson, Tennessee.

Julie hoped that she wouldn't slip and call her *Angie* in public. She needed to start thinking *Heather*.

"So, tell me a little about yourself, and please call me Shannon," Mrs. Hutchins said.

Shannon had curly red shoulder-length hair and freckles. She smiled easily, but seemed sensible. She looked to be in her late 20s. She had two children, two boys. Julie was in a personal conference with her since she had missed the open house a month before school started.

"I'm not sure there's much to say. I'm a single mom and just moved here—trying to make a new beginning." She saw compassion in Shannon's eyes. "I clean houses and do any odd jobs I can find. While

I have some free time, I could help out in the classroom in any way you need me."

Shannon expressed appreciation for the offer and suggested that Julie try out the church's "Mom's Day Out" Tuesdays. "It's a great way to get to know other moms. I obviously can't go, but I know many of the ladies who do go, and I think you'd really like them."

Julie thought she'd like that. She needed to blend in more. She was feeling that her guarded life was a little too isolated. Actually, she just really missed her mother. She hadn't realized how fortunate she was to be so close to her mom and be able to tell her anything. Now she didn't have anyone to freely talk to.

That night, before they went to bed in the two-bedroom apartment the church owned, Julie asked Angie if she had a happy day.

Angie thought for only a moment. "I had a very happy day. Bethy let me slide down the slide with her, and when we got to the bottom, we splashed into the ocean and swam away from the sharks."

"Did any of the sharks get you?"

"Of course not. Then I wouldn't have a very happy day."

"Oh, you are a funny girl," Julie said, tickling her.

But Julie wanted to know more about how Angie really felt. "Who do you wish you could see more than anyone else from back in Kansas City?"

"I miss Grandma," she said with a pouty lower lip.

"Do you miss Daddy?" Julie ventured.

"No, Daddy hurts me when he goes like this, and this." She acted out some of the abuse she had received. "I don't want him to do that to me anymore."

"Pookie, I made a promise to you. Do you remember what that was?"

"Yes. You said I wouldn't have to be alone with him anymore."

"And I mean that. That is why we are living here, and you can't tell anyone about what your daddy did to you and why we don't live in Kansas City any more. We don't want anyone to find out and tell daddy where we are. Do you understand that?"

"Yes. But can Grandma come and visit us?"

That was an idea Julie hadn't thought of. "I'll have to consider that. I don't really know right now. We wouldn't want anyone, like Daddy, to follow her here and then he would find us."

"Is this like hide and go seek?" Angie asked.

"In a way. And we'll be playing that for a long time." *I wonder how long? I suppose until she turns 18, if we have to.*

Julie read her *Jack and the Bean Stalk* from the school library until Angie went to sleep.

Then Julie took out her journal. She had to find that verse. There it was: *When my father and my mother forsake me, then the Lord will take me up. Teach me thy way, O Lord, and lead me in a plain path, because of mine enemies.*

Her mother hadn't forsaken her, but she was certainly missing from their lives. *Then the Lord will take me up.* Julie wrote a prayer before she went to sleep and thanked God for that promise. "Lord, I'll hang on to that. Show me the way I'm supposed to go, and keep me from making bad mistakes along the way. Thank you for my little innocent angel. Please protect her, and allow her to see that you are taking care of her. Please take away any fear she might have."

The next morning as Julie got out the cereal for Angie, she asked her if she slept well.

"Yes. And I saw Jesus. He held me on his lap."

Julie stood there with the refrigerator door open. "Oh really? What was he like?"

"He had a beard and a white robe. He said he loved me. Oh, and he also said for me to tell you not to worry."

Julie almost dropped the milk. "Did he say anything else?"

"Umm. I can't remember."

Julie made a mental note to write that conversation in her notebook after the prayer she wrote. She suddenly felt peaceful, like a cloud had lifted. She realized she didn't need to focus on the disadvantages of her circumstances anymore. God was completely aware and was taking care of her. She could go on building a new life. It would be okay. She didn't realize how much the whole situation had burdened her heart. But that burden was gone now, and she didn't want it back.

"Pookie, let's have a great day today, okay?"

CHAPTER 15—MAY 1988

Taking a big deep breath of the fresh morning air, Julie rang the doorbell and waited. It was already bright out at 7:30, and the birds were cheerfully singing. She thought it would be a great day to take Angie to the park after she got home from school. They might even round up a few of her friends and any other mothers who wanted to come along.

What was taking Mae Bentley so long to answer the door? Julie rang again. Mae and her husband, Robert, were shut-ins. Their daughter, Dorothy, didn't want to put them in a nursing home, but neither could she take care of them. So she hired Julie to come each weekday morning to check up on them, clean the house a little, and prepare their lunch. Dorothy always stopped over in the late afternoon with their dinner.

Finally Julie heard the click of the lock and Mae finally opened the door. She was still in her nightgown, which was unusual. "Good morning, Mae. I brought you some cinnamon rolls this morning. You're still in your nightgown."

"Come on in. We're having a bad morning," Mae said. "I can't seem to get Robert out of bed. He just lays there and doesn't act like he even wants to get up."

"Well, let me see what I can do," Julie said. She was confident she could get him up. Robert loved her because she listened to his stories and challenged him with an artful wit.

She went into the bedroom and whisked open the curtains. "Good morning, Robert. Guess what, I brought your favorite for breakfast this morning. Cinnamon rolls."

But he just laid there unresponsive. His eyes were

open, and he looked at Julie. But he didn't say anything and had no acknowledging expression. This was very unusual.

"Robert, can you say something to me?" Julie asked.

"He's been like this since I woke up," Mae said. "I'm not even sure he hears us."

Julie asked Mae if he'd ever been like this before.

Just then, he groaned, then closed his eyes. There was no movement. Both women gasped.

"Honey, wake up!" Mae said, shaking him. Still no movement.

Julie took his hand and felt his wrist. She couldn't feel a pulse. "I'm calling 911," she said.

"Hello, 911. What's your emergency?"

"Hello, I'm a caretaker for an elderly couple, and I just arrived at their house, and I think the husband just . . . well, I don't feel a pulse. Something is seriously wrong," Julie said.

"Where is he?" the operator asked.

"He's in bed and he's not moving. When I got here he was awake but unresponsive."

"What's your name and give me the address."

"Uhh." In her panic Julie forgot her new name for a second. She also didn't have the address memorized. "I'm Brenda Mathews. I'm on 32nd Street." She asked Mae to remind her of the house number.

"I must call Dorothy," Mae said.

"Of course." Julie went back to Robert's side and stroked his forehead. "Oh Robert. Please wake up. Don't leave us." She couldn't bear the thought that he might be gone. She didn't want him to be gone. It was a horrible, abrupt thought. "Tell me again how you used to milk the cows and churn butter when you were growing up. Or, I know, tell me how you built the fence around your property when you and Mae were first married and the two of you spent a week painting it—and repainting it when it rained too soon."

But there was nothing. Julie heard sirens. An ambulance, the police, and a fire engine came. The house filled with men in uniforms who took over next to Robert and performed CPR on him. But nothing worked.

Mae stood on the other side of the bed in her bathrobe, looking pale as she watched, with her hand over her mouth.

Julie felt like she was watching a drama from the outside. There was nothing she could do.

Dorothy showed up soon and came in the room. She and Mae hugged as Mae explained that he was unresponsive when she woke up and how she just couldn't get through to him, and how he gasped and closed his eyes.

"Ma'am," one of the paramedics said. "I'm afraid there's nothing we can do. I think he probably suffered a stroke. I'm very sorry."

Dorothy and Mae held each other, crying. Julie felt completely helpless, without even an idea of what to do.

"What can I do to help?" Julie finally asked as the activity and squawking radios continued.

A uniformed man with a clipboard wanted to take down Julie's information. She diverted his attention to Dorothy—the daughter. "We'd like to get everyone's information that was here. It's just procedure," he said.

Julie guessed it was okay, but she hoped there was no cause to check her social security number in all this. She didn't have one to match her name. She felt guilty, in a way, for even thinking that at such a time. She told him her Brenda Mathews name and her address along with her description of events that morning.

When she was finished, Dorothy told her she might as well go home. "I'll call you and let you know what's happening and what we decide to do next."

"I'm so sorry," Julie said sincerely, giving Mae a hug. "I'll be in touch soon, and please call me if you need anything."

She drove home in a daze. Mae and Robert had become like family over the past several months. She had finally felt stable and in the groove of a normal life again.

But most of all, she felt sorry for Mae. At least she had Dorothy. And maybe they would still need her. If not, Julie would need to find another job, besides the few cleaning jobs she had rustled up. She was limited as to the types of jobs she could take, mostly cleaning and homecare since she couldn't produce a valid social security number.

If this was a normal life, she thought, cleaning and homecare wouldn't be her ideal career. But under the circumstances, she just needed to make some money to support them and live under the radar. Any job that allowed that was perfect for her.

Kindergarten was out for the year, and Julie was happy for Angie's progress. Shannon Hutchins said great things about Angie. Actually, Julie loved this age. Angie was so trusting of those around her—amazing considering the circumstances of her earlier life. Anyone her age was as good as a best friend to her. She seemed not to struggle too much with lingering effects from her abuse. She did occasionally have nightmares about mean men. Julie would sing to her—calming her and assuring her that no mean men were around. She would protect her from them.

With summer officially starting, Julie realized Angie didn't have a swimsuit. In fact, neither did she. Julie picked her and all of her school supplies up from her last day of school. She announced the plan for the evening.

"Pookie, how would you like to go to McDonald's for dinner tonight to celebrate finishing kindergarten? And then we'll go to Sears and buy swimsuits?"

Angie was thrilled. They never went out to eat, and Julie knew she thought McDonald's was the best. They would share a chocolate milkshake. Ice cream was definitely their thing.

"What would be the funnest thing you could imagine doing this summer?" Julie asked Angie as they sat next to each other in the booth finishing their french fries.

"Going to Cassie's house and playing in her backyard. She has a fort with a roof and chairs. Debra and Lindsey told me about it," she said.

Julie couldn't place who Cassie was, even though she had helped out in Angie's classroom a time or two for holiday parties.

"What does she look like? I don't think I know who she is."

"She's in the other class. I don't know her," Angie confessed.

"Well then. Let's think of something else that would be really fun to do this summer."

When they finished, they jumped in the car and headed down the street to Sears. Julie knew they usually had a good selection of swimsuits for a decent price. To get to children's clothing, they had to pass through appliances and electronics. There were always salesmen standing around rocking back and forth, heal to toe, with their hands behind their backs and trying to make eye contact with anyone who walked by to see if they might need a new stove or refrigerator.

The stoves were on the left side of the aisle, and the TVs on the right, all tuned to the same channel, which happened to be showing *America's Most Wanted*. Julie looked over and suddenly stopped with a gasp. Her heart started pounding. She grasped Angie's hand. Though the volume wasn't turned up, the pictures were screaming—images of her and Angie with flashes now and then back to John Walsh talking. Angie, who hadn't been paying attention to anything in particular looked over at the TVs. "Hey, that's me!" she said.

"Shhh!" Julie said, as she looked around. No one had heard her as far as she could tell. Julie leaned over and in a soft voice said, "Sweetie, I want you to be very quiet for Mommy right now. We are going to casually turn around and walk out of the store. I'll explain why later after we get in the car, okay?" Angie seemed a little startled. She obeyed, and the two of them turned and walked back to the car.

Oh my gosh, they really are serious about finding us. Now everyone in the country knows what I've done and what we look like.

As Julie put the car in gear to rush back to the apartment, she quickly had to think of how to collect herself and avoid upsetting Angie any further. Angie was clearly confused by the whole situation. "Honey, you're right. That was us on TV. We are on television all over the country right now. They are showing us because we ran away from home and some people who know us, like Daddy, don't know where we are and they want everyone to look for us—and turn us in to the police."

Julie hoped the car wouldn't give them away. She no longer had Kansas plates on it. Elizabeth had seen to that. They were Michigan plates.

"As soon as we get home, we will put everything we want to keep in our plastic bags and we will take a long drive. Okay, Pookie? Can you begin thinking of all the things you would like to take with you?"

Julie's heart was racing, but she was careful not to speed. She couldn't afford to attract any attention. The light in front of her turned red.

"Mommy, am I in trouble?" Angie asked.

"No. You're not in trouble, Sweetie. But this light needs to change fast!"

"Where will we go?"

"I'm not positive. But we will pack up so fast and start driving. Can you be really fast?"

The light finally turned green after what seemed like 10 minutes.

Dear Lord, please help us get out of town without being noticed, Julie prayed silently.

Then she marveled at the unusual circumstance for her to see that program that she never watched at the exact moment she and Angie were featured. It was mercifully miraculous given the fact that she had failed to follow one of Elizabeth's bits of instruction. She had told her to get a pager and give out her number to key people who could alert her when there was danger. She just hadn't gotten around to it and had become lackadaisical with how smoothly things were going. She determined that she needed to take care of that—if she got out of this situation.

She finally pulled into the apartment at 7:25. She scanned the area for anything unusual, especially police cars. Everything seemed normal. She instructed Angie to quickly go inside and load garbage bags with anything she wanted to keep.

"We only have about 5 minutes," Julie advised.

Once inside, Julie went to work. She was

organized enough to have documents all in one folder, which included reports from Angie's teacher. Julie loaded as many clothes as possible into bags. She added her *Thoughts & Prayers* journal and her recipe notebook. She looked around the kitchen and wished she could take everything. She wanted all their dishes. She decided she could take some of them. In the bathroom, she took her toiletries. Then she decided to go help Angie.

She found her taking the sheets off her bed and stuffing them along with her pillow in a bag. Julie scanned Angie's room for anything else she should be sure to take.

Julie felt an overwhelming uneasiness. She was compelled to stop packing and start loading the car. "Come on, Sweetie. Let's take these bags to the car."

It took three trips, and Julie felt she couldn't afford to go back in one more time. Instead she ordered Angie into the car. They got in, slammed their doors and Julie threw the car in reverse, then into drive and screeched out of the parking lot.

With no real aim as to where to go, she turned left onto 32nd Street and got moving. She looked in her rearview mirror and saw flashing lights several blocks down the street behind her.

Oh great. Wouldn't you know, she thought.

Then she noticed that the police car turned left into what appeared to be her apartment complex. Her heart nearly beat out of her chest. Had she come that close to getting caught?

She looked ahead and tried to concentrate on where she should go.

"Chatty Cathy!" Angie shouted. "I left Chatty Cathy in the closet. We have to go back and get her."

"No. We can't go back. You should have put her in the bag!" Julie snapped.

"But I was going to carry her."

"Well, I'm sorry, but we can't go back. The police are there right now. Honey, I need you to be strong right now, okay? Mommy has to figure out where we are going, so I need to think. Can you be strong and not cry right now?"

"Okay, Mommy." Angie said.

"Thank you." Then Julie had two ideas. *Elizabeth. I need to call her. I hope she has some ideas of where we can go now. I guess I should get out of Tennessee first. I wonder if there is some other road less traveled. I know, I'll go south on Highway 45 down to Mississippi.*

It was starting to get dark enough to turn on the headlights. She was thankful for that. Any passersby wouldn't easily spot her.

She couldn't decide where they should spend the night. For now, she would just drive as long as she could. They could be well into Mississippi by daybreak.

After a few hours on the road, Angie woke up from dozing and announced that she had to go to the bathroom. "Okay, we'll find a place to pull over, and we'll have to go outside."

She was so thankful that when they had first run, she had thought to put a roll of toilet paper in the corner of the trunk. She found a one-lane road off the highway and pulled off, shining the headlights off the side of the road in the place she chose for them.

Once they were on their way, Julie decided maybe they should try to find a motel. *I'm so tired, this is dangerous.*

Then she realized something else. When Robert

had died and the police and ambulance came, they had taken down her information. So they knew her current latest name. Actually, come to think of it, anyone the police would talk to in Jackson, Tennessee, would know her fake name. Now that she had been on television, they would all know her real name and tie it to their fake names. She would have to come up with new names for them. *We'll do that tomorrow.*

For now, she would just give some other fake name and pay for a motel room with cash. She had plenty of money saved for occasions like this.

It was about 11 o'clock, and Julie decided to take a chance. They were coming to Columbus, Mississippi. Once in the city limit, she looked for a side road that might have a motel. She found Main Street and just hoped no one had watched *America's Most Wanted.* But just in case, she did have glasses without prescription lenses and a red wig—another ingenious piece of instruction from Elizabeth.

She found another side road off of Main Street and took that for a few miles until there were hardly any more buildings. She decided she had better turn around and head back to Main Street before she got them really lost. But then she saw a tall orange neon *Motel* sign with a burnt out "o." It was on the edge of the road. She turned into the drive and followed it as it wound around through a wooded area. She heard dogs barking. There were no street lights, and Julie felt uncertain about this as the road narrowed and soon ran out of pavement. She was on a dusty rock road.

"I don't know about this, Sweetie. I think we should go back," Julie said. But there was no place to turn around. Finally, she came to two white buildings with a small parking lot and a dim street light. One looked like an office, with a light inside. A covered walkway connected it to the other longer, single-story building that looked like it had rooms on both sides of it. Each motel room door looked thin and beat up, most with gold-lettered numbers on them, though not all. They each had a little cement stoop. All were cracked and crumbling.

What have I gotten us into? Though she felt entirely uneasy, Julie decided that at least it was off the beaten path. She reached for the glasses and wig in the glove compartment. She tied up her hair and pulled on the wig, looking in the rearview mirror, though she couldn't see well. This would have to do.

"Pookie, I'm not sure about this place. I don't want to take you in there. You stay here with the doors locked while I go in and see if they have a room for us." She guessed that was the best plan for a situation like this.

She tried the office door, and it opened. Inside she saw an older, voluptuous bleached blond woman sitting behind a counter watching television. She was chewing her gum vigorously. There were no lights on in the rest of the room, though Julie could tell there was a couch and cushioned chairs.

"Yeah?" the woman barely looked up.

"I'm wondering if you have any rooms available." The woman raised her eyebrows, shifting her attention from the TV to look Julie up and down without saying anything to her.

"Frank!" she shouted. From a back room came a big, bald, black muscular unshaven guy in jeans and a white t-shirt. "You wanna show this lady to room 8?"

"How're you gunna pay?" the lady asked.

"Uh. I'm not sure. I think I'd like to see the room first," Julie said, feeling positive she wouldn't get a wink of sleep here and that the better deal might be to run while she still could.

"Follow me," the guy said. Julie opened the front

door and looked at the car to make sure Angie was okay. She didn't want to leave her in the car alone, but neither did she want her to get out. Julie's stomach felt twisted. How she wished she were anywhere else.

The man followed Julie's gaze, and she noticed he saw Angie. Julie thought about what she might have in her purse that could inflict harm if she needed to. A ballpoint pen?

The man led Julie to the back of the motel.

"Uh. I don't know about this," Julie said instinctively.

The man glared at her and led her down the sidewalk anyway. She could hear wicked laughter coming from one of the rooms. *What is that horrible smell?*

Her knees shook. She wanted to bolt back to the car and rescue Angie. Who knew what might be happening to her.

He finally reached the next to the last room and put the key in the door. It stuck. He kicked it open. Then he flicked on the light. Julie could see bugs scurry under the single bed, which had an ugly dirty blanket on it. The room looked like it previously had carpet, but it had been torn up, leaving a textured finish no one would leave in their house.

The man walked into the room, but Julie stayed outside. "Uh, I think I've decided we won't be staying here."

"Okay," he said in a coming-to-terms way. "Let me give you a little piece of advice. If I was you, I'd git in that car and drive away from here. This really ain't a place for a lady like you with a kid."

"Oh, thank you!" she said. "I believe I'll do just that," and she turned around and ran. With shaking hands, she unlocked her door, jumped in, started the engine and jammed the car into reverse, turned and skidded out of the parking lot.

Breathless, she asked, "Are you okay, Sweetie?"

"It was scary in here alone," Angie said. "A lady came out and asked me to roll down the window. But I didn't."

"Very good, Sweetie."

"She asked me if I was on television."

"What! What did you tell her?"

"Yes."

Oh dear God!

"Hello, Elizabeth? This is Julie."

"Julie! Where are you? You know you were on *America's Most Wanted* last night?"

"I know. It was a miracle that I saw it at Sears and ran home to pack and leave, just before the police got there." She was talking to Elizabeth from a payphone at a convenience store.

"You didn't see the whole program, then," Elizabeth stated. "You're going to have to choose new names. They said you might be going by Brenda Mathews and living in Jackson, Tennessee. Apparently the police learned about you as a caregiver for a man who died.

"What is your pager number? I realized last night I don't have it, and I should," Elizabeth said.

"I hate to have to admit it, but I don't have a pager. I know, I need to take care of that. In the meantime, I don't know where to go. I'm just driving through Alabama right now."

"I know just the place for you right now. It's in South Carolina. It's my second cousin and her husband and five kids. They live in the country. It's a little rustic, but it would be perfect for you right now."

Elizabeth took out an atlas and asked Julie if she had paper to write on. "Find your way to I-85 and take it east through Georgia into South Carolina. Then find I-26 South." As she continued on with the directions, Julie began to feel a little better. She had a goal now.

"While you're there, I'll arrange to get you a pager," Elizabeth said. "You have to have one. You're one lucky person, I have to tell you. Let me know when you think of new names for yourselves."

When Julie hung up the payphone, she just sat in the car. "Mommy needs to think for a second here," Julie told Angie. She wanted to think of names for them, but instead she marveled at how that television program knew so much about her.

We are so vulnerable. I had no idea how hard this would be. How could I be so naïve? I thought we could just run away from it all and start our lives all over again.

She looked up and saw a police car coming toward her. The policeman pulled into a parking space in front of the convenience store and went inside.

It was time for her to pull herself together and go find I-85.

CHAPTER 16—JULY 1988

Julie wished she had a camera. Angie was racing through the pigpen trying to catch her favorite pig, Lucille. She would get close while the robust sow rooted and snorted around, but seemingly with eyes in the back of her head, Lucille ran squealing away whenever Angie got within arm's length. It was as much fun watching Angie's antics as Lucille's.

On one of Angie's tries, she fell headlong into the mud. Julie laughed hysterically.

She and Angie had plenty of fun around Sarah and Mitch Laflin's vast country property that rested in a valley meadow between two mountains. It couldn't be more beautiful or rustic, as Elizabeth had said. Yet, in spite of the reprieve from city life, Julie didn't know how long they would be able to survive without air conditioning and with laundry allowed only every other Monday. The washing machine was on its last leg, and the Laflins didn't have any spare money sitting around in case it broke down. Plus, they just didn't care if they or their kids wore dirty clothes. Julie went along with it because she had no choice, and dirty clothes made little difference to Angie. Julie did hand-wash a lot of their clothes, though. They didn't have enough for either of them to have clean ones each day for one week, let alone for two.

Right now, the Laflins were gone on their grocery store journey. It was usually a three- to four-hour affair. They did everything as a family, and there was no room in the car for Julie and Angie. Unfortunately, that was the case for every outing, including church. Julie had parked her car. She didn't want to drive it and possibly raise any suspicion with her Florida plate, which Elizabeth had just sent to her. Since the plate had no connection with Julie's name or car, if she was caught, consequences could be disastrous.

At 10 a.m., the day was cooler than it would be later, so Julie decided to pick some tomatoes, zucchini, and spinach. She would use them to make salad and spaghetti sauce for the family. She loved preparing supper. It made her feel useful. Plus it filled some of her time. She couldn't sit around watching television. The Laflins had an old black and white TV that only got three channels—which they never watched.

Julie washed a few things and was hanging them out on the line to dry when the Laflins finally returned home.

They all piled out of the car. Each kid had a brand new 50-cent paddleball and immediately began learning how to play with them. Angie, now seven, looked at them enviously. She wanted to play with them. But they hardly noticed her.

"Here, let me help you bring in the groceries," Julie said as she grabbed a bag. Sarah and Mitch followed her in the side screen door with their arms loaded.

"I'm glad we're in here alone," Sarah said. "We all ran into Cousin Elmer and his kids in town, and our little Bucky told them that we have a television star at our house. Well, Elmer was puzzled because he knows we don't even watch TV. Bucky said you was on some crime show. I tried to get him to shush, but he wouldn't. Elmer thought for a spell and asked if it was *America's Most Wanted*, and Bucky said it was."

Julie's stomach sank. "What did you say to him?"

"We just told him Bucky has a big imagination. We didn't know what else to say really."

Julie felt like she'd been punched in the stomach. She sighed, walked into the living room, and paced back and forth.

They would have to leave as soon as possible. She had the pager now, but still needed to give the number out and devise a plan for how to use it best. She still wanted to pick a new name for Angie. For herself, she had chosen Linda Herman. She had looked through one of Sarah's books that listed baby names and was considering the name Gabrielle for Angie, because it meant *angel*. But she needed to run that past Angie.

She considered their just-washed clothes out on the line. There was no time to wait for them to dry.

"Sarah, we'll have to move right away. I'm wondering if I can make a long-distance phone call. I need to talk to Elizabeth."

"I'm so sorry this happened, Linda. Bucky's always talkin' before he thinks. Sure, you can call Elizabeth."

"Hi Julie. How are you? How have you all been getting along?" Elizabeth asked.

Julie assured her that they all had gotten along well for the last two months, but a situation had come up.

"Ugh. What a disappointment. Wow," Elizabeth said. "I'll need to do some checking and get right back with you."

Then Julie called Angie in from outside. "Let's go to our room. I want to tell you something." With all the cheer she could muster, Julie told her that they were moving to a new place.

"Why? I really like it here. I have lots of fun," Angie whined.

"Well, we have to move. We are in danger of being found out. So I need you to start filling your plastic bags with your things. I'll do the same. Here, let's get going."

About 15 minutes later, the phone rang. It was Elizabeth.

"Okay, I was thinking. You have a Florida license plate, so it makes sense to send you there. I know of a very good church with a Christian school near Jacksonville. One of my closest friends lives there. I asked her if she could find a place for you to stay. She's checking into it. She doesn't know your situation. She just knows that you are a friend of mine. So you'll be starting fresh there. She's single and very friendly. I think you'll love her. I told her you are going to go ahead and start driving. In the meantime, she will find a place." Elizabeth gave her Gloria Miter's phone number and address with directions. "Give her a call when you get close, and if she hasn't found a place, she said you can stay with her until she does."

Julie thanked her, not knowing how she could ever repay Elizabeth for all her efforts.

Now, you have a pager," Elizabeth said. "You need to give that number to family and anyone else you trust. Then you need to devise a plan where they enter a certain number to alert you of danger or to the fact that you need to call them. And I want to be at the top of that list. In fact, let's figure this out right now. If there's danger that I'm aware of, I'm going to page you and enter my phone number because no one would connect me with you. You might want to give your pager number to a neighbor or two wherever you are and tell them you are always concerned about safety and if they are aware of any danger or police activity around your place to enter 911. You'll know it's a neighbor. Then you might want to give your mom a different number to enter, which will mean you need to contact her somehow."

Julie decided to choose those numbers on the spot and ask Elizabeth to call her mom and give her the number. With the thought of choosing three numbers, she had an idea. What if she used the beginning verse number on the inside of her journal. It was Psalm 27:1. *The Lord is my light and my salvation; whom shall I fear? The Lord is the strength of my life; of whom shall I be afraid?*

She wondered if her mom would recognize the significance of 271. If so, it might encourage her as it had encouraged Julie many times. She asked Elizabeth if she would call her mom and give her the pager number and code number, explaining when to use it.

She went back to their room and had Angie help her clean it before they left.

"Okay, I think we're done. Let's go out and say goodbye."

Julie was surprised at how tearful this parting was. Maybe it was because they had the opportunity to actually say goodbye, and weren't sprinting to the car and pealing out. She wished she had a gift to leave with them for all their trouble.

About an hour down the road, and with Angie very much alert, Julie tried to warm her up to the idea of starting all over in another location. She told her that there was a great school she could go to, and there would be lots of kids her age she could become friends with . . . she hoped. And the weather would be warm all year round, so they wouldn't even need coats.

"And we will change our names. What name would you like to go by?" She thought she'd give Angie a chance to make the first suggestion.

"Gabrielle," Angie said without hesitation.

Julie's jaw dropped. She looked over at Angie. "Why did you pick that name?"

"A few days ago I had a dream, and my name was Gabrielle, and I loved that name. I woke up sad that Gabrielle wasn't my real name."

"Well, I think this is a miracle, because that's the name I was thinking I'd like you to have," Julie said. She made a mental note that she would have to write this down in her *Thoughts & Prayers* journal.

"I have a treat for us tonight," Julie said, feeling confident that no one was trailing them and that enough time had passed since they were on *America's Most Wanted*. She was sure they wouldn't have to be so reclusive. "It's about 4:15 now. How about if in another hour, we find a K-Mart and buy those swimsuits, since we didn't get to do that before, and then we'll find a hotel and go swimming? We can also eat somewhere near the hotel."

Angie definitely approved, and Julie couldn't wait to take a long shower. She looked at the highway signs and decided Augusta, Georgia, would be their destination for the day.

"I like you," Angie told Gloria Miter. She was sitting next to Gloria in the front seat of her Pontiac, Ventura. Though Julie couldn't recall Angie ever saying that to anyone else, she totally understood. Gloria was a relaxed, light-hearted person, and Julie could see that Angie was enamored with her. Gloria liked ruffles and red lipstick and had curly brown hair. She was spunky for her 30-something years, and from what Julie could tell from staying with her for a few days, she didn't have a mean side to her.

"Well, I like you too. You're a very smart little girl. I wish I had been like you when I was your age," Gloria said. "Instead, I hid from everyone and sucked my thumb."

That made Angie laugh.

It was Wednesday, and Gloria was showing them

around Middleburg. Their agenda included driving by the church and school. Gloria had called her boss at the mortgage company that morning and told him she'd like to take a personal day off to spend some time with her houseguests.

"I'll show you the best places to shop, the library, a couple of wonderful grocery stores, and for lunch, I'm taking you to my favorite pizza place. It's on me."

"We get pizza?" Angie asked with wonder.

"We don't often get pizza," Julie felt she had to explain from the back seat.

"I'll bet you don't get enough ice cream, either. I know the perfect place for that too." For sure, Gloria had just made a new best friend. Angie clapped her hands and said how happy she was.

Julie lounged in the back seat soaking in the sites and loving the fact that someone else was in control for a few hours. *I wonder what it would be like to live here for a long time. I think I like this city. It's the perfect size. But I better not get my hopes up.*

Gloria had found them a place to live in a fourplex, which wouldn't be ready for them to move into until Saturday. It was owned by a church member, and with Gloria's recommendation, Julie was able to get it for cheaper than she thought possible. The landlord was a Christian, and he liked to give a break to those he felt reasonably sure would be good tenants and wouldn't destroy the place. Gloria had assured him that they would be perfect tenants. And that was not an exaggeration. Julie was a homemaker at heart. She would probably keep the place cleaner than anyone else ever had.

Julie had only breezed through the home for a few minutes. The current tenants and their three kids hadn't moved out yet, so they all stood around gawking as Julie and the landlord toured the place.

With so many eyes on her, she hadn't felt comfortable looking too closely. It seemed okay. She wasn't going to be picky. She did notice, though, that there weren't any curtains. Only blinds. She could definitely make some improvements. If she could borrow someone's sewing machine, she would dress up the windows.

They pulled into the church parking lot of Faith Believers Fellowship Church with its Faith Christian Academy attached on the west end of the building. The white church was a two-story A-frame building with a single-story attachment that looked like a later addition. The school was attached to the addition lengthwise, so the back of the church formed a T. A giant wooden cross was affixed to the upper part of the A-frame.

"How long have you gone here?" Julie asked Gloria.

"Oh, my goodness. I would guess 11 or 12 years," she said. "It's like home to me. Here, let's run in and see if the pastor is here."

It turned out Pastor Blum was indeed there and greeted them with a handshake and a smile. "This is Linda and Gabrielle Herman," Gloria said. The names certainly sounded foreign to Julie. She just hoped she could keep her ears tuned in and respond whenever anyone called her Linda.

"Gabrielle, that's a beautiful name. Do you know what it means?" he asked Angie.

"Yes. It means *angel*," she said. "There's a Gabrielle in the Bible, but it's spelled different than my name."

He chatted with them about where they came from, and Julie told him that she had a tumultuous marriage and was making a new beginning. It made her feel good to be ever so slightly transparent so people could get to know the real her as much as comfortably possible.

"So, I'm new in town. I'll be looking for a job, perhaps house cleaning or home care," Julie said.

"I'll certainly keep that in mind," the pastor said, squinting and with his arms crossed, rocking back and forth. He looked like he was already thinking about it.

"Who do we talk to about enrolling Gabrielle in our school?" Gloria asked the pastor.

"You're thinking of going to school here?" he asked Julie with a smile.

"We sure are. Gabrielle loves Christian school, don't you Sweetie?"

"You will want to see Tabby Cabello," he said.

"Okay, great. I'll call her and get them set up," Gloria said.

Before long, they were on the road again, headed for pizza. Julie felt like things were falling into place quickly, and she was so grateful. Only four days earlier their lives had been upended again, and here she had a new fourplex to move into, a delightful new friend, a church, and a school. At least she hoped she had a church. She hadn't heard the pastor preach yet, but from what she could tell, he was genuine, and Gloria had assured her that he was a great Bible teacher.

I wish I could call Mom and tell her everything. But I better not. I'm sure the police or FBI are all over her phone calls right now.

"I know something you might enjoy," Gloria told Julie. "Each Monday night, some ladies from church go to Tilly's Bakery for pie. It's just whoever can make it each week, and they have so much fun."

"Can I come too? I like pie," Angie said.

"Well, I'm afraid it's for adult ladies only, but you could stay with me while your mom goes," she said.

Julie thought that might be a real possibility.

CHAPTER 17—AUGUST 1988

Julie was startled with a loud banging on her front door. She was in the bathroom washing her face and looked at the clock. It was 9:05 on Saturday morning, two weeks after they had moved into the fourplex. She felt alarmed. This was no ordinary knock. It was loud and long and sounded like it was made with fists.

"Angie, hide in your closet while I check this out," she urged.

She tiptoed to the front window and saw a group of women at her door, and several cars and trucks parked out front. At first her heart pounded, but then she saw Gloria. She also recognized a few other ladies she had met at church or at Monday night pie night. They all had their arms full of things. She opened the door and everyone shouted, "Surprise!"

"What?"

"We're giving you a welcome shower." Gloria announced. "Can we come in?"

Julie opened the door wide, and they all filed in bearing gifts and smiles.

"I'm sorry, I don't really have anywhere for you to sit," Julie said. She only had two folding chairs and a tiny table. In their bedrooms, they each had a swimming pool air mattress to sleep on. Julie had planned to go shopping for a few household goods in a few hours.

"This is such a surprise," Julie said. "Gabrielle, come see who's here."

Angie beamed when she saw Gloria.

One at a time, the ladies presented what they had brought. One lady had a box of dishes. Another a box of silverware. A few had beautiful lamps.

This is amazing. What did I do to deserve this? They hardly even know me.

Julie's cheeks hurt from smiling. After each lady showed what she had brought, she set it in the corner where a useful pile was accumulating. Gloria presented her with a vacuum cleaner, which Julie was most grateful for.

One lady, Mrs. Gray, whom Julie had sat next to at pie night, said that her husband would be there soon with his truck. He was bringing some furniture.

In a matter of hours, Julie had two living room chairs, a couch, coffee table, kitchen table, two twin beds, two night tables, and two dressers.

She was speechless. All she could say was "thank you so much," and that just didn't seem like enough. She started to cry as everything she could possibly need came through the front door. Many of the ladies were complete strangers to her.

Before noon, nearly everyone was gone except Gloria and the pastor's wife, Jean. Gloria said, "No shower is really complete without food. Margaret is getting you some Kentucky Fried Chicken. She should be back in a minute."

"I don't know what to say," Julie told Gloria. She hugged both women.

"You don't need to say anything," Jean encouraged. "We admire what you're doing to make a life for Gabrielle. It's not easy, we know, and we all agreed that we really wanted to help you."

"I think any of us would be willing to watch Gabrielle for you if you need to get out sometime," Gloria said. "At least I know I would."

Soon Margaret was back with a bucket of chicken and a bag with some side dishes.

Before they left, Jean handed Julie a sealed envelope. "Now, get yourself settled in. We'll see you at church tomorrow."

"Goodbye!" Angie called as they left. "Thank you for the stuffed animals!"

They stood outside on the front step, waving goodbye as the last ladies drove away.

"Pookie, can you believe this!" Julie said, hugging Angie. "We are so blessed."

Once settled back inside, the first thing Julie looked for was the new dishes. Otherwise, they would have eaten on paper plates. She admired the beige plates with their blue rims and thin strip of red flowers and green leaves around the edge. They were non-breakable, which Julie loved.

The flatware was shiny and smooth with scalloped edges on the handle, mimicking flowers. Julie felt they were a pattern she would have bought herself.

"Let me wash these," she told Angie, who was looking through the bags of chicken side dishes. Of course they were her favorite—mashed potatoes and sweet corn.

As they ate, Julie remembered the envelope Jean had given her. She got up, washed her hands, and opened the envelope. She read it aloud to Angie.

"Linda and Gabrielle, we are blessed and humbled to know folks like you who live unpretentious lives. Not many of us would be willing to sacrifice our comfort to start a new life—among strangers no less. Please consider us your friends, and let us know any needs you have. We want you to feel like we are your family. It may take you awhile to trust us completely, but we have your back."

They don't know how much that means to me, she thought. She continued reading. *"Linda, we know you are looking for work so you can support Gabrielle. Two ladies at church are looking for house cleaners. We will set you up. Also, when school starts, we have a part-time secretarial position open. Would you be interested in that? We will talk more later. Jean and your church friends."*

Julie put down the card. "Wow." She slumped down in her chair. "This is unbelievable. After we eat, I'm going to write all this down in my journal."

Maybe this will be the place we can settle into for years.

CHAPTER 18—OCTOBER 1990

"Try to hold still," Julie mumbled with pins in her mouth. She was hemming a floor-length pink and purple princess dress for Angie. Mrs. Kerns from church was loaning her a sewing machine so Julie could make Angie's Halloween costume.

"It's taking so looong," Angie complained.

Julie took the pins out of her mouth. "That's because you won't hold still. And we want this to be perfect, don't we?"

She also planned to make a cone hat with pink, purple and yellow ribbons draping from the top. A matching wand with ribbons streaming from the end would make the costume simply regal, in a little girl way.

Julie had recently bought a Polaroid camera. She'd dreamed of sending photos to her mom, who had loved to spend Halloween with Angie. She'd have to think of a safe way to get the photos to her.

Rita had already missed so much of Angie's growing up. She was nine years old now, doing well in school, with many friends. Slumber parties were regular events—usually occurring whenever one of her friends had a birthday party.

"Can I go over to Pixie's after this?" Angie asked. She hardly needed to ask. Pixie lived in the fourplex. She was a bit younger, but they enjoyed pretending together. "Pixie is going to be a star for Halloween."

"Which movie star will that be?"

"Not a movie star, silly. A star star."

"Hmm. I wonder how her mom will pull that one off." Julie said. She was friends with Pixie's mom, Beth. She had given Beth her pager number and told her to type in 911 if she ever saw any unusual activity around their place.

So far she had lived more than two years in Middleburg, Florida, with no close calls. She was cleaning houses, and loved being a part-time secretary at Angie's school. She had asked them to pay her in cash and, with no questions asked, they did it.

The phone rang, and it was Gloria. "I was just calling to tell you I can't watch Gabrielle next Monday night. I need to go to a family party. Can you find someone else to watch her?"

"That's okay. I think I'll stay home from pie night next week. I need to watch my weight and this will be a perfect excuse not to go," she said, and she meant it. Living a more relaxed life, Julie was gaining weight.

She had become such good friends with Gloria, living through her hard times as her mother had just passed away. In fact, Julie had felt completely comfortable telling Gloria her situation. She remembered Gloria's reaction.

Julie had marveled that Gloria had told her about the physical abuse her mother had experienced from Gloria's father, and about a car accident her mother experienced that affected her mentally, causing her to treat Gloria like a child, often meanly.

"I want to assure you that you aren't alone in living a strained life," Julie had said. She wanted to console Gloria, but she had also wanted to tell someone so she could hand over some of her valuables for safe keeping in case she had to leave home suddenly and couldn't assemble all the important documents in a hurry.

"I'm not really Linda, and Gabrielle isn't my daughter's real name. Remember I said we had to leave her father and move? Well, he was abusive to her, and the judge was giving him opportunities to be with her and abuse her more. I had to run away with her, and we've been living on the run ever since."

Gloria had just stared at her. "Of course . . . " she had said in a daze. "That explains why you know Elizabeth. Why didn't I put it together before? She helps people like you. Oh my goodness. I'm best friends with a fugitive!"

Gloria vowed never to tell a soul, and the two of them became even closer. So Gloria also had Julie's pager number. She was allowed to enter her own phone number since no man-hunter would tie Gloria and Julie together.

Though everything was going wonderfully, Julie was feeling extra cautious lately and couldn't figure out why. Maybe things were going *too* well.

That night about 8:30, after Julie had put Angie to bed, she turned off the lights and peeked through the living room blinds. She just felt something was going on. She had heard footsteps running a few minutes earlier and then some sort of a thud and a car door slam. She didn't see or hear anything now.

She went back to her bedroom to read. But soon she heard sirens getting closer and closer. In fact, they stopped right in front of her place, and she heard a loud knock at her front door.

Julie's heart thumped. She could hardly breathe.

This is it, she thought. *I can't believe it will all end, just like this.*

She put on her green cotton bathrobe and slowly went to the front door, turned on the porch light, and peeked outside. She dreaded what she saw and started shaking so badly she could hardly unlock the door. Angie came out of her room and stood behind Julie. Should she try to hide Angie? Oh, what was the use? She had been caught. This was bound to happen sooner or later.

She opened the door to two tall policemen. "Is

Angie here?" one of them asked.

"Uhh." Was all Julie could say. Her voice was weak.

Angie peeked out from behind Julie and said, "I'm Angie."

They looked at her for a few seconds with furrowed eyebrows.

"Oh. Sorry about that. We must have the wrong place," the other policeman said. "We're looking for someone a few years older. Do you know any teenage girls named Angie around here?"

"No, I don't," Julie said.

"Okay. Well, sorry to bother you. Good night ma'am."

Julie closed the door. Her knees buckled and she slumped to the floor, breathing hard, trying to catch her breath. Her heart continued to pound in her throat.

"Oh, that was close," she gasped.

"It's okay Mommy. God takes care of us," Angie said.

"Yes, he does. And once I settle down, I'll write about this in my journal."

Two hours passed before Julie's heartbeat returned to normal and the adrenaline rush subsided.

###

"I think we should send a note home with the kids to their parents and ask them to collect shoe boxes. We'll never be able to find enough on our own before Valentine's Day," Marsha said. She was the full-time secretary at the school and leading a meeting with Julie and a few teachers.

"Why don't I stop by a few shoe stores and see if they have any?" Julie suggested. "They usually have boxes they would otherwise throw away."

The group was ironing out the school Valentine's Day party, and they planned to have each child decorate a box as a Valentine's card mailbox. They would use wrapping paper, doilies, and anything else interesting they could find.

Julie had also volunteered to find volunteers to make cookies. Angie would enjoy helping her with that. Next on the agenda was games.

Suddenly the ladies heard a muffled beeping noise and looked around. The sound came from Julie's purse.

"Oh, it's my pager," she said. She pulled it out and looked at the number: 271.

"Uhh. It's my mom. I need to call her. Excuse me while I find a phone."

"You can use the one in my office," Marsha said.

Julie felt sick to her stomach. Her mother had not paged her before.

Her hands trembled as she dialed the phone.

"Hello?"

"Hi there. It's me," Julie said.

"Great. In 10 minutes, can you call me back at you-know-where?"

"Yes. Bye."

That was their game plan. The closest pay phone to her mom's house was a few minutes away. This way they could be sure no one was listening. Julie went back to the meeting and told them she needed to call her mom back in a few minutes.

"Hi Mom. Is everything okay?"

"Well, I'm not sure. I received a call from Trudy at the shop this morning. She said that while she and her kids were eating breakfast, they saw Angie's picture on the milk carton as a missing child. I rushed to the store and looked at the milk cartons, and sure enough, they all had a picture of Angie with her date of birth and the date she went missing. There's a toll-free phone number to call if anyone thinks they know where she is."

Julie fell back in her chair. She wondered if Angie's picture was on milk cartons in her area. She groaned and ran her fingers through her hair.

"I think you should go to a store right away and see if the milk cartons show her picture," her mom said.

"I just can't get away from this, can I?" Julie said, discouraged. "You know what this means. I'll have to pack up and run again."

"Well, you don't know for sure. Maybe these pictures are regional. But if you have to run, do it quickly. Can you call me back at this number in about 20 minutes after you've had a chance to go to the store, and we'll see what needs to happen?"

"Okay. I'm leaving now," Julie said, looking at her watch.

She returned to the ladies discussing the Valentine's Day party. "I'm sorry, I need to leave. Can I check back with you tomorrow on whatever you decide for the party?" she asked.

"You look as white as a sheet," Marsha said. "Is everything okay?"

"Yes, yes. Everything is fine. My mom just reminded me of something I need to take care of."

She ran to the car and was so lost in her thoughts that she didn't even know how she got onto the busy street. Once again, as always happened in her crisis moments, her heart pounded wildly. She drove on automatic pilot to the Safeway and headed straight to the dairy case. *Why do they always put the milk in the very back?*

She turned around a milk carton and didn't see anything unusual. She felt quick relief. But there was another brand of milk. She turned that around and there it was. Plain as anything. Angie's picture. It looked exactly like her. Julie gasped. How many people had seen that?

She saw the restroom sign and took refuge. She went into a stall and locked it. She leaned against the stall door. "No, no, no," she said. "This can't be happening!"

Then she caught herself. *Calm down. Let's see. I need to call Mom back. I need to get hold of Gloria. I need to pack. I need to pick up Angie from school. Do not panic.*

She thought it all through, just as she always did.

What do I need to buy? She decided she had better buy some snacks they could eat on the road. She also thought she should buy something to disguise Angie. She looked for red hair dye. She was pretty sure she could find Angie's sunglasses at home.

Julie called her mom back. "Oh, Mom. Her picture is on the cartons here too. We'll have to leave. I don't know where we'll go, but probably to a hotel until the milk cartons don't have her picture on them anymore."

She decided to keep Angie in school for the rest of the day so she wouldn't raise suspicions. She went home and called Gloria at work.

"Oh, shoot. That's awful," she said. "Let's see. Why don't you pack quickly and go to my place. That way if the police look for you, they won't find you home."

Julie liked the idea and packed as many of her and Angie's things as she possibly could fit in plastic bags in her car. She wanted to take so many things, such as two beautiful lamps that had been given to her. But it just wouldn't make sense to take those. She had also been given some large picture frames she had filled with pictures of Angie. She took the photos out of the frames. Should she take her silverware? She wished she could. But what sense would that make? Maybe she could take a few pieces. One of the church ladies had made Angie a quilt, probably feeling sorry that she didn't have a grandmother around. Julie decided to take that.

This time there were so many sentimental things Julie wanted to pack, and she realized how much of a home this was to the two of them. But there was no time for nostalgia.

At 4 o'clock she picked up Angie. "Let's go to the park for a few minutes, okay? Let's go watch the ducks," Julie suggested. Finally she told her nine-year-old that they would have to move.

With tears in her eyes, Angie looked at Julie.

"No. Why?" she pleaded. "I like it here."

Tears ran down Julie's cheeks too. *I hate to uproot her. She is so well-adjusted and has such a great school and friends she loves. I must seem so mean to her.*

"Let's sit at this picnic table. Can you look at me and listen carefully for a few minutes?"

Angie sighed, crossed her arms, and glared at Julie.

"There's an organization that tries to keep track of children who are missing. One way they do it is to get milk companies to print pictures of missing children on the back of milk cartons. That way when people sit, eat their breakfasts, and look at the milk cartons, like we do, they might recognize the child. Then they call the phone number on the carton and get the police involved in finding that child. Your picture is on milk cartons in grocery stores right now."

Angie quit glaring as her jaw dropped. "*My* picture is on milk cartons?"

"Yes. And no doubt people all over this town are looking at your picture when they eat their breakfasts.

I'm actually a little surprised that none of them have called the police to say they know where you are. We have to go hide for awhile and then move to where no one knows us."

Julie waited for Angie to complain, but she seemed lost in her own thoughts and may have even comprehended the seriousness of the situation.

"Maybe we can take some of our friends with us," Angie volunteered.

"How I wish we could," Julie said. "Now, I have already packed, and we are going to Gloria's house to pick up some of our remaining things. We may even spend the night with her."

Angie seemed satisfied, and they drove to Gloria's house where she'd already come home and made dinner.

"Hi you two." She hugged Julie and Angie, but had a sad face. "I'm so sorry you will have to leave. I've already called Elizabeth. She doesn't think you should take your car, Julie."

Elizabeth had explained that when milk carton alerts come out, the FBI is particularly attuned to leads that come in and can easily track down cars.

Julie's pager went off. She looked, and the number was 911. That meant it was Beth in the fourplex. Julie was afraid to call her, figuring the police were there looking for her.

"Let's put your car in my garage," Gloria suggested. "And why don't you call Elizabeth. You'll probably have some questions you want to ask her."

A few minutes later, Julie heard Elizabeth's voice.

"I've seen Angie's picture on the milk cartons," she said. "It was bound to happen sooner or later. Listen, I know some guys in your area, and I'll have them pick you up tonight and take you to a motel in Tifton, Georgia. You'll need to stay there for a few weeks. Do you have enough money?"

"Yes. And I think the police are at my place right now."

"They probably are. Don't worry. We'll get you out of there." She explained that the people would come to Gloria's around 11 o'clock and would drive them all night.

In the meantime, Julie dyed Angie's hair red.

Julie and Gloria kept peeking out the front door, waiting for a car to pull up, hoping it wouldn't be the police. At 10:55, a long, black, beat up Chevy pulled into the driveway. Gloria opened the door and motioned for the man to turn his car around and back in. Then she ran to open the garage door.

He turned out to be a large, lethargic, poorly dressed black man. A buxom black woman with a low-cut blouse, short skirt, and high heels popped out from the passenger side.

"Danger, what you doin'?" she asked.

"She's wantin' me to turn the car around."

"Oh my God—can't we just git outta here?" she whined.

Julie hoped this was a mistake. Surely these two wouldn't drive them to Georgia.

Gloria spoke sharply.

"Will you lend us a hand here?" she asked as she removed some black plastic bags from the trunk of Julie's car in the garage.

"I might break my nails!" the woman complained.

"Dear Lord, please help us," Julie prayed out loud.

"That's what I always say," the lady agreed in her high-pitched voice.

Fortunately the Chevy had a large trunk.

Unfortunately, there were already a few boxes taking up space. But most of the bags fit. The rest would have to go in the back seat with them.

Julie and Angie clung to Gloria as they said goodbye.

"Call me when you get to your motel," Gloria urged. Julie could tell she was about to cry too.

"Can we go already?" Danger pleaded, rolling his eyes.

Julie and Angie slid into the back seat with a few of their bags and Angie's quilt. The back seat was ripped, and smashed paper cups, napkins, and empty chip bags filled the floor. The car reeked of cigarette smoke. Still, Julie was glad they were getting out of town. She had felt increasingly uncomfortable throughout the evening, knowing the police were looking for her. She just wanted to get as far away as possible as fast as possible.

She tapped the woman on the shoulder. "What's your name?" she asked.

"You don't need to know!" she proclaimed.

"Her name is Tosha," the guy said. He lit up a cigarette.

"Can we roll the windows down?" Julie asked.

He obliged, and turned the radio to a blues station.

It could be worse, Julie thought.

"Here Sweetie. Why don't you lay your head on my lap and go to sleep," Julie told Angie.

The longer they drove with the steady rhythm of the road and the periodic flash of street lights streaming in the window, the more relaxed Julie felt. She dozed on and off. No one talked.

After a few hours, Julie heard Tosha tell Danger she needed to use the restroom. He said he'd pull off at the next rest stop. Julie was glad—she could use the restroom too.

In about 10 minutes, Danger exited to a rest area. Julie noticed a police car with a policeman inside parked in front of the building.

"Can we please pass this one?" Julie asked.

"Why? I gotta go!" Tosha glared at her.

Julie realized that this chauffer couple didn't know anything about her or why she would be concerned about the police. She decided to keep her mouth shut.

The parking lot wasn't exactly well lit. In fact, it was pretty scary with tree shadows dancing and people milling around, some with dogs.

"Pookie, do you need to use the bathroom?" Julie asked.

"Yes."

"Okay, let's go."

They got out while Julie watched the police car. The policeman didn't appear to be paying any attention to them. They went inside the girl's room.

Julie gasped. There stood a man with a scruffy face, but wearing a wig and red lipstick. He wore a tight black skirt, a shiny red blouse, and carried a purse. He was looking in the mirror.

"I'll stand outside the stall door while you go," Julie whispered to Angie.

When it was her turn, she made Angie come in the stall with her.

Then Julie heard a scream outside.

"Come on. Let's get out of here," Julie said.

Outside, she heard a woman in the van parked next to them yelling, "Where's my purse? It's gone! It was here a minute ago!"

The policeman got out of his car.

"Let's go!" Julie urged Danger.

"What is your big deal?" Tosha asked Julie, glaring at her once again.

"I'm just ready to get going."

Danger willingly complied.

Julie turned around to see if anyone followed them. She breathed a sigh of relief. She leaned forward to watch out the rearview mirror. Then she saw it. An aqua purse was sitting on the floor of the front seat. It wasn't Tosha's because hers was black patent leather.

Oh my goodness, Julie thought. *What kind of a man is this? How does Elizabeth know him?*

She decided not to say a word, but silently begged God to quickly get them wherever they were going.

CHAPTER 19—MARCH 1991

"**D**inner will be ready in about 10 minutes. Go wash your hands," Julie announced.

"Can I wait until the next commercial?" Angie asked.

"What are you fixin'?" Eight-year-old Marvin asked.

"Chili."

"I don't like chili. I'm not eating."

That figured. Julie didn't know how he survived. After living with Sandra and her son in the spare bedroom of their house for six weeks, she'd only seen him eat a full meal maybe twice. She'd seen him eat plenty of potato chips, donuts, candy bars, and French fries.

"Well, come in here and eat a few bites anyway, okay?" Julie said. "We need to put some meat on your bones."

"No. And you can't make me!"

"If you don't eat chili, you don't get any dessert. It's as simple as that."

"I'll just wait till my mama gets home," he announced.

"You might be asleep by then."

Actually, Julie didn't know what time Sandra would be home. She regularly left the house in the evenings to party with friends since Julie was there to watch Marvin. It was a living arrangement sparked by an ad in the small-town Georgia newspaper.

Plenty was wrong with the arrangement, but Julie determined to just be thankful that she had a cheap place to stay for however long she needed it. She hadn't let on that it probably wouldn't be for more than a few months.

"I don't really feel like chili either," Angie announced.

"What do you mean you don't *feel* like chili? You love it, and that's what we're having, so you'll eat it." She was irritated and afraid that Marvin was rubbing off on Angie—in many ways. He watched too much TV, so Angie did too. He was mouthy, and that was something she would not tolerate in Angie.

Julie heard the garage door open. It was only 6:15. Sandra had only been gone for a half hour. Soon she burst through the garage door into the kitchen with a grocery bag.

"I decided I'd rather be at home tonight. So I thought I'd buy us some treats," she declared. She unloaded packaged cinnamon rolls, a large bottle of Coke, a can of smoked almonds, and a block of cheddar cheese.

"Didn't you buy me any Cap'n Crunch?" Marvin asked.

"Oops I forgot." Then she pulled that cereal out of the bag, and Marvin enthusiastically showed his approval.

"He doesn't like chili, so I think I'll give him some cereal for supper."

"I love Cap'n Crunch," Angie exclaimed. "Can I have some too?"

"Why don't we make this cereal and cinnamon roll night!" Sandra suggested, obviously thrilled with her irresponsible idea, as were the kids.

"I'm sorry, but I just can't go along with that for us. I don't want this chili to go to waste, and it's better for us."

Sandra rolled her eyes for Marvin to see, who then rolled his eyes.

Confrontations and undermining were normal around there.

Marvin had already gotten under Julie's skin earlier in the day when he teased Angie about her red hair, which she was sensitive about anyway. He couldn't be reprimanded without his mother backing him up.

Supper was quiet that evening as Angie was upset to be eating chili while Marvin smacked his lips through his much sweeter meal. Julie was perturbed to have to play the "bad guy." Sandra sat in front of the television with her junk food watching *Cheers*

After cleaning up the kitchen, Julie told Angie to take a bath. Then she went into their room to clear her mind and write in her journal.

She re-read the passage in the front of her journal. Some of the words jumped right out at her as if they were put there just for her. *I had fainted, unless I had believed to see the goodness of the Lord in the land of the living. Wait on the Lord: be of good courage, and he shall strengthen thine heart: wait, I say, on the Lord.*

She closed the journal and let the thoughts of those verses wash over her tormented mind.

Her life certainly was turning out differently than she had imagined years ago.

So much for becoming a children's book or cookbook author. Maybe when my life settles down, I can take culinary classes and have some kind of career baking, catering, or writing.

But not now. Tonight she relished her verses. *I had fainted, unless I had believed to see the goodness of the Lord.* God must surely understand everything she was going through.

Then she had a random thought. *I'm done here. I don't need to live in this house anymore.* She had no idea where to go next or what to do. But she felt she was finished with this living arrangement. She almost

168

audibly heard a voice say, "Call Elizabeth."

Just then, she was startled to hear her pager beep. She looked at the number. It was Elizabeth wanting her to call.

This is amazing, she thought.

She dialed the phone in her room.

"Hey there, I was just thinking about you," Julie said.

"Well, you've been on my mind a lot lately. I just learned about a great place you could go. It's a Christian complex with a church, school, and apartments. One of my former clients lives there and told me about it. It's near Indianapolis. I think the time is right for you to move on. The milk carton alert passed long enough ago. I'm thinking you should take a bus there. I can contact my former client, if you'd like."

"Oh, wonderful! I was just thinking that it's time for me to move on right when you paged me. I can't tell you how good that sounds to me," Julie gushed. "Sometimes I think God works through you. I'm going to find a bus schedule and make plans to leave here as soon as possible."

After the 10-minute conversation, Julie sighed and thanked God. Then she took out her pen and started writing in her journal.

Just when I thought I couldn't take it any more here, God opened a door for me to leave, and he let me know just seconds before the opportunity opened up. He put Elizabeth on my mind, and just then, she paged me.

I'm amazed at how God takes care of me, even though what I did in running with Angie was illegal. How could anyone doubt God's goodness? I'm getting ready for the next chapter in my life passage.

CHAPTER 20—JUNE 1991

Julie woke up and looked at the clock. It was 5:25 a.m. on Thursday, June 15. *Oh good*, she thought. *I have plenty of time to decorate the living room before Angie wakes up.* She had crepe paper, balloons, and a colorful, plastic *Happy 10th Birthday* banner. Fortunately, she had been able to blow up many of the balloons the night before in her bedroom after Angie went to sleep.

Angie was growing up so quickly, she thought. They had moved around so much, she was afraid Angie might become withdrawn and have a hard time making friends. But that wasn't a problem. Julie was most amazed at how Angie could keep their secret life so confidential. As far as she knew, Angie had told no one of her true past and identity. She was quite used to being called Gabrielle. In fact, she was better at responding to her fake name than Julie was at recognizing that people were talking to her when they called her *Linda*.

Julie used clothes pins to attach the banner to the vertical blinds covering the sliding glass door in the living room. She stuck thumbtacks into the end of the balloons and tacked them to doorframes and the ceiling here and there, with sprays of red, blue and yellow crepe paper.

She was long finished decorating by 7 o'clock and went to wake up Angie. She was surprised to find Angie standing at her window looking out.

"Good morning Pookie. Happy birthday! What are you doing?"

"I'm just looking at the school," Angie said. "I can't wait to start back there."

She'd only been out of school for a few weeks, but

she already had some great friendships.

"I know, Sweetie. Why don't you come out and get some breakfast."

Angie's eyes lit up when she saw the birthday decorations.

"You're in the double-digits now!" Julie exclaimed. "I don't have any work today, so I'm taking you anywhere around here you'd like to go."

"Can we get donuts?"

Yes, they could, and they did.

As soon as they returned home, the phone rang. It was Mrs. Sutherland, the church and school secretary.

"Hi Linda," she said. "I have some bad news and some good news."

"I'll take the bad news first," Julie said instinctively. *What could it be this time?*

Mrs. Sutherland explained that some missionaries were coming back from Argentina the following week and would need the house they were living in. That meant Julie and Angie would have to move.

Oh, that's all? Julie wasn't surprised. The church had allowed them to move in with the stipulation that they might have to move out in a moment's notice if a missionary needed the home. After all, it was designated as missionary housing, fully furnished. It had been perfect for the two of them, who had absolutely nothing. But it was only temporary.

"Okay. I understand. What's the good news?"

"Well, we're going to let you keep using the car. The Murreys already have a car. Also, we'll probably have an opening in the apartments we own pretty soon."

This church, like Faith Believer's Fellowship, was very good about taking care of them. For some reason, they had a heart for a struggling mother trying to raise her daughter on her own with hardly two nickels to rub together.

"Wow. That's really good news. We'll just sit tight, then. Really, Gabrielle and I are quite used to feast or famine."

"That's easy for us to believe," Mrs. Sutherland said. "We all really admire you, and we want to help any way we can."

When she got off the phone, Angie asked if they would have to move again.

"Yes. But it won't be so bad. We'll stay in this area, and you can still go to school here."

The next morning Julie was collecting her supplies for her cleaning job when the phone rang.

"Hello, Linda? This is Pastor Frank. I was wondering if you could come to my office this morning."

Julie figured he must have an idea of a place she could rent or that he had a cleaning job offer. He had told her when she moved into the missionary house that they might be able to hire her to clean the church.

"I'd be happy to stop by. Do you want me to come over right now?"

She only lived across the parking lot from the church and school, so it was no big deal. They agreed she could just pop on over, and no need to bring Angie.

When she got over there, Pastor Frank invited Mrs. Sutherland and the school administrator, Mr. Sharp, to sit in.

The pastor sat behind his desk, while the three of them sat in leather chairs arranged in a semi-circle around a dark wooden coffee table. Once they were all settled with chit-chat out of the way, the pastor looked at Mr. Sharp.

"My wife collects containers that we can use in the classrooms to start plants in," Mr. Sharp began. "We keep them in the basement. Last night I was down there looking for something and I noticed some empty milk cartons."

Caught completely off guard, Julie immediately tensed up. She looked down as he finished what he had to say.

"I saw a picture of a little girl on the milk cartons, and it caught my attention." He looked at the pastor, who reached beside him behind the desk and picked up a milk carton.

"This is Gabrielle, isn't it?" Pastor Frank asked.

Julie looked up and nodded. Each one of them gave her a questioning look.

The pastor continued. "What can you tell us about this?"

Julie had no choice. *Here goes*, she thought.

"I knew this would happen sooner or later," she said. "I was married when I was 21 to what I thought was a wonderful guy. He was a security guard where I worked, and he loved children. I had big dreams of having our own happy family, but after we had Angie, er, I mean Gabrielle, it was anything but happy. He became abusive. Then I discovered that Gabrielle had been sexually abused.

"At first I didn't realize it was Terry molesting her, but as soon as I suspected, I divorced him and filed for legal custody. But instead, Terry got custody."

It was painful for Julie to recount. She had successfully put the events behind her, and now she had to drum them up again.

"I took her to the hospital several times to have her molestation confirmed, and the hospital reports always came back with the words *likely molested*."

Mr. Sharp interrupted her. "If your husband was molesting her, why did the judge give *him* custody?"

"That's a very good question," she said. "First, there was no legal proof Terry did it. Then, the judge didn't like me and thought I was abusive for subjecting her to hospital tests. But also, Terry's dad is a respected policeman and is personal friends with the judge. In fact, the judge was at our wedding. It's very sickening to think of.

"So anyway, when Terry had custody of her, he kept abusing her. I fought with everything in me to get her back, and I eventually did.

"I wish the story ended there. But I watched Gabrielle disintegrate a little more each time she went to see her dad for his supervised visits.

"Gabrielle looked me in the eyes one day and begged me to not make her have to go with Daddy any more. I promised she'd never have to see him again without someone else around. When Terry's parents got visitation rights, it became apparent that I couldn't protect her any more. And I simply could *not* let my little girl be alone with that monster again.

"The decision to run with her when she was five was very easy."

Julie looked around the room at each one, hoping they could understand. They each leaned forward, listening intently.

"I've left a lot out and probably haven't done a good job of explaining it. But I'm begging you to please believe me. I did what I had to do. You can't possibly know what it's like to have your little girl abused and have no power to stop it. The only power I had was to take her and escape. So I did."

Julie sighed, relieved that she had gotten all that out. But she couldn't know what the repercussions would be for telling these three, any of whom could send her to another state with one phone call.

"It's been hard living on the run, but at least I know Gabrielle is safe. I know I did the right thing, and God has helped me, confirming all the time that He is with us. And Gabrielle is doing very well. Please believe me, and don't turn us in."

All three sat there, speechless.

"Well, I don't really know what to say, maybe for the first time ever," the pastor said.

"How many places have you lived since running away?" Mr. Sharp asked.

"Oh. I don't know. I haven't counted."

"Well, I'll tell you what," Mr. Sharp said. "I have about five of these milk cartons. When I go home, I'll rip them to shreds, throw them away, and pretend I never saw them."

Julie noticed tears streaming down Mrs. Sutherland's face.

"You did the right thing," she said, dabbing her eyes with a tissue. "I'm amazed you've been able to go this long and not be caught. God must really be watching out for you. I won't tell anyone," she promised. "I just can't imagine what I'd do if my little Gretchen went through what your child has been through."

The pastor finally spoke. "Well then. You have our confidence. We will just keep this information to ourselves. Does anyone else here know your story?"

"Well, as you know, I found out about this church and school from an acquaintance of Donna Blake's. Donna was my first contact here, and she told me how nice you all are, and to be honest, that's why I moved here. I needed to start all over again around some supportive people. So Donna knows my story to a certain extent. I don't think she'll tell anyone."

With all that out of the way, Julie was ready to get

up when the pastor spoke up. "Please, before you leave, can we just pray with you?"

They all bowed their heads.

"Dear Father, thank you for bringing Linda into our lives. We feel enriched knowing the story of how you have guided her and Gabrielle and how she's remained strong. You have been so faithful to her. Please use us here at New Life Bible Church to be a blessing to them. Please provide for all their needs and keep them safe. We would be honored if you would use us to help both of them remain free from their enemies. And please use their testimony to make us stronger in our faith."

Julie felt a peace she hadn't experienced in a long time. She just wanted to sit back and soak in more of it.

The pastor asked her how she would know when she could stop running.

"Well, I'm not really sure. I suppose at the worst, I will raise her like this until she turns 18, when custody will no longer be an issue."

Mrs. Sutherland spoke up. "I'm just curious. What has all this done for your faith in God?"

"Oh my goodness. Well, I came to know Jesus Christ as my personal savior in Sunday school when I was about eight years old. After that, I always went to church and lived a Christian lifestyle. But looking back, I was pretty shallow, obviously. I married Terry, didn't I? But when things got really hard, I learned what it really means to turn to God. I found that He is just what He said He is… a rock.

"My mother gave me a journal several months before I left with Gabrielle. In the front cover is the passage Psalm 27. I'd have to say God has used those words to stabilize me more times than I can count."

She thought for a second and felt she couldn't

leave without finishing that part of her story. "You know, you all can count on your families and your church. I envy you for how comfortable you can be here. I wish I could be that comfortable. But I can't really trust anyone. I've tried, but I always end up having to leave those I get close to. I can only trust in God. He's the only one who won't let me down. I hate to say it, but I'll probably have to . . . " She stopped. She didn't want to burden them with her insecurities. They probably wouldn't understand. "Never mind. At any rate, thank you for listening to me ramble."

"Oh no. We're completely moved by your story," Mrs. Sutherland said.

Julie realized she'd been gone longer than she expected. She needed to get back to Angie.

CHAPTER 21—OCTOBER 1991

The doorbell rang at exactly 5:30 p.m. Julie quickly turned off the oven and took off her apron. The house smelled so good, she thought. This would be a fun evening.

Mrs. Sutherland, whom Julie now had the freedom to call Rebecca, stood at the door with the prescribed cream cheese Danishes. Just then another lady pulled up. Shirley and her daughter, Pippa, bounded to the door with an apple pie.

"I think Courtney will be a bit late. I saw her going in the store as I was leaving," Shirley said, handing the pie to Julie.

Angie ran to the door when she heard Pippa's voice. "Oh good. You brought her," Angie said, referring to Pippa's Skipper doll. "I'll show you my dolls." And they were off to Angie's room.

Julie was living on the first floor of the church-owned apartment since the missionaries had moved back into the missionary house. The church gave Julie a generous monthly discount. Julie knew Pastor Frank was behind that.

"I'm sorry there's not much room in here," Julie apologized. "But I thought we could eat on these card tables, and then clear them off to work on our project."

She knew her mother would be so proud of her. After all, she was the inspiration behind the craft for the evening.

"We must be having something wonderful for dinner!" Courtney said when she arrived. "I can smell it outside."

It was Julie's first attempt at a sausage, squash, and apple casserole, in keeping with the fall season. "Well,

I thought I could hardly go wrong with sausage," Julie said. "To tell you the truth, I've wanted to make some of these recipes I've collected, so I'm thrilled to have some guinea pigs to try this one out on."

They all sat on folding chairs that Julie had borrowed from the school. She'd also borrowed a card table and found some decorative fall paper tablecloths with matching napkins and paper cups.

They all enjoyed their dinner, especially with the tasty additions the others brought. Courtney had brought apple cider.

"It looks like apples are the theme tonight," Shirley said, as she cut the apple pie.

After clearing the tableware and tablecloth, Julie brought out four sturdy, blank notebooks and explained the project.

"We're going to make decoupaged notebooks that you can use for anything you want. Mine is called *Thoughts & Prayers*."

"Why don't you show us yours?" Rebecca suggested.

Julie felt a little thrown off by that. She didn't want anyone reading even a page of her journal. But she guessed she could show it if she didn't let go of it.

She went to her room and grabbed her journal.

"Here it is. My mother gave it to me." She walked in front of each lady so each could see it more closely. Then she opened the front cover and showed the passage.

"That's a beautiful idea… and a beautiful notebook," Rebecca said.

Julie brought out decorative paper of all colors and patterns along with some magazines they could cut headline words out of. "We will use sponge pieces and Mod Podge glue to get the paper to stick, and you can also use the glue as a sealer. I'll show you."

179

Before long, they all had sticky fingers and piles of paper scraps in front of them and on the floor. Julie paid attention to how each lady was doing and offered compliments and suggestions.

"Your notebook looks so much better than mine," Shirley said to Julie. "Do you actually use it? I'd be afraid to write in one that beautiful."

"I actually do write in it, quite a lot. I like to write my prayers and what God is teaching me," she said. "It might sound kind of funny, but my journal is like a best friend. I can tell it anything."

"Oh, I completely understand that," Shirley said. "I used to have a diary that I wrote in every night. But after I got married, I quit writing in it so much. I guess then I had someone to tell all those things to."

"Yeah, Doug would probably rather have you keep it to your diary rather than tell him everything," Courtney joked.

By 8:15 they had finished their notebooks. Each looked unique and beautiful. Shirley was the first to look at her watch and suggest that she and Pippa should go. They were the first to leave. Courtney followed.

Rebecca volunteered to stay back and help clean up while Julie encouraged Angie to take a bath.

As she took a wet paper towel to the card tables, Rebecca told Julie how she admired her cooking and craft aptitude. "You're such a well-adjusted person, in spite of everything you've gone through. Has . . . ." She hesitated. Julie could tell she had something on her mind. "Has living like this been hard?"

"Um, in some ways, I suppose."

Rebecca stopped cleaning and the two of them sat down.

"Well, I mean, living a nomad lifestyle and never letting people in on your real life."

"I guess I usually don't think of it as difficult because I don't have any other choice. In fact, in one way, it's a really good thing. I'm truly thankful every single day that we're not caught and that Gabrielle gets to live a normal life without any fear that her father will hurt her."

"I'm sure that must be true," Rebecca said with a wistful look. "Well, I guess I'd better get going. Jack probably isn't paying any attention to Gretchen's bedtime."

"I should know, but what does Jack do, by the way?" Julie asked.

"He manages a hardware store. But I think his real vocation is watching TV," she sighed.

Julie didn't know how to respond to that. She looked around the kitchen. "Oh, here, take your leftover Danishes. Gretchen might enjoy them."

After she left, Julie leaned against the door. *That sure was a fun night. It felt so normal. I just love it here.*

Then she turned her attention to Angie, hearing about the great time she had playing dolls with Pippa.

###

"Hello little girl. Can I put some Jell-O on top of your green beans today?" Julie asked.

Angie rolled her eyes. "Mom, don't be silly," she said as she went through the school lunch line. Julie was working part time at the school as a lunch lady. She actually loved being around all that kid energy, to say nothing of being around food. Maybe this would be a springboard some day to a food career. Maybe she could write about food for kids.

As she was cleaning up Pastor Frank stopped by the kitchen.

"Hi Julie. How's it going today?"

"Just great. Any day with tater tots is a wonderful day. Especially if they have cheese on them."

His laugh seemed forced. Julie noticed he wasn't very cheerful.

"I'm wondering if you can come by my office when you get off work. I have something to discuss with you."

She agreed, but definitely didn't like the mystery.

She scooped leftovers into containers and washed pots and tray pans. She was done in half an hour and crossed the parking lot to the church and into Rebecca's office, which was just outside the pastor's office. Rebecca wasn't there, so Julie knocked on the pastor's doorframe. He was at his desk.

"Come on in," he said. "Have a seat."

She sat in one of the leather chairs.

"We have a situation you need to be aware of," he started. "A couple in our church just started divorce proceedings. They have a young child, and the husband is going to try for legal custody."

Julie felt bad for whoever it was. She could certainly relate, but couldn't figure out why that couple's private affairs should be any of her business. *I hope he doesn't want me to talk to them.*

"One reason he plans to give for appealing for full custody is that if his wife has any contact with their little girl, she is likely to take the girl and kidnap her—like you have done with Gabrielle."

"What? Kidnap her like I did? I don't get it. How does anyone know that I ran with Gabrielle?" She felt her blood rush to her face. "Who told these people about me?

"Well, actually, it's the Sutherlands. Rebecca told me that she told Jack about your situation and how she admires you for what you did.

Julie's mouth hung open. *Rebecca! What? Surely she and Jack aren't getting a divorce.*

The pastor seemed to read her mind. "They've had problems for some time. I've been counseling them, but they can't get past some of their challenges. I'll not go into details. But Jack is very much aware of you and how much Rebecca looks up to you. He is convinced that she will try to take Gretchen, and he's planning to testify about it in court and give you as his case in point."

Julie sat back in her chair, flooded with emotions. *I shouldn't have told these people about running away. But I didn't have a choice. I never suspected Rebecca was having problems with her husband. I should have known my story wouldn't stay within these walls.*

"Oh my goodness," she sighed. "What can we do? Do I need to go talk to them?"

"No. Don't do that. I've talked to Jack at length. He said he's going to cite you as an example and a bad influence on Rebecca. He really is obsessed with the idea that she will take Gretchen and run."

This will be disaster if lawyers and a judge find out my story. I bet they would investigate me and all the names we've had. We're going to have to leave and change our names again.

"Have they already met with lawyers?" Julie asked, wondering how much time she had.

"I'm not positive. I talked to Jack yesterday and tried to tell him that it wasn't a good idea to bring your name into the trial. He wasn't convinced. I think he'll meet with his lawyer this week."

"Well, I'm glad you told me as soon as you did."

"I wish I could tell you everything will be okay. I know God takes care of you, but I knew you needed to know about this."

"Thank you. I need to go now."

She looked at her watch. Angie wouldn't be out of school for another few hours. She knew what she needed to do.

Julie went back to the apartment and started filling plastic bags with important possessions. This time adrenaline wasn't leading her. In fact, she felt deflated. She picked out photos, clothes, and a few kitchen appliances. Then she sat on her bed with her journal and turned to the inside cover. This time the words that spoke deeply to her heart were, *Deliver me not over unto the will of mine enemies: for false witnesses are risen up against me, and such as breathe out cruelty. I had fainted, unless I had believed to see the goodness of the Lord in the land of the living.*

"Oh Lord. You know I don't have the strength for this," she wrote. "My enemy is someone I haven't even met yet, and he is planning to ruin my life. Please help me not to faint. In fact, I choose to trust that I'll see your goodness in the land of the living soon. Once again, I throw myself at your mercy."

Her mind felt clearer after she wrote that. She looked up at the ceiling. "And God, I mean it."

Then she went into Angie's room to pack.

She knew that when she decided it was time to go, she couldn't take the car because it belonged to the church. She didn't feel that she was ready to move out of town yet, but she knew she couldn't stay in the apartment, not knowing when some lawyer would find out about her and put someone on her trail.

She came up with a plan and dialed the phone.

"Hello, Shirley? This is Linda. Hey I'm fumigating our apartment for bugs, and I was wondering if Gabrielle and I could come to your place to escape the fumes this evening."

"Ah, having problems with bugs? That's the

problem with apartments. Your neighbors probably don't clean up their kitchen and they are attracting roaches for everyone. Yes, come over. Why don't you bring your pajamas and spend the night?"

Julie was relieved that Shirley suggested spending the night. She didn't want to have to ask. "Oh, thank you so much. You're a saint. Gabrielle and Pippa will have a great time."

Next, Julie had to pick up Angie from school. She wasn't sure if she was ready to break the bad news to her. So she decided to buy a bug bomb and set it off in the apartment so she wouldn't have to lie about why they weren't spending the night at their apartment.

The plan worked like a charm, and Julie had some time to devise her next move. She was starting to hatch an idea. This time, she wouldn't need Elizabeth's help, she hoped.

Early the next morning, Julie went to the trunk of the car to get a change of clothes for the two of them. They all got ready to start their day, and Julie planned to drive Angie and Pippa to school.

After she deposited the girls at school, she ran to the church to use Rebecca's phone. Once again, Rebecca wasn't there. Julie was glad. She could hear the pastor on his phone in his office.

She picked up Rebecca's phone and dialed. It rang five times. "Come on. Pick up!" Julie stood on one foot and then the other. She hung up and wondered what to do next. The pastor ended his call and came out of his office.

"So, now that you've had some time, what do you think?" he asked.

Julie didn't feel prepared to discuss her plans with

him. Certainly she wouldn't tell him everything, but she felt she did owe him some explanation, given that she was driving a church-owned car.

"I'm not sure how long Gabrielle and I will be around. Probably not much longer. But I'm going to leave the car with you when we go."

He looked her in the eyes. "I know that trust is a huge thing to you, and it's been shattered—once again. I just hate that it had to happen here. I'm sorry it turned out like this. You've been such an asset to our church and school. I wish I could do something to erase this whole . . . thing."

Julie gave him a half smile and hugged him. "Thank you," she sighed. "Now I better get over there and start working on lunch. Can I come back later and make a phone call?"

"Yes. Do whatever you need to do."

This time, when Angie came through the lunch line, Julie felt nostalgic. Her daughter was growing up so quickly, and it was wonderful to see all the friends she had made and to see her do so well in school. She didn't seem to suffer any insecurities from all their moves. One thing she knew. This next move would be a pretty easy adjustment. It might not even be hard to break the news to her. But she couldn't just yet.

After she finished cleaning in the kitchen, Julie went back to the office to try the call again.

The phone rang three times, and Julie thought she would pop with frustration. But then she heard, "Hello?"

"Oh my gosh, Melanie, I'm so glad you're there."

"Julie? I can't believe it's you! Oh wait. Is everything okay? Are you and Angie alright?"

"We're fine. There's nothing to worry about. Yet."

"Well, the girls and I miss you guys so much. We wonder about you all the time."

"I know. I'm such a horrible sister—and aunt. But I'm going to do better. First I have to ask, is everything okay around there? I mean, do you ever see police or detectives or anyone like that snooping around trying to find us there?"

"No. It's been pretty quiet. Nothing like the first year when it was still fresh."

"Good. You know, Angie and I need to move from where we are. Long story. I was trying to think of where to go next; what if we came to your area?"

"Wow, that would be incredible." Melanie paused. Would you, could you, really do that?"

"Well, yes. But I kind of need your help."

They discussed how they could be secretive about it, and where in Omaha or the surrounding area she and Angie might live. She asked Melanie to scout out locations and to think of any jobs Julie could do to support herself. After all, this move was different in that she wouldn't automatically have a church to help her out. But she felt compelled to be close to family again. Certainly Angie was ready. And maybe her mom could visit now and then, and they could have some real family time.

As they were discussing things, Rebecca walked in.

"Oh. I have to go. But be thinking. I'll be in touch later."

Rebecca looked as if she had been through a war. Gone was her pleasant, proper persona. Her eyes were red, her shoulders drooped, and she wasn't wearing her usual bright lipstick.

"Oh Rebecca. I'm so sorry. Pastor Frank told me. He kind of had to tell me."

"I know. I'm just sick about . . . everything. I guess I'm here to pack up my things."

"What do you mean?" Julie asked.

"Well, surely I can't be the church secretary with everything that's going on in my life right now."

"I don't know about that. Have you talked to Pastor about it?"

She plopped down in one of the armchairs. Julie was already sitting behind the desk. "No. I haven't talked to him. But what's the use? It would probably be better for me to quit than for him to have to ask me to leave.

"This job is just one thing. I can't tell you how awful I feel that you've been dragged into this. Gosh, if anyone doesn't need any more upheaval, it's you."

Julie could see why Rebecca would feel that way, so she couldn't blame her for that. But she didn't feel nearly as badly about it since she had a new plan—a plan she wouldn't tell a soul.

"Rebecca, I know this whole thing stinks. But I don't want you to give my concerns another thought. Don't feel guilty. I will be just fine. For the most part." Julie realized that another goodbye was coming, but that was for another time. Not this moment.

"I know you didn't plan this. You, or actually both of us, have to realize that God is bigger than this circumstance. In another year, maybe we'll both look back and realize how God led us, even though it doesn't make sense and feels awful."

"Maybe. But I sure can't imagine that happening. Dear God, what will become of Gretchen?" Then Rebecca started crying.

The pastor walked in. "Uh, do I need to leave?" he asked, looking at both of them.

"Well, actually, Rebecca needs to have a conversation with you," Julie said. "Do you want to do it now?" she asked her.

Julie stayed for the discussion, and when it was all over, they decided Rebecca should take a leave of absence, and then they would revisit her employment later.

Julie was glad to get out of there. But she could have kicked herself for not asking Rebecca if Jack had already talked to his lawyer. She guessed she should assume so.

She went to the store before picking up Angie, still trying to decide if they should spend the night at the apartment or beg for another night at Shirley's.

Realizing she was about out of gas, Julie pulled into the left turn lane leading to the gas station. As she waited for the traffic to clear, she looked at the gas station and saw a man pumping gas who reminded her of her father-in-law. She focused in on him, and a chill went up her spine. The car had a Kansas license plate. It *was* him. She nearly lost her breath, and quickly veered out of the turn lane and kept driving down the street, her heart racing.

How did he know to find me here? Or is this a coincidence? It couldn't be. How much does he know? Julie turned and went back to the school.

She went to Angie's classroom, knocked on the door and asked if she could speak with Gabrielle.

"Hi Mom. Why are you here?"

"Hey there, Pookie. I'd like you to go to your desk right now and quickly and quietly take your things out of it and then come with me. Okay?"

Angie looked into Julie's imploring eyes.

Julie continued. "I can't answer any questions right now, but I need you to be cool about this, and after we get in the car, I can tell you everything."

Angie's shoulders drooped. "We're moving again, aren't we?"

"I'm sorry Sweetie. We really need to, and we need to right away. I'll wait outside the room, okay?"

Then Julie thought hard. *Should we take a bus or a*

train? I guess a bus would be better. She imagined the route to the bus station, which she had thought through months earlier in case a time like this ever came. She already had all their things in the trunk. She would drive them to the bus station, buy the tickets, and just before getting on the bus, she would call the pastor or Rebecca and tell them where to find the car.

Just then her pager beeped. Maybe it was her sister calling with some living arrangement details. She looked down. It was 911. That meant one of her neighbors saw something suspicious at the apartment.

Julie slipped into the classroom to help Angie quickly pack.

Julie coaxed Angie down the aisle. "Let's go to the back, Sweetie."

They managed to maneuver themselves and five black garbage bags to the back of the bus. They put their bags in the back seat and on the floor and sat in the seat in front of them. That way they could be sure no one would disturb their things without their knowing it.

Soon the bus was moving, and Julie felt that familiar relief as they pulled out of yet another city uncaptured by their pursuers.

She looked carefully around the bus to see if there were any suspicious-looking people, like detectives, police, or FBI agents.

Truly, none of them could possibly be professionals. Julie determined that she was the best-dressed person on the bus, and she was wearing jeans and a sweatshirt.

"Okay. We're off. Now I can talk to you. Sorry I haven't focused on you enough since we left school,"

Julie said.

"I know. And I was too scared to ask what's going on."

Julie almost asked her why she was scared, but decided it must be because she acted scary. No need to rehearse that.

"Goodness. Where should I begin?" *This time I can't tell her a lot. She doesn't need to know about the divorce.*

"Maybe you could tell me what happened," Angie suggested with raised eyebrows.

"Good question. I suspected that we were about to be discovered. That's really why we didn't stay in our apartment last night."

"I thought it was because you used bug spray."

"Yes. Well, I did that as an excuse to get us out of the apartment. I had a feeling the police would come knocking on our door.

"So, this afternoon I was about out of gas. I was getting ready to pull into the gas station, and you'll never guess who I saw."

"Who?"

"Guess."

Angie thought. "The police?"

"No. Well, actually kind of yes. I saw your grandfather. Terry's dad."

"You did? What is he doing here?"

"I don't know!" Julie caught herself. Her voice was rising, and she didn't want anyone on the bus to hear them. "What do you remember about your grandfather?"

"He was kind of mean. He wouldn't let me eat cookies out of the cookie jar."

"Well, he's a policeman, you remember? And he vowed that he would find you and get you. So somehow he knew to come here to find you. Pretty scary, don't you think?"

"Would he make me go back to Daddy?" Angie asked.

"He would, and he would also make me go to jail for taking you away. That's why we have been so careful not to tell people who we are. The wrong people could find out, and I don't even want to think about what would happen then."

"I know. I don't either," Angie said. She put her hand on Julie's leg. "Then I'm glad you came and took me out of school."

Ohhh. That is so sweet. She's getting to be so mature.

They were quiet for a minute.

"Oh, but let me tell you where we're going!" Julie suddenly remembered. This was the best part. "Guess."

"To Grandma's?"

"No. But close."

"To Hawaii."

"Now you're getting silly."

She whispered into Angie's ear.

Angie squealed. Several passenger's looked at them as Julie giggled with her.

"Just think of it. Soon you'll get to see Lexie and April and Aunt Melanie and Uncle Steve."

"Will we live with them?" Angie hoped.

"That wouldn't be a good idea. We'll have to find a way to be extra careful that people don't find out we are related to them. People around there know she has a sister who's wanted by the police."

Then Julie thought more about it. *Is this such a good idea? I wonder what Elizabeth would say. I'm probably a moron for not calling her. Maybe I will a little later. But we have to go some place. We'll just find a way to make this work.*

They sat quietly. Julie decided to pass the time by reading. All she had was her journal, so she took it out of one of the bags. Actually, she thought, this would be a good time to write down another miracle. She had narrowly escaped getting caught—once again. *This will sure be a good book in a few years. I wonder how it will end. I hope it will be the kind of thing I can read to Angie's kids some day. It would surely keep them fascinated. How could anyone know our whole story and not believe in God? Well, they would just have to be hopeless.*

"There is one more thing to think about," she told Angie. "We will have to come up with new names."

CHAPTER 22—NOVEMBER 1991

Julie woke up naturally, enjoying the cheerful sun streaming through the orange curtains in the cabin bedroom. The muted sound of young girls playing Yahtzee on the other side of the door was music to her ears. Julie sat up in bed. She smelled bacon and heard her mother tell Melanie to wake her up.

Julie got up and swung open the door. "I'm alive, I'm awake, I'm enthusiastic!" she proclaimed.

"I haven't thought about that phrase in years," Melanie said. Their father had always said that to them when they were little girls as he came in to get them up in the morning before he left for work.

"I'd forgotten too," their mother said. "You girls want to help me get breakfast on the table?"

While eating eggs, bacon, and English muffins with grape jelly, they discussed their plans for the day. First, they thought maybe they should go in the woods and find some logs for the fire, or make some logs. An axe was in the little mud room for just such a need.

"I know, can we go fishing?" Cousin April asked. She was 11 years old, just a year older than Angie.

"Yeah!" Angie agreed.

"I think that requires worms. Why don't we wait until Daddy is here and let him decide if that's a good idea," Melanie suggested.

Steve was checking into apartments for Julie and Angie. It was just a girls' weekend at Steve's parents' lake house. They all thought it would be the perfect place for them to reunite, unnoticed by suspicious eyes.

Lexie, now 14, reminded them that they hadn't all been together for four and a half years.

"It seems longer than that, doesn't it?" Rita asked.

"Why don't all of you go on a hike. Melanie, how long does it take to walk around the lake?"

"Only about 45 minutes. Why don't you come with us?"

She insisted she would stay in the cabin and clean.

Once the dishes were cleared and everyone was bundled up and off on their outing, Rita got out a bag of crepe paper, balloons, scissors, and tape.

A few minutes later, Rita heard a crunching sound outside, and a slow engine. It stopped. She peeked out the window. It was Steve's car. She swung open the door.

"You're here early. We weren't expecting you until this evening."

"I found them an apartment and signed the papers yesterday afternoon. So I thought I'd just come down here early and help celebrate."

"Good. I'm not sure I can blow up and tie all these balloons before they get back from their walk."

Julie found herself out of shape. The girls were running ahead, and she and Melanie were trying to keep up with them.

"I hate to be such a sap, but I'm really glad you decided to move here," Melanie said. "Lexie has been talking about you two a lot lately. I think one of her most vivid childhood memories is the day we all went to the zoo six years ago."

"Wow. You remember it was six years ago?"

"Lexie reminds me. She has quite the memory for dates and numbers. Anyway, through the years, whenever we've seen clowns, she has always reminded me how Angie doesn't like clowns. She also remembers not getting to see elephants at the zoo because we had to take Angie to the hospital."

They walked silently for a few minutes. Julie would never forget that day either. "Well, now the girls will get to be together for happier times, hopefully," she said, adding, "I've missed you guys so much. You have no idea what it's like to not be really close to anyone because you can't let people know who you are. In the places I've stayed, I've had to build a new life based on whatever was around me. And just when I'd get comfortable with my new identity, I'd have to run again."

Melanie listened carefully. "I truly don't know how you did it."

"You could do it too, if you were in my shoes."

They were almost back at the cabin with the girls ahead of them.

"Hey, Daddy's here!" they heard April shout.

When Julie and Melanie walked in the cabin, everyone was facing them and shouted "Happy birthday!"

Julie was amazed to see streamers, balloons, and a Happy Birthday sign.

"Happy 33rd birthday," her mom said, and held out the birthday cake she had managed to smuggle in. They lit the candles and sang to her.

"I already know what I wish for," she said. "But I can't tell you." She blew out the candles.

Out came a few presents. Julie felt like a kid again. "You know, in all this time on the run, we haven't celebrated my birthday. I forgot what it's like."

She opened a box from Melanie and pulled out a pink fluffy bathrobe. "Oh, I love it. I would have never bought myself something like this."

"I thought that was probably the case. I guess what I was thinking when I bought it was—relax! Oh, and there's something else in the corner of the box."

Julie found a box of chamomile tea. "Well, I guess that about completes the idea, doesn't it?"

Her mother handed her a neatly wrapped box with

instructions to open it carefully. She found a white silk blouse—far fancier than anything she would have ever bought herself. There was also a glass mug with Psalms 27:1 printed on it. "Oh my goodness. It's our verse!" Julie blurted. She quoted it aloud, not needing to look at the mug: *The Lord is my light and my salvation; whom shall I fear? The Lord is the strength of my life; of whom shall I be afraid?*

"That verse has gotten me through a lot," she said.

"Me too," her mom added.

She also found two books, *In His Steps* and *A Shepherd Looks at Psalm 23.*

"Have you read those yet?" Rita asked her.

"No, but I've heard of them."

Melanie spoke up. "She gave them to me a few years ago for Christmas. I think you'll love them, and maybe even more than I did, given what you've been through."

Julie admitted her love of reading, but added that she hadn't really done much of it, even though she had access to such books when she worked at Christian schools.

"I should be reading more books. After all, someday, somehow, I'll write a book myself," Julie said.

"I know you will, Dear," Rita responded.

"I don't have a present to give you," Steve said, "but I have good news. I found an apartment for you two."

He explained that it was nearby in Council Bluffs, Iowa. He thought that living across the state border from them would provide some safety—given it would be a different police jurisdiction.

"And, I found you a job. Or actually, my dad did. One of his friends runs an insurance agency, and he needs a receptionist. So he agreed to hire you."

Julie felt butterflies. Usually she was in charge of getting work that she felt comfortable with.

"Do they know anything about me?" she asked.

"The agency owner knows about you. He's actually known about you for several years. My parents and he and his wife are good friends, so they know your situation, but he isn't telling anyone else at the agency."

A stranger knew about her? Who else knew? But Julie also felt slight relief that at least her boss wouldn't be caught off guard if she suddenly had to leave.

"A receptionist, huh?"

Julie took a bottle of Clorox and paper towels to the surfaces of their new apartment. It would have been wonderful if her mom could have been there to help. For some reason, this felt like a new and permanent destination.

She was thinking about what names they should switch to, pondering the name *Tina* for herself. She would have to remember to have a serious conversation with Angie soon about what her name should be.

Julie thought the apartment was perfect—something she would have picked herself. It was on the second floor and had two bedrooms, one with a master bathroom. She loved the kitchen. It was at an angle and opened into the living room with a bar area separating the two rooms. The carpet was new, and the walls were freshly painted an eggshell white. It had a sliding glass door in the living room with vertical blinds. It also had a door leading outside from the kitchen. Both doors led to a private balcony. She imagined the plants she could put out there. The view was the best part of all. Some of the units faced the parking lot, but hers faced a wooded hill. Because her balcony had walls on both sides, she felt perfectly secluded.

The closet in Angie's room was standard-sized, which was more than enough since the two of them hardly had anything. Julie stood on a folding chair to clean the closet shelf. As she swiped, a piece of paper fluttered down. Julie picked it up.

She gasped. It was a birth certificate. At first glance, she saw the birth state was Washington. She looked at the name. It said Victoria Ellen Morgan. And the date of birth was August 18, 1981. So close to Angie's!

Julie stared at it, blinking, with her mouth open. She felt a powerful sense of peace and assurance that this was for them, and this was to be Angie's new name. She repeated the name over and over. She also rolled the name Tina Morgan over in her mind and said it aloud a few times. She liked it as much as she could like a fake name with no built-in personality. She would define *Tina Morgan*.

Angie was out back exploring the woods. Julie went to the balcony and spotted her. "Pookie!" she shouted. "Come here. I want to show you something."

When Angie got inside, Julie asked, "So, what do you think of the name Victoria Ellen Morgan?"

"Who's that?"

"That's your new name." She showed her the birth certificate that fell from the sky. Angie agreed that this was amazing.

"Victoria," she stated. "I don't know anyone with that name."

"Oh, you probably do. That's where the name Vicky comes from. We could name you Vicky for short, if you want."

"No, I think I like Victoria," Angie decided.

Once again, Julie was grateful that the naming conversation turned out easier than it could have. She always dreaded renaming Angie. After all, a name was such a personal thing.

"And you can call me Tina Morgan."

"Well, you'll always just be 'Mom' to me."

And that suited Julie just fine. This was something to go in the journal. God miraculously dropped an identity down from heaven for Angie.

Just then, the doorbell rang and Julie's heart skipped a beat. It was an automatic reflex that had long ago become normal. She peeked out and saw a lady about her age with a girl about Angie's age. She opened the door.

"Hello there. I'm sorry to bother you, but my name is Dottie and this is my daughter Angie. We saw you two move in, and Angie was so excited to see someone her age that we thought we'd stop and introduce ourselves."

Julie and Angie looked at each other, and Julie took control with, "Oh, thank you. This is Victoria and I'm Tina Morgan. Would you like to come in?"

"Oh no, we'll let you get settled, but I thought we could meet so if the girls play together, we won't all be strangers. Are you new to the area?"

"Yes, we are. Brand new. But we look forward to getting to know the area and meeting new people," Julie said, not really prepared for an in-depth conversation.

Angie eyed her new potential friend who was wearing blue jeans and a pink coat. "I'm ten years old. How old are you?"

"I'm eleven. In the fifth grade."

"I'm only in fourth grade."

"We have a playground behind that building," neighbor Angie said.

"I saw. Maybe sometime we can play together over there."

Dottie piped up. "That would be very nice. Well, we better get going and let you get back to work."

"Thanks for stopping by and introducing yourselves," Julie called after her.

Julie closed the door. "Well there, Pookie, I don't know about you, but I think we got our new names just in time."

"Yes, and what do you think about her name?"

"This will be hard for you when someone calls for Angie, don't you think?"

"I guess I'll get used to it."

During the brief encounter, Julie realized she would have to figure out what she could tell these people in Council Bluffs and what she couldn't—especially about having family in the area. For now, she would err on the side of caution and not admit that her sister lived 15 minutes away and that her mom lived three hours away.

Maybe I should call Elizabeth now and tell her what we've done.

"You're kidding me, right?" Elizabeth responded.

"I just feel right about this. I want to be close to family," Julie replied.

"Oh my gosh. I don't think that's very smart, Julie. The FBI doesn't give up. I really think they will find you in no time." Elizabeth's words sounded so foreboding.

"I know it sounds reckless. But let me tell you how we came up with Angie's new name." Julie told her the story.

"Okay. Well, you're there, so we'll just have to hope for the best. But do be careful. I mean it."

CHAPTER 23—MARCH 1992

Wanda and Lydia stood giggling at the copy machine, which was in the corner of reception area next to the water cooler. Julie heard them talking about their weekends. She was battling a cold and had a headache. She decided she'd better take some cold medicine, so she took her cup to the water cooler.

Wanda and Lydia stopped talking and glared at her.

"How was *your* weekend? Did you do anything fun?" Lydia half sneered.

It wasn't a genuine question, but an assumption that Julie hadn't done anything fun. She was used to the inevitable Monday weekend update conversation. Normally she would have politely named a few interesting things, but today she wasn't in the mood. "I fried a few eggs, washed a few loads of laundry . . . you know, the usual."

The two gave a taunting laugh. Julie went back to her post to answer the phone and type some auto insurance claim forms.

"She's so boring," she heard Lydia say.

"I know, and look how she dresses."

Julie was wearing a light blue A-lined skirt and a dark blue knit sweater, which she suddenly felt self-conscious in. She didn't have many clothes. Back in her mall-job days, she dressed as stylishly as anyone else, but her priority had long since shifted away from fashion.

But she was no shrinking violet and decided to get up again for a little more water in her cup. They stopped talking again.

"Excuse me," Julie said, "but I think you left your manners outside."

The two girls went back to their offices.

Her phone buzzed, which meant her boss wanted to see her. She took her notebook and pen with her.

"Here, I've got a few homeowners' insurance quotes I'd like your help with. I know I haven't spent much time teaching you how to do those, so I thought I'd show you how."

"Okay," Julie said, blowing her nose.

"But first I should ask, how's it going?"

"How's what going?"

"Well, this job? Are you getting more comfortable with it? I know insurance is a new field for you."

"It's a challenge for sure. There are so many things to learn and companies and people to keep track of. I guess I should ask you how *you* think I'm doing."

"It takes a long time to learn everything. I'm just glad to have someone conscientious like you. It's hard to find someone like you these days."

"Hmm," was all Julie said.

"I notice you don't pal around much with the other girls."

"Oh, they are so much younger. And I'm a mother. We don't live in the same worlds."

Mr. Bogart leaned forward in his chair, folded his hands together on top of his desk and spoke more quietly. "I know. I want to ask you to hang tight and not get too upset with the girls. Lydia won't be a problem for much longer. I won't say any more, but relief is on the way."

His cryptic comment intrigued Julie. She hadn't realized how obvious it was that she didn't get along with the two women.

"Oh, I don't hate Lydia or anything. It's probably normal office stuff I'm just not used to. I just try to ignore her as much as I can . . . sorry to say," Julie responded.

"There are other issues, so don't worry," he said.

The phone rang, and since it was Julie's job to answer, and she was in Mr. Bogart's office, he took the call.

"Yes, she's right here." He put the caller on hold.

"It's for you. You want to take it out there?" he asked.

She did.

"Mom!" she said. "You're calling me."

That was not normal. They both still vigilantly lived under the assumption that her mom's phone was bugged.

"I know, Sweetie. I'm calling from a pay phone. I'm sorry to bother you at work. That was your boss, wasn't it? I don't want to make him mad. Please apologize for me."

"Mom, what's the matter?" Julie could tell that her usually calm mother was rattled.

"I was watching the early local news this morning and your father-in-law was on. He said they almost tracked you down in Indianapolis. He said an Indiana couple is getting a divorce, and the husband is filing for custody of their child, fearing that the mother will run with the child like you did."

Julie felt the bottom fall out of her stomach. She asked if they said where she might be now.

"No, but they named cities you have lived in and names you have gone by, so they know quite a bit about you."

"Oh dear, Lord," Julie said as she thought about what she should do.

"I'll have my prayer group pray for you today," her mom said. They all knew the real story and had regularly prayed for her since she originally left with Angie. "I don't think they have any idea where you are, but be careful, and you should be very careful about contacting Melanie. I'll call her next and tell her. And don't forget Psalm 27:1."

"I won't forget it. Thank you." Julie hung up the phone and put her head on her desk.

"Dear Lord," she breathed. "Please help."

She had a small Bible in her desk and thumbed to Psalm 27. She came across verses 11–12. *Teach me thy way, O Lord, and lead me in a plain path, because of mine enemies. Deliver me not over unto the will of mine enemies: for false witnesses are risen up against me, and such as breathe out cruelty.*

She was so thankful that in her and Melanie's ecstasy at being near each other, they were smart enough to not be in the same church, though she and Angie hadn't settled in on a church yet. Also, the girls were not in the same school—or even in the same state, thanks to Steve's wisdom.

While her head was still on her desk, Mr. Bogart came into the reception area. "Are you okay?"

She looked up. "Uhh. I think I'll be okay. I think I'll go home for lunch today. Do you think someone can cover the phones?"

I just don't have the energy to deal with anything today.

"Let's hurry up and eat," Julie told Angie. She had heard about a terrific church with a wonderful youth program on Wednesday nights, and Julie decided they would try it out that night.

"What's wrong with the church we've been going to?" Angie asked.

"Well, you haven't really gotten to know any of the other kids very well, and I don't think I can sit through another sermon of Pastor Mike's where he says 'Amen?' after every sentence. So let's try Redeemer Covenant Church tonight."

Julie dropped Angie off in the church basement after meeting the adult leader couple, who assured her that Victoria would be well taken care of and would have a wonderful time.

Then Julie went upstairs. The pastor's wife greeted her. "I don't think I've met you before. My name is Sylvia."

Julie felt under-dressed in her jeans. Sylvia wore a green, belted shirt-dress and a floral scarf.

"Let me introduce you to a few other ladies."

Soon Julie felt more at ease, especially since other women wore jeans.

The pastor gave a short message about prayer, obviously picking up from where he had left off the previous week. He talked about the importance of faith when praying, and that without faith, there would be no hope of answered prayer. Julie agreed with him. *If only he knew!* she thought.

Soon he asked everyone to break up into small groups of six or seven, and he wanted couples and singles in each group, so everyone felt included.

Julie didn't have to wonder what group she would be in. A small group gathered around her. *What friendly people,* she thought.

Her group included another unattached woman and two couples. She, being a new face, was asked to introduce herself. She gave her name and explained that she had a daughter downstairs and that she was new to the area. She couldn't decide if she should say where she worked, but she didn't have to decide, because the girl next to her jumped in and introduced herself as Goldie. Julie wondered how she got that name since she had long, straight black hair. The other two couples introduced themselves briefly and then everyone gave their prayer requests, which were mostly about the health of someone they loved. One man asked for prayer regarding his job, while Julie discreetly fished around in her purse for a mint.

"I should find out in a few days if I get a new position as the police chief," the man said.

Julie froze. Someone asked him how his interview went, and he explained that he felt confident he would get the job since he had longest tenure.

One thing Julie knew, they needed to bow their heads soon so he wouldn't have any more chance to examine her face. She took charge, looking at her watch.

"Oh look at the time. Maybe we should start praying."

They all agreed and bowed their heads.

Julie didn't hear a word anyone prayed. She imagined how she would break away from the group as soon as the last amen was said and go get Angie. She prayed silently and earnestly that Angie wasn't in the basement giving away any secrets.

How do these things always happen to me? What are the chances that I would run into this guy and be stuck in a group with him?

Before long she felt a nudge from the girl next to her. "Would you like to pray next?"

"Uhh, no, I'm a little shy. I think I'll pass this time."

That apparently was it, then. Everyone looked up. Fortunately, they didn't all focus on her.

"Excuse me, I've enjoyed praying with you guys. But I really need to get going." Then she went to the basement. The kids were all in small groups, each with a leader, quoting memorized Bible verses. Julie found Angie.

"Hey there, Sweetie." Then Julie addressed the

leader. "I hate to interrupt. But Ang . . . Victoria and I need to go now."

"Well, sure. Victoria, we enjoyed having you tonight. I hope we see you again next week."

"Thank you," Angie said and jumped up to go with Julie.

Julie took her hand and encouraged her to go straight out the door to the car.

"I'm sorry, Sweetie, but we can't come back to this church," Julie told her once they were in the car. "We will try another church Sunday morning."

She decided not to tell Angie the reason, but she did ask her about her conversations with others. It turned out that Angie had no personal conversations, because the children mostly played games, listened to a lesson, and reviewed memory verses.

She had one other church in mind to try out, and if that didn't work, she just didn't know what she would do.

The next Sunday morning, they visited Life Hope Church. She knew about this one from a newspaper ad. It claimed to be a church centered on the Bible and its application to life. She didn't hold out much hope that it would particularly strike her fancy, but she just couldn't give up finding a church yet.

Julie liked the hymns they sang. She knew them by heart . . ."Wonderful Grace of Jesus," "How Firm a Foundation," "The Bible Stands." For some reason those songs put her at ease, even though she was in an unfamiliar place.

After announcements and a time where everyone greeted those around them, the pastor asked everyone to open their Bibles to Psalm 27.

Oh good. This should be interesting.

"Let me give the background to this," he said. "It's a Psalm of David, and he wrote it when he was facing conflict with King Saul, who was hunting him down unjustly to kill him. David had to run for his life with no place to call home, since his home had been with King Saul, who was now suddenly his enemy.

"How could he get through a time like that? He did it by comforting himself in God. He rehearsed everything he knew about God, and wrote about it."

Julie barely breathed. Every word he said touched her heart to the core. It underscored everything she knew about God and His faithfulness through her situation. She wanted to stand and shout, "Amen!"

The pastor continued. "David was a solitary man. But he was used to that from his years as a shepherd in the field with nothing but sheep. To pass the time, he wrote and he sang. The words he wrote speak to us today. We should all leave a legacy in words as David did."

That's exactly what my journal is for! I want Angie to have it as a legacy of what God has done in our lives. I don't want her to forget. I want this faith to be her faith, not just mine.

Then the pastor went through the comforting, self-encouraging lessons David penned in Psalm 27.

She took notes on the back of her bulletin and had soon filled all of its empty space. A woman nearby noticed and gave her a piece of paper from her notebook.

People take notes in this church? She marveled. *These people are really serious about the Bible.*

The verses that stood out the most from Pastor Brad's sermon were *For in the time of trouble he shall hide me in his pavilion: in the secret of his tabernacle shall he hide me; he shall set me up upon a rock. And now shall mine head be lifted up above mine enemies round about me . . . .*

He asked, "How many of you have ever

experienced that?"

Julie raised her hand. So did others. "All of you should experience that, because that is what God is like. He will hide you when you need to be hidden. He will set you upon a rock. That rock is Christ. We sang 'How Firm a Foundation' this morning. We should all know Him as a rock and a firm foundation. If you don't, you don't really know Him."

Julie didn't want the sermon to end. No sermon she had ever heard had meant as much to her. When it was over, she sat and wept while the final hymn played, which was "I Surrender All."

She had to shake the pastor's hand afterwards. "I can't tell you how much I needed to hear that. God really used you this morning. This is the church my daughter and I need to be in," she said.

"Well, we're glad to have you. Thank you for your kind words."

As she walked away, Julie heard another woman tell the pastor, "This is my first time here. I have to tell you, that was the best sermon I've ever heard."

After the woman was finished talking to the pastor, Julie introduced herself to the woman. "Those were practically my exact words to him," she said. "My name is Tina, and this was my first Sunday here too."

She found out the woman's name was Beth Crowly, and she was a single mom too. The two decided they should have lunch together that very day.

It turned out to be one of the best Sundays Julie could remember—one she immediately wrote about in her journal.

CHAPTER 24—JULY 1992

Julie finished brushing her teeth, put on her nightgown, and went to the kitchen to get a glass of water. She noticed light coming from under Angie's door. She opened the door to turn out the light and found her 11 year-old lying there staring at the ceiling with her arms behind her head.

"What's wrong, Sweetie. Can't you go to sleep?"

"No," she sighed.

"Is something on your mind?" Julie sat on the floor beside Angie's bed—a hand-me-down from her cousin Lexie.

"I miss Daddy."

Julie's jaw dropped. "You do?"

"Yes. Do you think he's still trying to find me?"

Julie knew that Terry was a very real enemy to Angie, and she thought Angie realized that. She breathed a quick prayer for help in handling this.

"What do you remember about Daddy?" she asked. "It's been such a long time since we talked about him."

"I remember that he likes cars. I remember that he likes to swim, and he likes to give kids swimming lessons."

"Do you remember anything about the way he used to treat you?" Julie asked, stroking Angie's wrist.

"Not really too much. I think sometimes he was mean. But maybe he has changed."

Julie remembered that her advisor Elizabeth had told her that over time Angie might forget the abuse. Stuffing her thoughts and feelings was a way of protecting herself, and it was okay if that ever happened. But some day she would have to face it all again.

"Well, Sweetie, you do remember why we have been on the run all these years, and why we've been hiding from police and not letting people know who we really are?"

"Yes."

"Okay. Then what I'm wondering is what makes you miss your daddy all of a sudden. Or is this something you've been thinking for a long time but you've been afraid to tell me?"

"No."

"You know you don't have to be afraid to tell me anything. I won't get mad at you for how you feel." *I hope I'm handling this right.*

"Well, you know at church they are planning a father and daughter banquet, and I heard the girls in my Sunday school class talking about it."

"Oh." Julie realized exactly what the problem was. "Do you feel a little left out?"

Angie nodded with tears in her eyes.

Julie got onto her knees and reached over and hugged Angie.

"You know, I don't see any reason why we couldn't ask Uncle Steve if he would take you to the banquet. I'll bet he would love to."

"Really?" Angie lightened up a little.

"Of course. Why don't I call him tomorrow and ask him? Or would you like to ask him?"

"Will you ask him?"

"I sure will. And Pookie, don't be afraid to talk to me about anything."

Their church was a regular smorgasbord of activities, for which Julie was grateful, since that's where they were used to making all their friends. She and Beth Crowly had become very good friends. She felt comfortable telling Beth almost anything, but not her biggest secret.

The singles at church unofficially took turns planning events. Beth and Julie decided it was their turn. Beth suggested they plan a board game night. Julie immediately started suggesting snacks they could make. She relished the thought of using her culinary skills on others again.

She planned barbecued meatballs, cheese and Rice Krispie puffs, Texas sheet cake, lemon poppy seed cake, Chex mix, and kettle corn.

They discussed what they would wear to the party.

"Don't laugh, but I want you to go with me to a thrift store," Beth said. "They have the most excellent clothes you could imagine, and for practically free."

"I can't argue with practically free. Let's do it."

She loved how unpretentious Beth was, to say nothing of adventurous.

Julie found a pair of perfectly fitting red corduroys, a black leather jacket and some boots, all for under $20. "I absolutely love this!" she told Beth. "I would have never thought to shop in a thrift store."

"Are you going to be okay without me for the evening?" Julie asked Angie later as she put on her earrings. She didn't often leave Angie home alone, but she knew Angie was capable of entertaining herself and staying out of trouble.

Julie had made plenty of extra treats for Angie and her neighbor friend named Angie. They were going to play together, and neighbor Angie's mother would keep an eye on her.

At the party, Julie set out treats while Beth put games on the various tables, and people began wandering in.

"Can I help?" someone asked. Julie turned and faced a skinny guy in faded blue jeans and a navy blue knit shirt. She'd never seen him before.

"Well, I guess you can help eat all this," she said.

"All this looks great. Is that kettle corn?"

"It sure is. I have the secret recipe they use at carnivals."

"I haven't had that since I was a kid—at the Omaha Zoo."

"Go ahead and try it and let me know what you think."

He took a handful and approved.

"Who was that?" Beth came over and asked after he walked away.

"Well. I don't know. I forgot to ask him his name. I guess that's fairly rude of me!"

"I think he's pretty cute. Why don't I go find out something about him?" Beth suggested.

"Yeah. While you're at it, ask him if he works for the FBI."

"What?"

"Never mind. Just kidding."

Julie cut the Texas sheet cake and the lemon poppy seed cake and then realized she had forgotten to bring napkins from home. She went into the church kitchen to find some.

Soon Beth appeared with the guy. "I told him he should properly introduce himself," Beth said.

He stuck out his hand. "Hi, my name is Peter Kowalski, and I work for the FBI."

Julie burst out laughing, which made Beth laugh.

He smiled, but with questioning eyebrows.

"Oh, it's just a joke," Julie said. Then she stopped laughing. "You don't really work for the FBI, do you?"

"Actually, no. I'm a high school English teacher."

"Oh good. Then we can be friends," she said. Then she looked around the kitchen. "Do they not have napkins in this place?"

All three busied themselves opening drawers and

cabinets. "It's official," Julie announced. "They don't have napkins."

"I'll go get some," Peter said.

"Would you?" Julie asked. And off he went. *Boy, he's pretty cute. And nice too.*

The rest of the night Julie alternated between game tables and hovering over the food table. The room was filled with 30 or 40 people, many of whom she had never seen before.

"Obviously there's a need for this kind of activity. It seems to draw people out of the woodwork," Julie told Beth as they collected dirty paper plates and cups with Peter's help.

"Yes, this was a lot of fun. Maybe I can help plan one," he volunteered.

Julie decided to make conversation with Peter as they cleaned up. *I think we should keep this one around.* "So, high school English, huh? Is that English literature or English grammar?"

"Both. But I really enjoy English grammar and creative writing."

"I like creative writing too," Julie said.

"Hmm. Well, I also teach adult creative writing classes at the junior college. They are non-credit classes. You should sign up for one."

"Well, maybe I will."

"One will start in September, and you should sign up soon because they fill up fast."

"That was interesting," Julie said as she hung up the phone.

"Who was that?" Angie asked.

"Peter Kowalski from church. He's painting houses this summer and he'll be close to my office tomorrow at lunchtime. He wanted to know if I'd like to meet him for lunch."

"He wants to take you out on a date?" Angie asked.

"Well, I wouldn't really call it a date. We're going to meet at Jake's Barbecue."

"You can't go out with a boy!"

"Ohhh, my little girl is jealous!" Julie teased, poking her in the belly button. "Well, you don't have a thing to worry about. We're just going to eat lunch. I know you haven't met him. But he's a high school teacher."

"You're going on a date with a teacher?"

"Okay, now stop it. There's absolutely nothing wrong with eating lunch with a guy."

It was true that she hadn't been on a date . . . since Terry. *This will be fun. An hour-long lunch isn't much of a threat. I just won't tell him much about myself. I'll keep the conversation light and focused on him as much as possible. Most people like to talk about themselves, so that should be easy,* she thought.

The next morning she stayed busy figuring auto insurance quotes and filling out a homeowner's application for an anxious pear-shaped man who came by the office. She was enjoying her job much more since her co-worker Lydia wasn't there anymore. One morning shortly after Mr. Bogart had told her that Lydia wouldn't be a problem for much longer, Julie came in and found that Lydia had been let go at the end of the previous day.

At 11:25, Julie headed out the door to the restaurant. Peter was already there.

After they'd sat and ordered their barbecue sandwiches, Julie decided she'd go ahead and steer the conversation. "So, how long have you lived around here?"

"All my life, though most of it in Omaha. My

parents still live there. They immigrated to the area from Poland before I was born."

"Oh, of course. Your last name. Kowalski," Julie said. "Have you ever been to Poland?"

He described the two times he had visited family there and why his parents had moved to the U.S. "My dad got an education in law here and worked for the Nebraska state court system as a judge. He's actually quite well known in legal circles. He's been extremely involved in the American Judges Association, and a number of years ago helped organize the American Academy of Judicial Education. But he's retired now."

Julie found that to be interesting, but actually, she didn't like to think about judges, thanks to her experience. *I better switch topics.* "So, how about your mother?" she asked.

Peter looked down. "My mother never really needed to work. She took care of my brother and me. After we were grown, she started volunteering at the hospital and other places. But right now she's very sick. She has lung cancer and has six months to live, at the most."

"Oh, I'm so sorry." Julie instinctively reached out to touch his arm. "That is so sad."

There was a short silence. "The saddest thing is that neither of my parents knows Jesus as their Savior. They are pretty much atheists, though I've told them many times about how real God is. My dad, being a judge, I thought would grasp the concept of God coming down to earth and taking our death sentence himself to make restitution for our sins. But it went right over his head."

Julie nodded. "I think it's hard for people to let themselves think seriously about what happens after death. It's the ultimate of *ignorance is bliss.*"

Peter agreed. "I wish I had some way to get through to them."

"Don't give up," Julie encouraged. "I'll pray for them," she sincerely promised.

"It's funny, though," Peter said. "My mother loves angels."

"So do I," Julie said. She almost blurted out that she named her daughter *Angie* because of her love for angels. She was so glad she didn't say it, though. That would have been a huge mistake.

Julie had a thought to encourage Peter. "You like to write. Do you keep a journal? It would help you sort out your thoughts. I keep one."

"Actually, I do keep a journal, and I love to go back through and read it. But I find that the things I thought were so important before always seem so silly later."

Julie laughed. "Me too." She told him about the journal her mother had given her years earlier. "It's a notebook decoupaged with purple and pink paper with flowers and gold foil glued into it. On the outside it says *Thoughts & Prayers*, and on the inside cover, whoever made it glued the scripture from Psalm 27. That chapter has become a huge part of my life."

I can't believe I'm telling him all this. But she babbled on. "The first sermon I heard at this church was the pastor explaining Psalm 27. It's hard looking for a new church, but that sermon told me this was the church for me. That's the day I met Beth."

"I remember that sermon," Peter said. "It helped me with what I'm going through with my mom. In fact, I memorized one of the verses he talked about. '*For in the time of trouble he shall hide me in his pavilion: in the secret of his tabernacle shall he hide me; he shall set me up upon a rock.*'"

Julie sat back, amazed. "That's the verse that

meant the most to me too!"

This is so refreshing. We have so much in common.

"I know it's a really tough time right now," Julie said before they left. "What are your parents' names and I will pray for them."

"My mom's name is Anna, and my dad has always gone by Judge, but his name is Leonard."

Before they left, Julie promised to sign up for his creative writing class at the junior college.

As Julie drove back to the office, she felt a warm peace. *He was so easy to talk to, and he thinks just like me. This is unbelievable.*

She decided to pray for him out loud in her car. "Dear Lord, please comfort Peter. He's really hurting." Then she thought for a second about his mother's dire circumstances. "And please speak to Anna's heart about her need to know you. Maybe you can bring someone or something to her besides Peter to explain what she needs to know. Open her heart to receive it before it's too late."

She was concentrating on her prayer so much, she didn't notice the light she was stopped at had turned green until the car behind her honked. "Oh, sorry," she said. "And speak to Peter's father too. They may be holding each other back from really taking you seriously."

She decided she would also write her prayers for them in her journal so she could look back on the date whenever God answered, if she was still around when it happened.

CHAPTER 25—SEPTEMBER 1992

Julie looked around nervously at the people in her creative writing class. She was ashamed to admit she'd never been inside a college before. But it was like any other classroom with the teacher's desk in the front center and four neat rows of chairs facing it, all of which were filled with adults, some older, some younger than she was. She noticed only two men were in the class. She knew women were more interested in creative writing, so she wasn't surprised.

She was surprised, though, when Peter got their attention and told them to make a giant circle with their desks. After the sorting and scooting, Peter stood and walked around behind the desks, changing positions so that everyone could see him at least now and then.

He asked everyone to one-by-one state their names and why they wanted to take creative writing. He also wanted to know any experience any of them had with being published.

Julie loved the class already. It was worth the hassle of making sure she got off work on time, rushing home to make something quick for dinner, making sure Angie was focused on homework, and dashing to class. It would only be once a week for 10 weeks.

One woman explained that she always dreamed of writing romance novels and had dreamed out loud at home so much that her husband signed her up for the class as a birthday present. *That is so romantic*, Julie thought.

Next to that woman was one of the two men in class. He gave his name and said he was her husband, and he signed up because his wife was too nervous to attend by herself. Julie wondered if he could have made up a better reason than that. She would have been mortified if her husband confessed that in front of everyone.

When it was her turn, Julie said she always loved writing and dreamed of writing children's books or some kind of recipe book—maybe one that combined party suggestions, including games and decorations. "I love to cook and entertain, so I thought I could combine it all," she concluded. Some of the other women nodded.

Many people told stories of their love of writing, so the introductions took up much time.

"Writing is our best form of communication," Peter said. "Think about it. What you write can last for centuries after you're gone. Think of the Bible and how it has endured and is still the number-one best seller.

"This is a creative writing class and not an English grammar class, so our main focus will be to express ourselves creatively. In this class, I'd like to help each of you determine your style—the way you like to express yourself—and then encourage you to develop your particular style further. Some of you may be humorous in your style. Some may be poetic. Others may be methodic and eloquent. I see my role as helping you figure out your style and encouraging you further in that."

He explained their first assignment was to write their autobiography in no more than five typed pages. "I won't tell you any more details about how to write it because I want to see your style."

Uh oh, Julie thought and raised her hand. "Will we read these out loud in class?"

"Good question," Peter acknowledged. "First I will read them all, and I'll pick out several to read out loud so everyone can get a feel for different styles. But how about if I ask the writer ahead of time before reading the paper to the class?"

Everyone nodded. Julie still felt conflicted. She wanted to participate, but she couldn't write her autobiography—unless she only focused on her growing-up years. Maybe he wouldn't mind that, since his goal was style.

She hung around after class waiting for him to finish answering others' questions. After everyone was gone, he thanked her for waiting for him.

"Don't you have a briefcase or anything?" she asked, noticing he only had a piece of paper with the class roster.

"Not this week. Next Wednesday I'll bring one to fill with all your papers."

"Oh, about that assignment. Can I write fiction . . . the way I wish my life had gone?"

He laughed.

"No. I'm serious. I want to write fiction anyway, so why not write a fiction version of my life?" She really hoped he would go for it.

But he didn't. "I like your creative thinking. But I want the truth. Besides, when we had lunch the other day, I feel like I didn't get to know your life as much as you got to know mine."

"That's because only one of us could talk at a time, and you had important things on your mind. By the way, I've been praying for your parents. My sister lives in Omaha and goes to a terrific Bible church there. Maybe someone from her church could invite them—or maybe even go Christmas caroling at their house this year. Where do they live?"

"They actually live a little south of Omaha in Bellevue. But I don't think they would be open to strangers inviting them to church."

"That's where my sister lives! Maybe the Christmas caroling idea would work better. They wouldn't have to know they were singled out."

He expressed appreciation for her concern. "Now, back to writing. You'll write a true story, won't you? You have one week to do it."

Julie agreed to write her autobiography.

She drove home deep in thought. Bellevue. She thought that was where her sister's church was too. Though Julie had never been to it, she knew they were big into Christmas caroling with a purpose and handed out Bibles when they went.

She also thought about her autobiography. *What in the world am I going to write? If he had asked us to write anything else, I would be thrilled. Actually, now that I think about it, how would he know if the story I turn in is real or not? In fact, he might even think the real story is fiction.* She laughed. She would come up with some way to get through this assignment without revealing anything and move on. She really did like the idea of discovering her personal writing style.

Julie sat at her desk with a mound of paperwork and a calculator. Her boss was taking a few days off, so auto insurance quotes were her responsibility—though she wasn't allowed to discuss the quotes with potential clients because she wasn't licensed yet. She had to give the quotes to one of the agents in the office who would pass them along to the inquirers.

Her phone rang. "Julie, I have to tell you something. I'm calling from a pay phone."

Julie's stomach immediately tensed up. It was her mother.

"One of my Bible study friends was at the

hardware store last night and saw Terry's dad. He was wearing his uniform and was talking to another man. She overheard him mention your name and Angie's name, so she inched closer. He told the other man that they are narrowing in on you and it's just a matter of time."

Julie put her head down on her desk and groaned, holding her stomach with her free hand. "Did she overhear anything else?"

"No. She had the impression that Bob doesn't know exactly where you are but is following some leads. I don't know if he was just being cocky, or if he really does have ways to find you. You need to keep your eyes open. I don't know what else to tell you. After we hang up, I'll call Melanie."

Julie knew, as always, she couldn't afford to panic and become incapacitated with fear. She had to think clearly. She felt ill, for sure. So she went to one of the agent's offices and told him she felt suddenly sick and needed to go home.

Angie was in her first public school, which may or may not have been smart. Julie knew she had to pick her up immediately. It was 10:15, and she went to the school office to ask if she could get Angie out of her classroom for a family emergency. They sent an office attendant to Angie's room to get her and her belongings.

Soon Julie and Angie were in the car on their way to the apartment. "I'm so sorry, Sweetie, but I talked to Grandma today, and it seems like we are on the verge of being discovered again. I needed to come get you, because you're in a public school where it's not so easy to hide you if they come looking."

Angie thought for a minute. "It's okay, Mom. I don't like that school anyway."

Julie explained that they would go pack their

garbage bags, and she would call Melanie to see if they could hide out at their house until she figured out their next move.

"Hi Melanie," Julie said with a sigh when her sister answered the phone.

"Hey, I talked to Mom this morning and she told me what she heard about Bob getting close to finding you. What do you think?"

"I don't know what to think. He's so arrogant that it's hard to say what he really knows. But I can't take a chance. Can Angie and I come over and hide out while we figure out our next move? I promise, we won't stay long. I know it's not safe for us at your house either."

Melanie agreed.

"Good. We're packing up now. We'll be there soon."

After they loaded their last bag, Julie looked around the apartment. She gazed out the back sliding glass door at the woods behind. This had been such a great place to live. "God, thank you for letting us live here. It was so perfect. Please help me figure out what to do next."

That night as they all sat around Melanie's big dining room table, Steve had a suggestion. "You know, Julie, whatever you decide to do, we need to get you your own car. I'm glad we had an extra one for you to drive, but you need your own now."

Julie was quiet.

"What's wrong?" Melanie asked.

"Well, I know you're right. I just haven't saved up enough money for one, and I think it would be hard to get one in my name since none of my personal information matches. I'm using a fake social security number, and so far, no one has said anything. But if I get a bank loan, all that will come up again."

"Julie, we've talked this through, and we'd like to get you a car. It won't be new, but we'd like to buy it for you. We'll even put it in our name," Melanie said.

"No. I can't ask you to do that. It's too much money."

"Just consider it an early birthday and Christmas present," Steve said. "You've sacrificed your whole life, and we want to help you."

"Really. Don't feel bad about it," Melanie said. "It's important for us to do this for you."

"Well, I'm very grateful," Julie confessed.

"Can we get a blue car?" Angie piped up.

"We won't be picky," Julie said, glaring at her.

Steve looked at Julie. "Tomorrow is Saturday. Why don't you and I go look at cars and everyone else can stay here and lay low in the house."

Melanie agreed, acknowledging how dangerous it was to be all together. After all, if the police suspected Julie was in the area, Melanie and Steve's would be the first place they would check. But somehow, Julie didn't mind the risk. Family was too important to her right then.

They agreed to all stay in that night and eat popcorn and watch the movie, "Sister Act." Lexie and April had already seen it and could hardly wait for Angie and Julie to laugh through it with them.

As they watched, Julie and Melanie sat next to each other. "The girls have missed out on so much growing up apart. I wish we could have been together more," Julie said.

Melanie looked sad. They both knew that moments like this probably wouldn't happen soon again, if ever. Time was running out again.

###

Julie had finally accepted that she was getting a car and no longer felt like she was imposing on her sister and brother-in-law. In fact, Steve was clearly in his element scoping out the lot and chatting with the salesman, Michael Brown, who thought they were husband and wife.

Steve went along with it, calling her "honey" and "dear." She followed his lead, finding it hilarious.

While Steve was talking to the salesman about a red Ford Mustang, Julie wandered over to a 1989 blue Ford Escort. She knew it was a '89 because the year was in bold print across the windshield. She peeked inside. It had a blue interior, and she could tell it was a manual. She hadn't driven a manual for awhile, but she liked how well they handled in the snow.

"Honey, I kind of like this one," she said to Steve.

"Ah, that's a good one," the salesman said. "We just got that in this week. It's only had one owner."

"Uhh, do you know how to drive a manual?" Steve asked.

"Well, Dear, you know I had a life before I met you." She smiled.

Steve looked at the price on the window: $3,000 even. Julie thought the price seemed very reasonable, but she wasn't paying for it, so she was more than willing to leave the price haggling up to Steve.

The salesman encouraged them to test drive it, with him in the front seat, of course.

Steve looked at Julie.

"Would you like to drive it, Dear?" Julie asked Steve.

"No, it's for you, Honey."

"Please, Dear. I insist."

Steve got behind the wheel and Julie in the back seat while the salesman went inside to get a tag to put on the back.

Julie was explaining how much she liked the car when her pager beeped.

"What was that?" Steve asked.

Julie pulled it out of her purse and saw "911" in the display window.

"Oh no!"

"What is it," Steve asked.

"This means a neighbor sees something going on around my apartment."

Melanie sat on the living room floor sorting and folding laundry from the dryer while the girls were in Lexie's room, drawing pictures on the windows with magic marker. She had long ago authorized that form of art, simply because it was easy to clean.

The doorbell rang, and Melanie looked out in the driveway to see a police car.

"Oh my goodness," she breathed quietly. She rushed to Lexie's room. "Girls, the police are at the door. I'm going to answer it, and Angie, I want you to hide in the closet. Lexie and April, you come out here, and we will act like we don't know where Angie and Julie are, okay? So if they ask, you haven't seen them and you don't know where they are. Act perfectly normal."

Angie opened the closet and had to push a few things out so she could fit.

Lexie and April went to the living room.

"Okay girls. Start folding clothes."

Melanie opened the door. "Hello there. Can I help you?" she asked. "Is something wrong?"

The officers introduced themselves and asked if they could step inside.

Melanie felt uncomfortable, but didn't want to act

suspicious, so she allowed them in.

"Do you have a sister named Julie Bradley?"

"Yes I do. Why do you ask?"

"Is she here? We'd like to talk to her."

"No, she isn't here. I haven't seen her in years."

"Are either of these girls Angie?" one of them asked, referring to April and Lexie.

"No, this is my daughter Lexie, and this is April."

The officers stared at Melanie. She knew they were trying to decide if she was telling the truth. She didn't want to say too much, but she wanted to assure them that she had no contact with Julie.

"Look. I don't know where my sister is. And what makes you think she's here?"

"We're sorry to bother you, ma'am. We're just following up on some leads we've been given," the tall one said.

The shorter one with a mustache ventured with a hint of sarcasm. "I don't suppose you would tell us if you had seen her, would you?"

Melanie glared at him, surprised at how rude he was.

"Where's your husband?" the short one asked.

"He's out running some errands. Sir, I don't appreciate you coming here to harass me."

The other one apologized and said they would leave.

After Melanie saw them out and closed the door, she sighed. "Wow. That was so close."

"I didn't like them," April said.

"Did you see their guns?" Lexie asked. "They could have shot us!"

Melanie went to the closet and told Angie she could come out. "Good job, Angie. They're gone now. That was so close!"

"Mom, look!" Lexie called out.

Melanie ran back out to the living room and saw Lexie staring out the window.

"Look over there."

She followed Lexie's gaze and saw a police car parked up the street and around the corner. Her heart started pounding. She saw a policeman in the car.

"Daddy will have to drive past them to get home. And Julie will probably be following him in a new car. This is bad!"

Melanie and Steve lived at the end of a cul-de-sac, so there was no other way for Steve and Julie to get home.

As the salesman came back with the car tags, Julie and Steve decided they would make this a quick test drive.

Michael Brown put the tag in the back window and jumped in the passenger seat. "Okay, let's get out on the road and turn right, and then we'll head for the interstate."

As Steve pulled onto the interstate entrance ramp, Julie's pager beeped again. She could see Steve look at her in the rearview mirror with wide-eyed interest.

She pulled out her pager.

"Hmm. I don't know who this is."

"Here, let me see," Steve said, reaching back for the pager.

"So, do you have any questions about this car? Doesn't it ride smoothly?" Michael asked.

"Yes. It's quite nice," Julie said flatly. *I wonder what's going on at the house. Is Angie safe? And who just paged me?*

"Umm hmm. Just like I expected," Steve said. "Why don't we head back now?"

"Oh no. We can go a few more exits," Michael

insisted.

"If it's alright with you, I'd like to get back. I can tell this is a great car."

As soon as he pulled into a parking space and stopped the engine, Steve said he'd like to buy the car but couldn't right then. He asked if he could give a quick down payment and come back later to fill out all the paperwork.

Julie could tell, he was as worried and anxious to get back to the house as she was. He didn't even try to come down on the price.

Ushering them into an office, Michael said he thought that would be fine, but he wanted to ask his manager.

Once they were alone, Julie was about to say something, when Steve put his index finger over his lips. Then it dawned on her that the room was potentially bugged so the salesmen in the other room could hear clients discussing potential sales.

"It's a nice car, isn't it?" he asked.

"Yes. I'd like it very much. And I wonder who that was. Can I have my pager back?"

"Well, let's get it. I will come back tomorrow if they are open, or Monday and finish the paperwork."

After Michael returned and agreed to take a $300 down payment, Steve took out his checkbook, wrote a check, and took Michael's business card.

Before long they were back in Steve's car.

"That was Melanie. I was going to tell you that we got her an unregistered cell phone so you can talk when you need to."

"When were you planning to give me that number?"

"I guess right now," he said.

"Here's the plan," he continued. "Let's go down the road a little further. I'll pull off and have you get in the back seat and lay down. I don't know why Melanie paged us, but between that and your 911 call, I'd say something is up. I didn't want you driving back to the house in a separate car."

Julie agreed.

Melanie paced in the living room, repeatedly peering out the window.

Why don't they call me? Have the police already found them? They will surely get her when she drives by in her new car.

Melanie looked at the clock again. It was nearly 2:30. *This is awful. I shouldn't have encouraged her to come here. Of course the police would look for her here. And now, I bet it's all going to come to a head today. I don't want to have to tell Mom.*

She had already put Angie and the girls in her own room with the shades pulled so no one would see them through any windows.

Melanie went to the kitchen to make some tea for herself and hot chocolate for the girls, just to keep busy. She thought she heard the garage door.

Melanie opened the door just as the garage door closed. She noticed Julie lying in the back seat.

"Are you okay?" she asked.

Julie jumped out. "I'm okay. Are you okay? What's going on? You paged me."

"Did the policeman see you?" Melanie asked.

Steve spoke. "Both of you calm down. I saw the policeman, but I know he didn't see Julie."

Melanie hugged Julie. "I'm so glad they didn't find you. The police came here and asked if you were my sister and if I know where you are!"

"Let's go inside," Steve urged.

"Yes, but let's stay in the kitchen. They can't see us in here," Melanie said.

She explained her conversation with the police and that after the visit, they parked up the street, probably waiting for Steve to come home.

"I'm so glad you didn't come home in separate cars!" Melanie said.

Julie explained the 911 page she received while they were out, and that when Melanie also paged her, they knew something serious was up and they better not spend any more time out.

"I'm going to the living room while you two talk. I need to figure out what to do here," Steve said.

Julie babbled on about enduring the test drive, and Melanie told how well the girls did while the police were there.

Eventually, Steve came back into the kitchen and informed them that the police car was still there and that he had a plan.

"Melanie and I and our girls need to leave in the car so the police can see it's just us here, living a normal family life. You and Angie stay in the house while it gets dark. Stay in our bedroom closet and I'll give you a flashlight. After it's dark—at 7:30—you and Angie leave the house out the back door with a flashlight. Jump over the fence and go through the back neighbor's yard to the front of their house. I'll have someone pick you up on their street and drive you to a hotel. You can stay there for a day or two until I get your car to you. Then you can be off. You will need to decide where you will go from there. But we need to get you out of here. Who knows, they may be getting a search warrant."

"You aren't going to make them go sneak around outside in the dark!" Melanie argued with him.

"Melanie! It's okay. We're used to this," Julie said.

At 3:45, the police car was still parked up the street, which made everyone very nervous. They gathered Julie's and Angie's plastic bags, taking out whatever they thought they could possibly live without to lighten their load.

"I'll bring whatever you leave behind when I bring you your car," Steve said. They made some sandwiches for the two to have in the closet while they waited for 7:30.

"If I need to call you, I'll call and let it ring once and hang up. Then I'll call again right away. That way you'll know it's us. Otherwise, don't answer the phone if it rings," Steve said. "And under no circumstance are you to answer if someone rings the doorbell or knocks."

"Okay, girls. Let's get in the car. We're going to the mall. I guess we'll eat and go to the movies," he said.

Before long, Julie and Angie were seated in the closet with a flashlight. Julie heard the garage door open and close with the sound of a car pulling away. Then silence.

"Well. I guess we could take a nap in here to pass the time," Julie said.

"I don't see why we have to stay in the closet."

"Steve just wants us to be hidden. If everything remains calm, maybe we can leave the closet, as long as it's still light outside and we make sure we don't walk in front of any windows. When it gets dark outside, we can't have a single light on in this house or we'll give ourselves away," Julie said.

"Do you think we're going to get caught?" Angie asked.

Julie sighed. "I hope not. We've come too far for it all to end today. But I have to admit, I'm a little concerned they might just break down the door and come in looking for us. After all, isn't this the most obvious place for us to hide? I'm afraid I got too comfortable being near family and forgot that our enemy isn't giving up."

"If we get out of here, you ought to write a book about all this," Angie said.

"Maybe so. I've certainly been making notes."

"You could call it 'How to Run Away From Home."

"Or, 'What Not to Do When You Run Away From Home," Julie responded. "What advice would you give to others about running away from home?"

Angie thought for a second. "Don't run away alone. Take your mother with you."

Julie laughed. "You silly little thing." She changed the subject. "It's about 5:30. Why don't we eat our sandwiches?"

Then they decided to doze in the closet. Julie awoke when she heard a dog bark.

Noticing that Angie was awake, she said, "You know, I just realized, I don't really know the layout of the backyard or how hard it might be to climb over the fence. And what if the back neighbor has a dog?"

It wasn't pitch black outside yet, so she got out of the closet and peeked under the drawn shade at the backyard. She saw a tall wooden fence with pointy posts. How was she supposed to get over that? She thought she could boost Angie over, but how would she get over? Maybe there was a chair out there somewhere that she could stand on.

She went back to the closet. "You know, Pookie, I think we need to pray."

"Okay. You pray," Angie said.

"Dear Lord, here we are again. You know we are in danger." Julie paused. She tried to think of some of the verses in Psalm 27. "We would faint unless we believed that we would see your goodness in the land of the living. We wait on you right now, and we get our courage from you. Please strengthen our hearts and help us to get away from here safely. That fence is tall. Please help us over it. We need you to come through for us again. Thank you in advance for how you are going to work this out."

She kept looking at her watch. It was finally 7:20. "Well, Pookie, in a few minutes, we need to make our move. Do you know what to do?"

"You've told me about five times. I think I got it," Angie said.

Angie was getting so grown up. She was also starting to develop a tiny bit of an attitude. Julie wondered if it was her age, or was it the kids at school rubbing off on her.

"Okay, time to go." They each grabbed two garbage bags of belongings and headed for the back door through the kitchen. Julie found some wrought iron chairs on the patio and whispered for Angie to help her drag one to the back fence. They left their bags on the patio while they dragged a chair, with a flashlight illuminating the way. They went back for their bags. Julie stood on the chair, and Angie tossed the bags over the fence. Then Julie cupped her hands and urged Angie to put her foot in her hands so Julie could boost her over the fence. Somehow, Julie found the strength to give her the needed push. Julie heard some rustling.

"Ouch!" Angie whispered loudly.

"Shhh!" Julie said.

"There are sticker bushes over here," Angie whispered. "One of the bags is caught in them."

"Well, try to get it loose without ripping it. I'll move the chair down. How far do I need to go?"

"Here, I'll jump up and touch the top of the fence

where you should move the chair."

Julie saw the spot and dragged the chair. "Dear Lord, I don't know how to do this. Please help."

Fortunately, there were cross boards on the fence at that very spot. Julie hoisted herself up. She put a foot on one of the boards and jumped up and over. The descent was farther down than she expected, and she ended up sprawled on the ground. She laid there a second feeling for any sharp pains. None. She had not hurt herself.

"Give me two bags," she whispered to Angie.

They ran across the neighbor's yard, not realizing they had another fence, which meant more scaling to get into the front side yard.

Just as Julie was trying to figure out how she would get over, she realized there surely must be a gate. It wasn't on the side of the house they were on, so it must be on the other side.

Julie could see lights on inside the house indicating the owners were probably home. She whispered to Angie that they would go to the other side of the yard to check for a gate. Angie got there first.

"There's a gate!" Angie said, this time not whispering.

"Shhh!" Julie urged. She opened the gate and they ran through with their bags.

Headlights came down the street toward them. Julie hid behind a tree. The car stopped in front of the driveway of the house. Somehow, it was lighter out. Julie looked behind her, and the backyard they had just run across was lit now. The neighbors surely heard them and were now investigating.

"Hello?" she heard a voice say from the lowered window of the car. "Do you need a ride?"

"Come on!" Julie told Angie. They ran to the car. Julie got in the front seat, and Angie settled in the back seat.

As the car pulled away, Julie looked back. Now the front porch light was on.

"Whew!" she said. "I can't believe we made it!"

Julie looked over at the driver, a Middle Eastern man with dark, neatly combed hair. He was wearing khakis and a dark green jacket. Fortunately, he wasn't nearly as anxious as she was.

"Do you know where to take us?" she asked.

"I certainly do. You can relax now. You're safe."

"Thank you so much for coming to get us . . . and right on time. Any later and I think those neighbors would have found us."

He drove on to the highway, got off in a few exits and went down three side streets before pulling into the Relax Inn.

"You've been so kind. Thanks for the ride. You can let us off at the front door," Julie said.

"No, I was instructed to check you in under my name and pay for two nights for you."

Julie was surprised. But knowing Steve, she realized she shouldn't be surprised. Naturally he'd thought of everything.

While the driver dealt with the lady at the front desk, Julie and Angie remained outside and out of sight, examining their plastic bags.

"Oh, Pookie, look at that bag. It has a pretty bad rip in it."

They examined the other bags. "It looks like that first one is the worst," Julie said. "I think we need to get some new bags."

The man came outside and handed the room key to Julie.

"You take care," he said. "And remember, wait on the Lord: be of good courage, and He shall strengthen thine heart: wait, I say, on the Lord."

Then he left.

Julie looked at Angie. "That was part of Psalm 27. That's very interesting."

Julie felt remarkably calm and protected—which was a strange feeling under the circumstances.

Julie searched for room 307, and once inside, she locked the door and looked around.

Angie started to root through the bags. "I'm putting on my pajamas and watching TV," she said.

Julie stretched out on the bed and put her arms behind her head. She thought about how smoothly the procedure had gone compared to how it could have gone. And what a nice man Steve had chosen to pick them up. She decided she would take a long shower.

A few hours later, as both of them were under the covers and engrossed in a movie, Julie's pager went off.

It was Melanie's new cell phone number.

"I can only imagine what happened after we left," Julie told Angie as she dialed Melanie's number.

"Julie, where are you!" Melanie shrieked. "I'm so so sorry!"

"What are you talking about? I'm at the hotel where I'm supposed to be."

"You are?" She paused. "How did you get there?"

Julie sighed. "Weren't you listening when Steve explained the plan? Some guy picked us up and took us to the hotel."

"He was *supposed* to come, but he was late and didn't find you," Melanie said.

"Of course he found us. He picked us up at 7:30 in front of the back neighbor's house."

There was silence. "Melanie, what's wrong?

What's going on?"

"I don't know. Steve asked his friend Mark to pick you up and told him where to go, but Mark couldn't find it and didn't show up to pick you up until 7:45. He drove up and down the street and waited a half hour, and you didn't show up, so he finally went home."

This time Julie was silent.

"Julie, who picked you up?"

"I don't know. Some guy who looked like he was from Iran or Egypt or somewhere like that came down the street just as we got to the front of the neighbor's house and asked if we needed a ride."

Julie thought through the rest of their time with him. "You know, he was very calm—and even peaceful."

"I don't know who he could have been. Just a minute."

A few seconds later she was back. "Steve says he didn't tell anyone else about meeting you."

"It must have been an angel," Angie piped up from in front of the TV.

"Did you hear that, Melanie? Angie thinks it must have been an angel."

They all pondered that idea in amazement. "Or could it have been the FBI?" Melanie asked.

"I don't think so. Before he left, he quoted a verse from Psalm 27. This may sound funny, but only God knows how important that is to me," Julie said.

They agreed it was a miracle she was at the hotel—the very one that Mark was supposed to drive them to. Julie didn't even know the man's name, and she didn't pay any attention to the name he used to check them in with.

They agreed to stay in touch regarding getting the car to her so Julie and Angie could be on their way. At least she had a plan for where to go next, thanks to her mother. She would be sure to call Elizabeth and fill her in on the latest and get her thoughts and advice on this next move.

After hanging up the phone, Julie sat in the chair next to the desk, leaned back, and thought about their driver and the ride to the hotel. She had felt so peaceful, and he had been so nice. She recalled that he told her she was safe now. "I've got to write this in my journal."

She went through the bags looking for it.

"Pookie, did you take my journal out and put it somewhere?" she asked Angie.

"No. It must be in there somewhere. I know you packed it."

"I know I packed it too. Let's see, which bag did I put it in?"

She remembered that it was in the same bag with her pajamas and robe. The ripped bag.

She dumped the contents on the bed and thrashed through them.

"It's not here. My journal. It's gone!"

"Maybe it fell out in the car," Angie offered.

"Oh, dear God, I hope not. If that's the case, I know I'll never see it again."

She had a thought. "Wait here. I'll go outside to the front of the hotel to see if it fell out down there when our angel checked us in."

She avoided people and looked around where they had stood. It wasn't there.

CHAPTER 26—SEPTEMBER 1992

Leonard Kowalski got up early. He went to the kitchen to get his wife's medications and start the coffee pot. While the coffee brewed, he followed his routine of opening all the curtains and blinds. He vaguely noted the blue cloudless sky and sunshine. No day was particularly sunny to him lately while the love of his life struggled every day just to get out of bed.

Anna didn't have many months left to live, he knew. The chemotherapy made her very weak and ill. He could barely stand to see her that way, but he was grateful she was at least still around. Maybe when the treatments were finished they would have some good days again.

Leonard noticed the red bird feeder on the back patio was out of birdseed. Anna loved to sit at the kitchen table and watch the birds. He took a cup out to the garage where he kept the birdseed and filled it, then went to the patio. Something caught his eye. He saw something colorful on the ground at the back fence line, under the bushes. He figured some wrapping paper must have blown into his yard. He went to pick it up and noticed that it wasn't wrapping paper at all. It was a purple and pink notebook with the words *Thoughts & Prayers* on the front. It looked homemade.

He filled the bird feeder, then took the notebook inside and opened it. The first thing he noticed was a typed passage on the inside cover. He sat down and read it while he waited for the coffee to finish brewing.

The Lord is my light and my salvation; whom shall I fear? The Lord is the strength of my life; of whom shall I be afraid? When the wicked, even mine enemies and my foes came upon me to eat up my flesh, they stumbled and fell. Though an host should encamp against me, my heart shall not fear: though war should rise against me, in this will I be confident. One thing have I desired of the Lord, that will I seek after; that I may dwell in the house of the Lord all the days of my life, to behold the beauty of the Lord, and to enquire in his Temple. For in the time of trouble he shall hide me in his pavilion: in the secret of his tabernacle shall he hide me; he shall set me up upon a rock.

He stopped and read that last sentence again. He had heard it before. Recently. Peter. His son Peter had read it to both of them several months earlier, thinking it would encourage them. It was a passage the pastor of his church had talked about in a sermon. It was just like Peter to read them Bible verses, even though he knew they questioned whether there was a God.

However, Leonard concluded that this must be a very important verse in the Bible for it to come up twice in just a few months. He went on and read the rest of the passage.

Whoever had written those Bible words was surely in some kind of trouble. The passage seemed pretty intense to put in the front of a journal. He thumbed through the pages and noticed it had dates and entries going back to May 1985. He flipped to the last journal entry. It was just a few days earlier.

"How did this end up in my yard?" he murmured.

"Leonard," he heard faintly from the bedroom.

He took the notebook with him.

"Can I please have a glass of water?"

"Yes. And let me bring you your pills. Look what I found in the backyard. I don't know where it came from, but it's very interesting." He handed the notebook to her and went back to the kitchen to count out her pills.

Anna sat up in bed and rubbed her weak hand across the front of the notebook, wondering where it had come from. It was beautifully made. She opened the front cover and saw the passage. Then she leafed through it. It was well worn and written in several colors of ink. Some entries were long, some were fairly short. There weren't many pages left to write in.

When Leonard returned with the water and pills, Anna asked where he'd found it.

He explained that it was in the backyard under the bushes.

"Maybe it has something to do with the noise you heard in the backyard last night," she said.

"That thought crossed my mind too," he said. "Did you read the Bible verses in the front? I recognized a verse Peter told us about recently."

Anna read it silently. "Hmm. This is very interesting. I don't know how we happened to get this book, but I'm going to read it."

"Let me know if you see anything to indicate who it belongs to."

Someone knocked at Julie's hotel room door. She peeked through the peep hole and then swung open the door.

Melanie hugged her as Lexie and April ran into the room to talk to Angie. Steve asked if they could come in.

"So, the car is in my name," he said. "It has temporary tags. When I get the plates, I'll mail them to you."

Julie hugged him. "You are the best. Thank you so

much. I guess God knew how desperately I needed this car—and right now. I don't know how I can ever repay you."

She looked at Melanie, who had tears in her eyes. "I promised myself I wasn't going to cry." She wiped away the tears. "I wish we had spent more time together. I guess I just thought you'd be here with us for years, and I took it for granted."

She plopped down on the bed.

"Well, it was nice living here and letting my guard down for awhile. For the past five years, I've lived always aware that any day I might have to move. While I was here, I felt as if I were living a normal, permanent life. I never would have considered taking a college class in any of the other places I lived."

"Do you know exactly how to get where you're going?" Steve asked.

"Yes, I've written out the directions, and almost have them memorized."

"I've been racking my brain trying to remember when I might have met Teresa," Melanie said. "Mom said we went to Teresa's mom's house for a Christmas party 10 or 12 years ago, but I just don't remember."

Teresa was the daughter of a woman in their mom's prayer group. She and her husband and their two kids lived in South Dakota. Teresa agreed to let Angie and Julie move in. They had built separate quarters downstairs for her husband's mom to live in, but she had passed away. The space would be perfect for Julie and Angie.

"I'll be okay," Julie assured Melanie. "God always takes care of us. And did you bring some garbage bags with you?"

"Oh, yes. Right here." She pulled them out of her waistband.

"You wear luggage well," Julie teased. "Actually,

it looks just like my last luggage."

Julie had already asked Melanie on the phone if she'd seen her journal. "By the way, did you look in your yard anywhere to see if my journal might be there?"

"I did. It's not there."

"That bothers me so much. It's like a piece of my life was ripped away from me. It's the record of the last seven years of my life, and somewhere someone is probably reading it. Who knows where it will end up." She thought for a second. "It's like I lost my best friend, who I tell everything to. Dear God, don't let them turn it into the police!"

Melanie suggested she get another journal.

"I probably will. But I've lost so much."

Julie placed her belongings from the ripped bag into a new bag. Melanie pulled some candy bars out of her purse. "Here. Take these with you."

"I can't wait to see our new car," Angie said.

"Well, are we ready to go now?" Steve asked. "It's blue, Angie. Just like you wanted."

As they got to the front door of the hotel, Steve told them to wait while he went to the parking lot to look around. Satisfied, he motioned for them to come on out.

They loaded the trunk of their new Ford Escort with their garbage bags. Angie, Lexie, and April hugged while Julie walked around the car with Steve. "I still love it. We didn't get to spend much time admiring it the other day," she said.

"I know. It drives really well. It has a full tank of gas."

"Well, I guess we should quit stalling and get on our way."

Melanie hugged her again and handed her an envelope. "This is from Mom. She wanted you to have some money for the trip."

As Julie and Angie drove away, her sister and family stood in the parking lot waving goodbye.

Anna had spent an hour cleaning up, dressing, and getting ready for the day. Though frail, she stubbornly refused to lie around in pajamas all day. She rubbed some blush on her cheeks, put on some eye shadow, and slipped on her wig. She felt nauseated, but tried to stay on top of it with medication.

She sat at the kitchen table coaxing a piece of toast down with black coffee. At least she had something interesting to look at today. She opened the journal, curious about what kind of life this mysterious person had lived.

Immediately she could tell it was a troubled life. The poor dear had a horrible husband and was filing for divorce and custody of their daughter, Angie. This struck a nerve with Anna—she had volunteered in a battered womens' shelter years earlier. She hoped leaving her husband brought some peace to Julie's life. She read on.

"What?" Anna was horrified. This father sexually abused his own daughter? She had never run into that situation in the shelter. She put her hand over her heart, knowing that if she was the mother, she might have killed her husband over that.

But it was worse. Anna felt her blood pressure rise when she realized this girl's father-in-law was a policeman, and he was backing his son in getting custody of Angie. It just couldn't be.

Leonard came into the kitchen to check on his wife, whom he could hear from the other room occasionally gasping and shrieking. "What is going on in here, Honey? Are you okay?"

"Oh dear, you have to look at this. But wait. Let me read a little more."

"If it gets you too worked up, I'll have to take it away from you," he warned.

Anna tried not to make any outward expressions as she read the journal, though she felt the kick in the stomach this woman must have surely felt with all the abuse and hospital visits to confirm it. And to top it all off, the woman's husband did get custody. She just didn't know how it could get any worse.

The cuckoo clock struck 11 before Anna looked up again. She realized she had sat there for two hours. That was too long.

"Honey, can you help get me up?" she called out. She felt stiff.

"Yes, Dear." He came into the kitchen to help her. "So, how is the journal?"

He walked her around the living room to help loosen her up. "Oh, I don't feel very well. Can you help me back to the room so I can lay down for awhile?"

As Leonard put her in bed, his heart ached. He so wished she felt better. She was due to have another chemo treatment in a few days, and if she didn't improve, she'd have to postpone it.

"For all the horrible things that woman went through, I'm amazed that she hung on to God. Some of her journal entries are prayers. And sometimes she went back to that passage in the front of the journal and talked to God about the verses—like they were written just for her. It's quite remarkable. She prays like God is right there listening to her and caring for her. It must have surely comforted her."

After Leonard left the room, Anna rested in bed with her eyes closed, wishing away the general physical, mental, and emotional malaise she felt.

She thought about the unbearable circumstances of the journal lady and envied the hope she seemed to have that kept her going. Her love for her daughter and her desire to protect her obviously drove the woman. But she had something, or Someone, in her life giving her a boost. She could only conclude how remarkable it was. Before long, she was asleep.

Leonard woke her up an hour later. "Could I interest you in a little tuna salad and some crackers?" he asked.

Groggy as she was, Anna wanted to get up and moving. But secretly, she wanted to read more of the journal.

"After lunch, I'm going to go to the store," Leonard announced. "Will you be okay here alone?"

"Oh yes, I'll be fine."

In another hour, he was gone, and she sat on the couch in the living room with the journal and some warm lemon water to soothe her.

When the time came for the journal lady to run with Angie, Anna felt a combined sense of grief for her—having to leave home, and relief for Angie. "Good for you," Anna said out loud.

She barely noticed the garage door open and close as she was on the part about the woman being featured on *America's Most Wanted*.

"How are you doing?" Leonard asked. Usually his wife greeted him at the door whenever he returned from being away.

"I'm doing fine. My goodness, Dear. You should read this. This woman has had the most remarkable life."

"I can tell that by the way you are devouring her journal."

"More than that, I think you would find this

interesting from your perspective as a judge," Anna said. "What happened here just isn't right."

"Yes, I'll have a look at it," he promised.

"You know, this woman sounds a lot like Peter in the way she thinks about God and the Bible, and in the way she prays. The next time he comes over, I think I'll talk with him about it."

She secretly wondered if an angel dropped the journal in their yard just for her. She was just almost ready to admit there was a God, in spite of horrible things happening to good people. That had always been a sticking point for her, along with seeing preachers on television who later were revealed as crooks. It made her think religion was just another business to make money and that no one really believed it deep down inside.

But Anna realized this journal lady, and her own son, weren't like that. Angie's mother was going through living hell, and she was hanging on to God. She'd have to think more about it later. She got up to see what Leonard had bought at the store.

CHAPTER 27—OCTOBER 1992

A nna sat in the hospital room with an IV dripping the chemo drugs into her veins. The doctor advocated listening to soothing music while going through the treatment, so the bed was tilted for her to sit up with earphones on. She loved classical music and sat there with her eyes closed.

Leonard sat next to her with the journal that had so intrigued his wife. He had heard enough from her to know this would be "quite remarkable."

After reading for an hour and a half, he had a completely different impression than his wife did. Something was wrong with how the entire situation had been handled. Gross negligence would be putting it mildly. With his background as a judge, he saw how he would have handled the legal issue completely differently, and he marveled at how the justice system in that area was apparently so corrupt. It was a sad commentary on his former profession.

He knew the hospital mindset well, and there was a desperate need for legislation that would require hospitals to report sexual abuse to law enforcement. The unwillingness of the hospital to definitively call it sexual molestation and report it was the first critical control point that had to be remedied.

He wasn't sure he needed to read the whole journal after the point where the journal lady fled with her daughter. This was something that happened too often, through no fault of the women, but rather the cracks in the system. It was the subject of investigative television shows now and then.

The obvious bottom line to him was that this situation—as well as others like it—was handled as a social rather than criminal issue. It made his blood boil.

Feeling driven to read further, he shook his head in disgusted disagreement with the incidences where law enforcement was used to track her down as a criminal when the real criminal was free and was no doubt out there committing these same crimes with other children.

He had an idea.

If it wouldn't have suffocated her, Julie would have held a pillow over Angie's head to block out the noise. Teresa and Bill were screaming at each other again. It always started over something petty. This time one of the kids had left a bicycle by the end of the driveway, and Teresa had driven by it and hadn't bothered to pick it up. Didn't she care that someone could steal it?

The day before, it was that Teresa let them run out of dishwasher soap when she had just been to the grocery store the day before. It would have been very simple for her to write it on the grocery list on the refrigerator right when she realized they were about out of it.

"I'm sorry, Pookie. I wish we had someplace else to go to get away from this, but it's too cold to hang out outside." Then she thought. "Why don't we go to the movies? We haven't been to a movie in I can't remember how long. Wait here. I don't hear any more yelling."

Julie was thankful that they were mostly self-contained in the basement apartment and didn't have to interact with Teresa and Bill much. Their basement living quarters had a small kitchen, a huge bedroom with two twin beds, a bathroom, and thankfully, the washer and dryer. But for now, she needed a newspaper to see what movies were showing.

Julie climbed the stairs, lightly knocked on the door at the top, then opened it and peeked around. Bill wasn't in sight, but she could see Teresa snatching up the kids' belongings from the living room floor.

"Hi there. Can I borrow the newspaper?"

"It's over in the magazine rack next to the chair."

Julie found it and didn't feel comfortable sneaking it downstairs, so she sat on the chair and looked for the movie section.

Teresa finally sat on the fireplace hearth. "So, do you hear what goes on up here from downstairs?"

Julie felt instantly awkward. "Well, a little."

"I'm sorry. Bill has been a little grumpy lately. He's not happy with his job and he takes it out on us—or rather, me."

Julie knew what it was like to live on pins and needles, and their fighting brought back her old memories and tense feelings. "I know it must be hard on you. Hang in there and try not to let it consume you." She could have talked at length, but didn't know Teresa well enough to intrude in her private affairs. "Hey, do you know of any good movies?"

"I took the kids to see *Home Alone 2* a few weeks ago. Have you seen it yet?"

Julie admitted that they rarely went to the movies.

"Well, I don't have anything to do. Would you mind if I went with you?"

"But you've already seen it."

"That's okay. I wouldn't mind seeing it again. It would be good for me to get out of the house. I'll drive, since I know where it is."

"Sure, but what about the kids?"

It turned out that they were spending the night with friends. Julie was glad they hadn't been around to hear the tirade earlier. She couldn't help thinking what that must do to their fragile hearts to have to regularly hear such harshness.

Soon they were driving down the straight stretch of road to the movie theater with Julie in the passenger seat and Angie in the back of the Nissan Maxima. Teresa talked about the movie and how much she loved *Home Alone 1* so much better, but that *Home Alone 2* was still funny. She recounted her favorite scenes, talking so much that Julie wondered if Teresa was starved for friends.

The sound of a siren interrupted her thoughts. She turned. A police car was directly behind them with flashing headlights signaling them to pull over. Julie tensed. This was closer than she wanted to be to a policeman.

"Oh no. He'll give me a ticket. Bill will kill me," Teresa said as she pulled to the side of the road. The police car stopped behind her.

Julie instinctively reached back and grabbed Angie's hand. "We'll be alright, Honey," she said. She didn't want Angie to panic and forget her fake name in case she had to come up with it. She rehearsed her own name in her mind and was so thankful she wasn't driving. There would be no need to produce her driver's license.

"Oh no. Where's my purse?" Teresa asked.

Julie gasped. "You don't have your purse?"

"It's back here," Angie said. "Both of you can calm down!"

Julie glanced back at Angie, who was looking at her with piercing eyes. "Really," Angie emphasized.

It was the first reaction like that Julie had seen from Angie. She was like a little adult scolding them. This child of hers was her own independent self. When did that happen?

###

"How's Mom doing today?" Peter asked his dad, who greeted him at the front door.

"She's having one of her better days. Look at those. She'll love them," Leonard said.

Peter had stopped by the grocery store after church and picked up some roses and a bottle of sparkling grape juice. Knowing his mom didn't have much of an appetite, he hoped this festive beverage would work for her. "Where is she?"

"She's in bed resting, but she'll be glad to see you."

Peter went to the bedroom. "Hi Mom. I brought you a little something." Her cheek was as soft as velvet as he kissed her.

"That is so nice of you. What beautiful roses! You shouldn't have. Now, sit down; I'd like to talk to you." She sat up in bed.

Her insistence made Peter dread that this might be the last will and testament conversation he dreaded having with her. He had only expected to show his love and interest. He wasn't prepared for a grave conversation.

"I'd like to talk to you about your religion."

"Oh?" Peter was taken off guard. "I'd be happy to talk about it. Where should I begin?"

"Well, you know your father and I are not religious people. Or I guess I should just speak for myself. When we sent you to college and you started going to church and talking about the Bible and all that stuff, we thought it was just a phase—that you would get over it and go back to normal after you graduated and started to work. Then when you didn't get over it, I have to admit, I was a little angry. We didn't raise you to be a fanatic or to be so narrow-minded that you

255

would think your religion was the only good one. Actually, that part still really puzzles me. But I guess I never paid attention to what made you change. So I'd like to try to understand now."

Of course. She was dying. She would naturally start thinking about these things. He should have guessed.

"Well, as you know, I'm somewhat introspective, and I feel things deeply. I never told you and Dad, but when I went through high school, I felt depressed—a lot of the time."

She interrupted. "It's hard to hide something like that from your mother. I knew something was wrong. I thought it was just your age, or that maybe you needed a girlfriend."

"No. It wasn't my age or girls." He moved from the chair to the edge of the bed. "I didn't feel like I had any purpose. No reason to live. It just seemed like every day was going through motions—and for what? When I look back on it now, the best I can describe it is that I was hollow and had nothing to hope in."

His mother looked at him with sad eyes.

"When I went to college, Jack, my roommate, was upbeat and cheerful. He went to Bible studies and invited me to join him several times. After watching his life for a few weeks and seeing that he was happy, and listening to him talk to people and care for them, I decided to go with him one time and see what it was all about. Everyone at that Bible study seemed . . . fulfilled. I'm not even sure what the Bible study was about that night, but afterwards, the leader asked me if I had the hope of eternal life. I thought that was an interesting question because I didn't have hope of anything.

"The guy told me that we all have a vacuum in our hearts. We were originally created to have a relationship with God. But after Adam's sin, the automatic relationship with God was broken, and everyone born since Adam is naturally at odds with God. We all live our own lives and neglect or reject God and his standard for our lives.

"I'll never forget. He told me that God fully recognized that broken relationship caused by our sin and loved us, his creation, so much that he put into action a plan to bring us back to him. He sent his only son from heaven to earth to live the perfect life we should have lived but didn't, and then he died on the cross, which was his destiny. He did it to take the punishment we deserve for our sins that keep us from having a relationship with him. But Jesus' death was different than anyone else's. He didn't stay dead. He rose again three days later and went back to God, having paid our debt.

"What the guy said made so much sense. He said the way for us to apply what Jesus did is simple. Just believe it and accept that our sins have broken us from a relationship with him, and pray and admit that He is the way, the truth, and the life. We simply give up and surrender our lives to him and admit we can't make it to him on our own."

Peter noticed his mother's penetrating eyes. She truly was listening.

"Do you understand what I'm saying?" he asked.

"Well, I think it's all very interesting. I never heard it like that before."

Peter continued. "So, that night I did surrender my life to Jesus. I told him I knew he was the only way and the only hope. I just asked him to forgive me of my sins, and I gave him permission to take over my life. I decided to trust him and not myself from then on. And that was the beginning of a whole new life for me. I had a purpose.

"I still have a purpose. It's to get to know him more and follow what he wants me to do. I don't have to rely on myself to figure out what is best for me to be or do. I just trust him to show me, and he does, through the Bible."

His mother interrupted. "Yes, the Bible. It's a very interesting book. I have some questions about that, like how you can be sure it's true. But that's a conversation for another time.

"You did tell me about a Bible verse several months ago. I was just reminded of it recently, and I wrote it down." She asked him to open the top drawer by her bed.

Peter found the verse written on a pink index card and read it out loud, "*For in the time of trouble he shall hide me in his pavilion: in the secret of his tabernacle shall he hide me; he shall set me up upon a rock.*"

"It's worded very beautifully," she said.

Peter remembered sharing it with her after he heard it in a sermon at church, hoping it would provide some kind of comfort. Obviously it had.

"Mom, can I ask what has made you think of all this recently?" Peter wanted to hear her reason, considering how negative she had been until then.

"I've been reading something lately that has caused me to think about these things. You know, I won't be around much longer, so I guess I'm trying to learn as much as I can."

Peter hoped she wouldn't give up interest. "I'm glad you're thinking about it. We should talk more about it again sometime soon."

###

Leonard sat in the living room reading the journal

while Peter and Anna talked. He had already marveled at the many times law enforcement had almost caught up to this journal girl. He was now at the part where she was in their area on the other side of the state line, but finally in contact with family again—her sister.

He got to the page where she had a lunch date with the nicest guy, Peter Kowalski, a teacher.

Leonard stopped and stared at those words. Peter Kowalski? How could all this be? He fought the urge to jump up and show the page to Peter, choosing rather to see what more he should know.

Tears came to his eyes as he read her prayer: "Dear Lord, you know the pain and heartache going on in Peter's family. Please comfort his mother and bring her merciful relief. You know she's dying of cancer and she doesn't know you. Please show her yourself. Bring someone to help open her eyes. If it's not Peter, bring someone or something else. And for his father, please comfort him as he watches his wife suffer. He's facing the challenge of his life, and he needs you. Help him to come to know you as his Savior. And for Peter, you know his tender heart and his inexperience with losing a loved one. He needs your grace and comfort as well."

Leonard closed the book, his head swirling. Had Peter planted this book in their yard for them to find? Surely not.

Leonard had already done some detective work, checking some of the sources he had access to. He had found out her real name. But how much did Peter know?

He decided he'd settle the questions.

"Peter, can you come in here?"

He extended the notebook to Peter. "What can you tell me about this?"

"I can't tell you anything about it. Why?"

"You don't know anything about this notebook?"

Peter took it from his father. Something seemed vaguely familiar, even though he knew he'd never seen it.

Tina Morgan. She had talked about her purple and pink journal with the words *Thoughts & Prayers* on the cover. He opened it to see the inside cover. Sure enough. There was Psalm 27, just as she said. He remembered their conversation about that passage and how heart-warming it had felt for someone else to have been so moved by it. He also remembered that someone made this journal. It wasn't mass-produced, so it probably really did belong to Tina.

"I think this belongs to Tina Morgan. She told me about it. But how did you get it? How do you know her?"

"I was going to ask you the same thing."

"I know Tina from church, and she's in my college creative writing class. Or she was. She dropped out. In fact, she vanished."

Leonard was now sure that Peter didn't have anything to do with the notebook.

"Well son, sit down." Peter sat on the footstool. "I found this in our backyard. I hate to admit it, and it might seem like an impropriety, but I've read through it. So has your mother, though neither one of us is done with it. Your friend has lived a double life, but she did it to protect herself and her daughter."

"What are you talking about?"

"Her name isn't Tina Morgan. It's Julie Bradley. She was married to an abusive jerk who molested their daughter. She divorced him, but he got custody of their daughter, Angie. He kept abusing her, so Julie essentially kidnapped Angie, left the state, and went into hiding. She has lived under several names and in many different places."

"You're kidding," Peter said. "How can that be?" He stared out the window in silence. "She's a really sharp gal. I don't think what you're saying could possibly be true about the girl I know."

"Well, that's the point. No one really knows her. That's the way she has lived. She had to do it, and it's not her fault. It's the system."

"I'm missing something here. I still don't understand. How do you know about it? How did you get her journal?"

Leonard figured he should tell Peter everything, given the relationship Peter had started with her.

He spent the next 15 minutes explaining what he learned about her from reading it.

"She's originally from the Kansas City area, and in here, she gives other people's names. Her husband was a security guard, and her father-in-law was a policeman and is now police chief."

"She never told me any of that," Peter said.

"Of course not. She couldn't trust anyone. I have to say, she really trusts God. It's good that she has her faith to lean on, because she has been through some harrowing times."

"Hmm. That explains why she didn't like my first assignment—to write a five-page autobiography. She wanted to write a fiction one." His mind was going in several directions. "She kidnapped her daughter?"

"I'm sorry to say the justice system has holes in it, and she was trapped. Whenever she took Angie to the hospital after she was molested, the hospital would not fully commit to the molestation diagnosis. They didn't want to get involved. The ex-husband's actions were never criminally investigated. So with no crime, he could just as easily get custody of Angie as she could. Only the judge thought she was abusive by subjecting Angie to invasive medical tests. He gave her husband custody. And the ex-husband kept abusing Angie.

"I'm checking into some things. It would be helpful to know a little more. She has family around here."

"Yes. Let me think." It was hard for Peter to think of her as *Julie* when he knew her as *Tina*. "I know she has a sister and family that lives here in Bellevue. They go to a church in the area."

"That would be Melanie and Steve," Leonard said. "She talks about them in her journal. But I don't have their last name. I'd like to find them. I think I can help her."

CHAPTER 28—NOVEMBER 1992

The house was quiet upstairs. Too quiet. Julie knew Teresa and Bill's routine, just from the sounds. Bill got up each weekday morning about 5:30 and ground some coffee beans. Then the front door always opened and closed twice as he got the newspaper. Around 6 o'clock, he would ring a hand bell, and that was the house signal for everyone else to get up. Soon Julie would hear running water, flushing toilets, and pitter-pattering feet.

But it was 6:30 on a Tuesday morning, and Julie hadn't heard any of that. Actually, it was her 34th birthday. But this year, she figured it would probably go unnoticed.

She finally gave in to her curiosity about the silence. She tapped on the door at the top of the stairs and opened it.

She glimpsed Teresa's bathrobe and slippers. She was sitting at the kitchen table. As Julie timidly inched closer to the kitchen, she saw the two kids eating bowls of cereal and reading their Fruit Loops and Frosted Flakes boxes, while Teresa ate powdered sugar donuts and stared into space.

"Good morning," Julie said.

The kids didn't lift their eyes from the cereal boxes. Teresa just looked at Julie. She saw dark circles under Teresa's blank eyes and white powdered sugar around her mouth. Teresa was quite a sight.

"Are you feeling okay?"

"Oh. Not really. Bill didn't come home last night."

Julie wanted to ask if they should be worried, but instinct told her it wasn't a safety issue. It was a choice.

"I see. Is there anything I can do to help?"

"Yes. Would you take the kids to school today? I don't think they'll be ready in time for the bus. And I don't have the energy to get them to hurry. I didn't sleep at all last night."

"Of course. I'd be glad to." Julie felt awful for Teresa. "I'll go downstairs and make sure Angie is getting ready. Kids, can you be ready in 15 minutes?" Julie asked.

"Ahh, can we stay home today?" one of them asked.

"No, now let's get going. We don't want to be late."

Julie was happy to take charge, given Teresa's emotional state. It was all she could think about as she drove the silent kids to school. Should she anticipate the worst? Did Bill have a lady friend? Did he have family around that he was staying with?

"I'll let you off here," Julie said as she approached the stop sign by the school. "If I go in the circle drive, I'll be here for another half hour."

The kids jumped out of the car. "Angie, you be good today, okay?" Julie admonished.

"Mom," she said sternly. "You don't have to tell me that."

Of course. She had forgotten that her little angel was growing up. She was practically a teenager, even though she was not 12 yet. "Be sure to ride the bus home, okay?"

As Julie pulled onto her street, a sheriff's car was leaving the neighborhood. That was odd. What was he doing on their street? Was he looking for her?

She watched out her rearview mirror as he turned left onto the highway. It didn't look like he planned to turn around and follow her. Still, she drove slowly, watching to make sure he didn't come back.

She pulled into the driveway and saw that the front

door was open, though the glass storm door was closed. This was also odd.

She walked into the unlocked door and heard sobs.

Teresa stood over the sink in her bathrobe, crying.

"Teresa, what's wrong? What happened?"

She waved papers in her hand and continued to cry, bending over the sink as if she was going to be sick.

"I've been served with divorce papers!" she wailed.

The phone rang. Julie looked at Teresa again and decided she should answer it.

It was Bill.

"Yes . . . she's here."

"It's Bill," she said. "I'll go downstairs."

As she closed the basement door, she heard Teresa sob "Hello" into the phone.

Julie's stomach was in knots. Old thoughts and emotions bubbled up inside her. Only this time, she was mad. She hated to see someone else go through marital anguish as she had. What would become of the kids? Would this be a fair divorce, or would Teresa get the raw end of the deal, as Julie had?

She half thought and half prayed. "Lord, what can I tell her to encourage her?" Julie wasn't sure if Teresa would accept any kind of spiritual help or guidance. The family showed no sign of interest in church or anything spiritual. Bill's language, especially, was less than godly. Maybe if the opportunity presented itself, she would share some verses with Teresa to see if Gods thoughts and words of love could comfort her.

Julie tip-toed up the stairs to see if the phone conversation had ended. It had, and she opened the door. Teresa was still in the kitchen, sitting down again.

"Can I ask you a question?" Teresa spoke first.

"How did you make it through your divorce? I

mean, you got Angie. Bill is telling me he will get custody of the kids. He says he'll also get the house."

Julie's heart fell into her stomach. She had many thoughts on the topics of divorce, custody, and surviving it all unscathed. Most of them, she dare not share. Julie remembered that Teresa's mom was in her mom's Bible study.

"How much of all this does your mother know?" Julie asked.

"She knows Bill and I haven't been getting along. I've talked to her about how I suspected it might come to this. But I never dreamed he would be so bold as to want or expect custody of the kids."

Julie knew Teresa needed to talk to her mother, who would then talk to Julie's mother, since they were in the same Bible study. She wondered how much of her own story would come out through all this.

"I do have something else I need to tell you," Teresa said, looking Julie in the eyes for the first time that morning. "He said you will need to move out. Soon."

Peter tried to think of the name of the church that Tina, or rather, Julie, had said her sister went to in the area. He remembered the conversation about Christmas caroling and getting someone to visit their home with the hopes of reaching out to Anna. He thought it was a Bible church.

"Dad, do you have a Yellow Pages around here? I think maybe I can find the name of the church she said her sister goes to."

He ran through all the Bible church names, and the one that seemed the most familiar was Calvary Bible Church. "Let's see if anyone is still there hanging around the office," he said as he dialed.

"Hello. My name is Peter. I'm trying to reach Melanie and Steve . . . uh, I can't remember their last name."

The lady who answered the phone paused. "We do have a Melanie and Steve who attend this church, but they aren't here right now."

"Oh, I understand. I can't think of their last names. Can you help me out? "

"Well, I'm not comfortable giving out their last name. Do you know them personally?"

Peter hadn't expected that response. "Uhh. No, I don't. How would you suggest I reach them? Can I give you my name and you could have them contact me?"

"We could do that. Or they usually attend on Sunday nights, so you could come tonight to get in touch with them."

"Okay, I'll be there tonight," Peter said. "I have the church address. What time is the service?"

"We start at 7 o'clock."

Peter hung up and announced that he would meet Melanie and Steve at church.

"Let me come with you," his dad said.

"You? Go to church?"

"Don't look so shocked. It wouldn't hurt me to get a little dose of religion—for a good cause."

The two of them were greeted by a man wearing a suit and holding the front door for everyone.

"I don't believe I've met you, my name is Max Chambers. How do you do? Are you new to the area?"

"No, I've lived here for years. This is my son, Peter."

They both instinctively knew it might be best if they met a few people and fit in a little before bringing up Steve and Melanie's names.

267

Peter led Leonard to an information table to look through the church literature and survey the group. Finally a woman greeted them. After introductions, Peter asked if Melanie and Steve were there.

"Oh, are you friends of theirs?"

"No. I'm friends with her sister."

"Well, I don't believe I've seen them yet, but they're usually late. If I don't see them ahead of time, why don't I introduce you after the service?"

They went on into the sanctuary where music was beginning. They sat in the third row from the back. Soon everyone was standing and singing a hymn, "Trust and Obey." Peter sang along while he held the hymn book for Leonard to follow along.

Peter was a little uncomfortable, not knowing how his dad would respond. But Leonard seemed to be going along without any problems.

After the congregation sang three more hymns Peter knew, the pastor said they would do something a little different.

"A lot of people have come to me in the past few weeks and told me stories of amazing things God has done in their lives. I thought it would be a good idea to have a testimony time before I share a few verses from Ephesians. We have a few microphones we can pass around, so if you would like to share something, raise your hand, and we'll get a microphone to you. Who would like to go first?"

After a short pause, a woman seated alone on the right hand side near the front raised her hand.

"My job has been in question. The boss told a group of us that he would have to lay off some people. So I prayed and told God that he knew how much I needed the job, as a single mom raising two kids. Still, I felt really worried. So one evening last week, I was reading through the Bible and I came across the verse that says, 'The Lord will perfect that which concerneth me: Thy mercy, O Lord, endureth forever.' I just prayed that verse and asked God to perfect what was concerning me. I had the most wonderful peace. I didn't worry about it anymore, and on Friday, my boss called me into his office and told me he wanted me to know I am very valuable to the company, and I don't need to worry about my job. In fact, he wanted to make me a supervisor over the rest of the support staff, which meant he was giving me a raise!"

Applause erupted as the pastor said, "Praise the Lord. Isn't God good? Gloria did just what God wants us to do, she trusted Him for what His word says, and He responded."

A bald, thin man sitting with a teenager on the back left side raised his hand.

"Jim, it's good to see you here tonight. How are you doing?" the pastor asked.

"Well, I've been better. As you all know, my cancer came back. I've been praying for God to take it away completely, and when I heard two weeks ago that it's back, I was angry with God.

"This week, I was driving to a doctor's appointment and I had the radio on the Christian station. The radio preacher talked about prayer, and he said the purpose of prayer isn't to get God to do what you want him to do. It's to get you to line up with what God wants.

"That's the first time I've ever heard that. I always thought we were supposed to pray to get our prayers answered. But he pointed out Christ's prayer asking the Father to let the cup of his wrath pass from him, but he said, 'Nevertheless, not what I will, but thy will be done.' The preacher pointed out that if Jesus submitted his will to God's will, surely we should. So I've surrendered my will to God. My cancer is His cancer, and He can do whatever He chooses with it. It's kind of funny. Now I don't feel like it's my problem anymore. The worst that will happen to me is that I'll die, and I'm ready for that."

Peter understood that man. He'd been anxious with his mother's cancer and felt it was his responsibility to make sure she was okay and that she was ready to die. He completely grasped the idea that changed that man's thinking. He had never thought of prayer as a means to submit himself to what God wanted rather than get God to do what he wanted. He breathed a silent prayer for God to forgive him for trying to be so much in control.

The service continued, and at 8:30, the pastor finished his message from Ephesians 6 and closed in prayer. Everyone stood to sing the final hymn.

The lady they had met before the service got Peter and Leonard's attention. She had a couple with her.

"This is Melanie and Steve," she said.

Steve took charge. "I heard you are looking for us? By the way, don't I know you from somewhere?"

"I don't know. My name is Leonard Kowalski, and this is my son Peter. And you know, you look familiar to me too? In fact, I think you live behind us."

"I think you're right. Do you have a red bird feeder?" Steve asked.

"Yes, we do. And do you have a sister named Julie Bradley?"

Melanie looked at Steve.

"Why do you ask?" Steve asked.

"Wait a minute," Melanie jumped in. "Peter? Peter Kowalski? Your name sounds very familiar. Honey, I think Julie has mentioned him."

###

Julie was at the car, arranging bags in the trunk. Angie was still inside.

"Well Teresa, I can't thank you enough for all you've done for us," she said.

"Oh, you don't need to thank me. I'm so sorry we had to kick you out like this. I'm just sick about it—and everything else right now."

"Don't worry about us. We'll get along okay. God will take care of us. He always does."

"So, where did you decide to go?"

"I'm not really sure. But we will figure it out. The main thing is that I want to make sure you will be alright. You'll need some help to get through this. Do you have a church you can go to?"

Teresa admitted that they had visited a few churches at one time, and that she kind of liked the covenant church, but Bill hadn't liked it. Maybe she would try that one again.

"That's a good start. Whatever church you go to, make sure it teaches the Bible. Some preachers talk about current events or comment on magazine articles. You don't want one of those. You need to hear the truth of the Bible."

"Just seeing the faith that you have, given your circumstances, lets me know it's possible to get through things like this," Teresa said.

Julie encouraged Teresa to page her any time, and she would call back.

Angie came out of the house and got in the front seat.

"'Bye, Teresa," she said. "You have a very nice basement."

Soon they were off. Julie had directions to I-90. "Here we go again, Pookie," Julie said.

"Mom, I'm glad we're leaving there. I didn't feel right there."

"How is that, Sweetie?"

"Oh, I don't know. It was Bill. He was mean. Sometimes I felt funny inside. It felt like I'd had those feelings before."

Julie realized Angie might be getting close to remembering some of the experiences she had as a very small child that she had hidden inside all these years. She couldn't decide if she should try to coax out more old feelings, or just let it go. This was all unchartered territory for her as a mother. She herself might need counseling to learn how she should handle it.

"Well, Sweetie, we are gone from there, so you won't have to experience that anymore."

"Where are we going this time?" Angie asked.

"This time? Well, I don't really know, for the first time. One thing I do know, tonight we will stay in a hotel, and I'll call Elizabeth and ask her for ideas."

CHAPTER 29—NOVEMBER 1992

"You found her diary?" Melanie asked. "No way! Are you sure it's hers? Where did you find it?"

Leonard explained how he had found it under some bushes in his backyard.

"That makes sense," Melanie said. "Julie said her bag had a tear in it, so she knows her journal fell out somewhere. It fell out in your backyard. We should have thought of that!"

"If you don't mind," Leonard said, "I think we should finish this conversation somewhere else. I want to talk to you about that journal. Since we're neighbors, can we meet over at our house?"

They agreed that Melanie would rush off and pick the kids up in the basement of the church, they'd all go home, she would get them settled, then she and Steve would head over to his house.

Within half an hour, Melanie and Steve were at Leonard's house, along with Peter. Anna sat in a cushioned chair with a footstool wearing her bathrobe, though she had on lipstick. She had a scarf tied over her head. She stood to meet the couple, who had been advised ahead of time that she had cancer.

"Hello Mrs. Kowalski. It's so nice to meet you," Melanie said, gently shaking the matriarch's soft hand.

"Oh, please, call me Anna. It's so good to meet you. I feel like I already know you a little." She looked at Leonard. "Should we admit we've read Julie's diary?"

"It's okay. I've already told them."

Leonard took charge. "Well, we don't want to keep you too long, but I want to explain who I am, and I'd like to offer my help in clearing Julie of the legal implications of what she is doing, if I might. Please, sit down."

He explained his career as a judge in the state of Nebraska and his interest in and connections with judges across the country through his former association days.

"Really, it's a small, connected community," he said. "At any rate, as I've read Julie's account of what happened, I see the injustice that she has lived with, in a legal sense. Obviously Terry molested Angie, yet the whole situation was treated as a social issue and not a legal one. Julie should have been instructed to work with the police for a criminal investigation. One change that is just now spreading across the country is that hospitals are being required to report molestation to law enforcement. I'm afraid in Julie's time, hospitals didn't want to get involved and swept these cases under the rug. They didn't want to face litigation for accusing individuals of sexual abuse. If what happened to Angie happened today, the outcome might be different."

"Really?" Steve said. "That's very interesting."

"What happened to Julie and Angie has happened too often. There have been television programs dedicated to this issue, which has helped raise public and legal awareness," Leonard said.

"So, I have done a little checking. I know Terry's father is a police chief, and that certainly hasn't helped anything. I'm thinking of taking a trip to Kansas City to do a little investigating of Terry and look through some records. It could be that he has a criminal record by now."

Steve interrupted. "What makes you think that? Are you thinking he might have speeding tickets or something?"

"No, I'm thinking that if he molested his own daughter, he may have molested other children as well. In fact, I'm almost certain of it."

Melanie was thinking like Steve was. "What makes you so certain?"

"His connection with children at Fantastic Fitness Gym. I doubt it is as altruistic as everyone thinks. The term we use these days is *sexual predator*. Now, he obviously doesn't love children, as he has led people to believe, when he's abused his own daughter. So there is something there."

Melanie and Steve looked at each other with mouths agape. "Of course," Melanie said. "Oh my goodness! We were so naïve!"

Leonard finally asked, "Where are Julie and Angie now?"

"They are living with a family in South Dakota," Melanie said.

"Well, I'd like to talk to her. But maybe you should talk to her first and tell her about our conversation—and that I have her journal. She can have it back."

Melanie and Steve agreed to get in touch with her as soon as they got home. They stood to leave, exchanging phone numbers.

Once home, Melanie made sure the kids went to bed and then paged Julie.

When Julie called back, Melanie was surprised to hear that she was in a hotel.

"We just got here a few hours ago. I was going to call you," Julie said. "I talked to Elizabeth to see where she thinks we should move to next, and I'm waiting for a call back from her."

Melanie ventured, "Why are you in a hotel? What happened?"

"It's a long story, but the couple we were staying with erupted. He wants a divorce and plans to get custody of their kids and the house. We had to get out of there."

Melanie admitted that she was surprised, but that she had a surprise too.

"A good surprise? What? Are you pregnant?" Julie asked, knowing that probably wasn't the case.

"No. But are you sitting down? Gosh. Where do I start?" Then she paused.

"Melanie. The suspense is killing me. What is it?"

"Well, I guess to start with, your journal has been found."

"It has! Where is it? How do you know?"

"Consider this. When you threw your bags over our back fence into the neighbor's yard, one of the bags ripped, right?"

"Yes. And so?"

"It fell out then, so it was in our neighbor's backyard under a bush, and the man found it."

"Tell me he didn't read it."

"Well, he did read it, and so did his wife," Melanie said.

"Oh no." Julie was sitting cross legged on her bed and fell backwards onto her pillow. "I knew something like this would happen."

"But it's not bad," Melanie said. "You know Peter Kowalski?"

Hearing his name in this conversation confused her. "Yes. But what does he have to do with this?"

"Well, his mother and father live behind us."

"Oh my gosh! Does that mean Peter has read my journal too?"

"I don't know. But now let me explain. If there

was anyone you would want to read your diary, it would be Mr. Kowalski."

"Oh no!" Julie interrupted. "I remember now. I wrote a prayer in there for Peter's mother, who has cancer, and his dad and Peter. Oh, and his dad used to be a judge."

"Really? He didn't say anything about you writing a prayer for them."

"How did you find out about all this anyway?" Julie asked.

"Peter and his dad showed up at church tonight looking for Steve and me. They were trying to get to the bottom of all this."

"Peter's dad came to your church?"

"Yes, now stop interrupting me. I'm trying to tell you something."

"Okay, you were saying that Mr. Kowalski is a good person to read my diary. I doubt it. But go on."

"Well, like you said, he used to be a judge."

"Yes, and I remember thinking he would be the last person I'd want to meet, under the circumstances."

"But you're wrong. He read your journal. He knows exactly what you and Angie have been through, and he's on your side! He thinks a horrible injustice has been done to you. You know what he said? He said that your case should have been treated as a criminal case, not a social case. There should have been a police investigation."

"Yes, but may I remind you who my ex-father-in-law is?"

"Well, Mr. Kowalski thinks a lot has changed since you ran away with Angie. He may be able to do some legal things. I don't know what, but he seems to think there's some hope."

"Hmmm. That's very interesting."

"He wants to meet you and talk to you. But first

he's planning an investigation trip to Kansas City in the next day or two."

"For me?"

"Yes, and he has a hunch. Let me run this by you. He is convinced that since Terry molested his own daughter, he's probably also molested other children."

"Well, I wouldn't put it past him. What makes Mr. Kowalski think that?"

"I asked the same thing. He reminded us that Terry works with children at the gym. He thinks something is up there!"

Julie had so much information swirling around in her mind that she hardly knew which piece to hang on to. "Let me think about this. If Terry did do anything to any of the kids at the gym, don't you think his dad would have gotten him off the hook?"

"I don't know."

"So, if Mr. Kowalski is going to Kansas City to stir things up in the next few days, I should probably stay right here for now. No one here knows who we are."

"You might be right," Melanie agreed. "I guess just do whatever you think is best. But I promise to keep you posted."

"You said Peter was at church tonight?"

"Yes. And then we went to Mr. Kowalski's house to talk more."

"How is Mrs. Kowalski?"

"She looks awful."

"That's so sad." Julie thought about the prayers they had surely read in her journal. *God sure works in mysterious ways.*

CHAPTER 30—DECEMBER 1992

Leonard Kowalski thumbed through legal records to see if he could find any charges filed against Terry Bradley in the past four or five years. He was disappointed when he didn't find any.

But he had another idea. He knew where Fantastic Fitness Gym was. He had already done his homework and learned that Terry still gave swimming lessons on Saturdays, and he found out the manager's name.

Now Leonard had a choice. He could pretend to be a potential employer doing a reference check, or he could trust his hunches and go in like a legal authority. He could pretend he knew something about Terry and try to get the manager to confess to anything he might suspect or know about. Leonard was leaning toward playing the authority.

Fortunately, when he asked the receptionist at the front desk, he learned manager Ralph Boxley was there. She called his office and said Judge Leonard Kowalski was there to see him.

Soon a short, muscular man with thinning hair appeared from an office. "I'm Mr. Boxley. You wanted to see me?" He looked Leonard straight in the eyes. He seemed like a confident, busy man. Leonard would match his confidence.

Leonard extended his hand. "I'm Judge Leonard Kowalski, I'm doing some background on a case that I can't discuss in depth, but I need some information. Can we go into your office?"

Mr. Boxley motioned with his head for Leonard to come into the office with him. Once inside the tiny room, he closed the door.

"I won't take too much of your time, but this involves a long-time volunteer of yours, Terry

Bradley."

"Yes. What about him? Have a seat."

"Thank you. I'll stand. This is in strict confidence. A charge might be filed against him for certain— indiscretions, shall we say. It involves children, and I know he works with children here. I am trying to find out if there is any just cause to make an official report with the prosecutor's office. Mr. Boxley, from your standpoint, is this man someone to look into, or just the opposite? I frankly have no desire to waste court time and resources based on unjust accusations." He looked Mr. Boxley square in the eye, waiting for a response.

"Huh," he stated. "An impropriety? Well, as most folks around here know, his ex-wife accused him of molesting their little girl years ago. She took off with the kid." He stopped and looked at Leonard with raised eyebrows, as if asking if he was already aware of that.

"Yes, of course. And naturally that bit of history weighs on the current investigation. But does anything else indicate he might have had inappropriate relationships with children?"

Mr. Boxley looked away, as if thinking. "And if there was anything else, what would my involvement be in a trial?"

Leonard was a bit surprised. "If there is anything else, I would think that your involvement in a trial wouldn't be as big of a concern as the lives of currently affected children, as well as future children. Wouldn't you think?"

"Well. There may be something to pursue, but I certainly won't be the one to rat on him. All I can tell you is that to save his hide, it's a darn good thing his father is who he is."

"If that's the case," Leonard said, "why do you

allow him to give children swimming lessons here? You could be just as liable as he is if it's found that you know something and you're not telling."

"Well then, that's all the more reason I can't talk to you anymore. Because I don't know anything," Mr. Boxley said. "Is there anything else, or are we finished here?"

"Nothing further," Leonard said. "But if you do think of anything else, let me write down my name and number, and you can give me a call."

After writing Leonard's number on his desk calendar, Mr. Boxley saw him to the door.

Walking to his car, Leonard was upset with how he had shut the man down. But he couldn't help it. Why *would* a man who suspects a volunteer of molesting children allow him to continue?

He drove around looking for a place to stop for a cup of coffee so he could think about his next move. He found a Winstead's restaurant and decided to go in. It was 10:15. As he sat at the counter, he rehearsed the information he had so far, which wasn't much. He could find no charges against Terry—which may or may not represent the truth, since his dad could have easily had his records expunged.

Mr. Boxley, with as little as he said, may have said just enough. What was it he asked? *If there was anything to report, what would his involvement be in a trial?* He must have said that for a reason. Leonard wrote some notes on his legal pad. Mr. Boxley had also said that there may be something to pursue, but he wouldn't be the one to expose it. Fair enough. At least that meant Leonard's hunch was correct. He wrote down the other comment Mr. Boxley had made. *All I can tell you is that to save his hide, it's a good thing his father is who he is.*

Leonard concluded that charges must have been

hidden.

After thinking long and hard, Leonard decided he had only one thing to do. That meant he wouldn't be home that night. He hated leaving Anna home alone. He found a pay phone and called Peter. He got his answering machine. "Peter, would you mind doing me a favor? It looks like I'll be in Kansas City over night. Would you mind spending the night at our house tonight? I don't want your mom to be left alone. I'll call her shortly to tell her you will be over later."

Next, he searched for a Radio Shack.

Someone was obviously home. Lights were on all over the house. Leonard was glad about that. He parked on the street and walked up the front walk to the door of the two-story brick home with colonial columns. He rang the doorbell.

A short woman with dark, graying hair answered the door. "Mrs. Bradley?"

"Yes?"

"I'm Judge Leonard Kowalski. I'm wondering if Mr. Bradley is home."

"I'm afraid he isn't home yet. Can I help you with anything?"

She looked concerned. Her deep wrinkles suggested that she may have had a life of concern. Leonard had already thought through every scenario of this visit, including this one.

"I'm working on a possible case involving your son. I think it's important to talk to Mr. Bradley."

Leonard knew her name was Gretta. But he refrained from calling her by her first name. "It's a very important case."

Gretta's heart appeared to sink. She sighed. "Oh, it

doesn't matter that he isn't here. Come on in," she said, opening the door wide.

They were in a formal living room. He could tell, it was fairly unused with barely more than two chairs, a couch, and a piano. She turned on a lamp.

"Have a seat and tell me about it," she said. She appeared to have no guard up. "What kind of a case is this?"

Leonard decided to go with as much as he felt safe assuming. "Well, I'm sure you are aware of the times that Terry has been accused of taking indecent liberties with children."

She hung her head. "Of course. You know I haven't seen my grandchild in years. I'm just so tired of this." She looked as if the weight of the world were on her shoulders. "I hate this so much."

Then she sat up straight. "I hear the garage door."

Leonard heard it too.

"He's home," Gretta said. "I'm glad. I'm ready to just give up. Bob needs to be here and own up to things."

Leonard knew he was on to something and realized he hadn't turned on the new thin tape recorder in his outside breast pocket. He would be sure to do that as soon as Bob came in. He didn't want to miss what was coming.

Gretta got up to greet her husband as he came in through the kitchen.

"There's a car parked out front," Leonard heard Bob say.

"Yes Dear. It's a judge. He's here to see you. He just got here."

"A judge?"

Bob and Gretta walked into the living room, and Leonard stood and held out his hand. "My name is Judge Leonard Kowalski. I'm here to talk about your son Terry."

"Yeah, what about him?" Bob was in his uniform.

"I'm working on a case about his involvement with children."

"I'm unaware of any such case," Bob stated.

"Oh, Bob. Stop it. Just stop it," Gretta said. "I've had enough of this."

Leonard felt his pocket, making sure his tape recorder was going.

"I'm working on a case, and I'm finding that charges against Terry have been erased from police records. I know a man in your position is concerned about the law, and I wonder what you can tell me about these charges."

"I have no idea what you're talking about," Bob said with firm conviction and fiery eyes.

"Well, if he won't say anything, I will," Gretta said. "It's bad enough that our own granddaughter has had to suffer, and who knows where she is and what kind of life she's living. We've enabled Terry, and we're still enabling him. And why is that, Bob? Is it because you are too proud to admit your son is sick in the head?"

"Gretta, stop it right now!" Bob demanded.

"What, are you going to hit me in front of this man? Go ahead, I dare you!"

Bob turned to Leonard, pointed at the door, and yelled at him. "Leave my house now! You have no right to come in and start accusing us and stirring up my wife!"

"No Bob," Gretta said. "I am sick of living this lie and covering up for Terry. He needs to be caught, he needs to be stopped, and he needs to get help. I want to see my granddaughter. I don't want her living like a fugitive any more. I won't let Terry or you continue to ruin my life and keep these lies going. It has to be stopped, and it's going to stop tonight!"

Bob was clearly stunned by his wife's outburst and started to respond to her.

"No. Don't say a word," she said. "Now, Judge, I am perfectly willing to answer any questions you have, but I won't do it in front of him. In fact, this might be the best time for me to leave him."

"So, what is she like?" Anna asked Peter.

"I think you have a better read on her, no pun intended," Peter said. "The girl I know is Tina Morgan, who isn't who she appears to be."

They both sat at the kitchen table eating the lasagna Peter had made, though his mother hardly ate a bite. "Come on Mom. Can't you eat a little more?" Peter knew she couldn't gain any strength like this.

She ignored the concern. "Okay, what is Tina Morgan like, and I'll tell you if Julie Bradley is like that,"

"Well, she's funny," Peter recalled. "Refreshingly funny. She doesn't take herself too seriously. She's deeply spiritual. And I guess I can see why, now. You know, that verse we all seem to have in common."

"Oh yes, that verse. I would like to hear it again."

The pink index card was on the kitchen counter. He grabbed it and read it to her: *"For in the time of trouble he shall hide me in his pavilion: in the secret of his tabernacle shall he hide me; he shall set me up upon a rock."*

They were both quiet.

"I guess I understand better why that verse meant so much to her," Peter said.

"I was thinking the same thing. I sure admire her faith," Anna said.

"I do too."

"You both are a lot alike in that way. I do want to ask you about the Bible. How can you be sure it's true? I'm sure much of it is true. But how do you know what is true and what isn't?"

"Well, Mom. It's either all true, or none of it is, because it claims that it's all true."

"Lots of writings claim to be true. What makes the Bible so special?"

"The thing that convinced me was when my college roommate told me about the hundreds of prophecies that the Bible tells in the Old Testament—which was written hundreds of years before Jesus was born. They were fulfilled in the New Testament. So many of them are about Jesus. The Old Testament told where he would be born, specifics on how he would die, and how he would be betrayed for 30 pieces of silver. It told how they wouldn't break any bones in his body when he was hanging on the cross, which was customary, and then they didn't break his bones. There are so many. It says in the Old Testament that Jesus would come riding into Jerusalem on a donkey, and that happened." Peter decided he would take it a little further.

"So, you know the Bible also talks about how you can know you have eternal life. I think it's very important that everyone knows that. We don't live here on this earth forever, but we live somewhere forever."

"I'm pretty sure I'll be going to a better place when I die. I'm kind of looking forward to it."

Peter hesitated. "Mom, are you sure you'll go to heaven?"

"I've certainly lived the best that I know how. I'm not perfect, but I've done pretty well, wouldn't you say?"

"I think you've done pretty well. But God's standard isn't 'pretty well.' He wanted us to live perfectly. But no one has lived a perfect life. Except one."

"I know enough to know that is Jesus."

"You're right. If God was going to base our entrance into heaven on the grading scale, we would have to make an A-plus. His standard is perfection. Only Jesus made that A-plus. He lived that perfect life God expects, but that you couldn't live. And as that perfect person, he took the death penalty your sin deserves. He took it for you so you don't have to. Then, when he died, death didn't defeat him. He rose again. He's not dead. He's alive, and he's in heaven preparing a place for you. All you have to do is believe that, trust it, and switch your faith to him. Turn your life over to him and admit he is the only way to God."

"That seems too simple."

"It *is* pretty simple. Here, I'm going to write down some verses on the other side of this card for you to read on your own. I really think you need to get this settled soon."

Anna admitted that she wouldn't be so interested in it all, except that she knew she wasn't going to live much longer, and Julie's journal got her curiosity up so much. "You know, she prayed for me—and you—in her journal?"

"That doesn't surprise me."

The phone rang. "Would you mind getting that?" Anna asked.

"Hello?" Peter answered. "No he isn't. Would you like him to call you back? Let me find a piece of paper."

"Who was it?" Anna asked after he hung up.

"Ralph Boxley at Fantastic Fitness Gym. He said

he has some important information."

"He does? We need to get hold of your father while he's still in Kansas City."

"It's boring here," Angie said. They had spent the past several hours laying on their beds watching random programs on television.

"I know. We need to get out and move around."

Walking out the front door of the hotel to walk laps around the parking lot, Julie asked Angie where she would like to go more than anywhere in the world.

"Australia."

"And why is that?"

"Because I want to see koala bears."

That made Julie think of the koala bears she once saw at the Omaha Zoo.

Julie had bad memories of their last trip to the zoo years ago, where she and Angie made a trip to the restroom that led to a trip to the hospital.

"You know, you don't have to go to Australia to see koala bears. They have them at the Omaha Zoo." She wondered what Angie might remember.

"Can we go sometime?"

"Do you remember that we went there with Melanie and Lexie and April when you were just four years old?"

"Oh. I forgot. Wait a minute. Was that when we saw a clown?"

Julie remembered that Angie was terrified of the clown and had said that clowns made her take her clothes off.

"Yes, we did see a clown. You didn't seem to like him."

"I know. For some reason, clowns are scary to me.

In fact, I start to breath really hard and my heart beats faster when I see one, even on television."

Julie prodded. "I wonder why that is."

"I don't know. I can't think about it for very long. It's just not nice."

Julie's beeper went off. She pulled her pager out of her pocket and noticed it was Melanie's number.

"Aunt Melanie must have some news for us. Let's get out of this cold and go back to our room and call her."

Melanie answered on the first ring.

"Hi Melanie. What's going on?"

"Well, I don't know exactly, but I think Mr. Kowalski has made some progress in Kansas City. He called us just now and said he's meeting with some people, and he'll tell us more later. But for now, he thinks you need to get into town here."

"Really? Does he think that's safe? I don't think it's safe to go to your house."

"He said he thought the safest place would be at his house. He said it would only be for a few days, and then circumstances might be far better for you."

That's interesting. "What did he mean by that?"

"I don't know. But something must be going well."

"How soon should I come?"

"He said right now. Why don't you check out of the motel and start driving. You know where he lives."

"Yes, I certainly know where he lives. I think before I go, I need to call Elizabeth. She's trying to line up a place for us."

"Don't let her talk you out of coming here. It sounds like it's important to Mr. Kowalski that he meet with you. I've called Mom and told her what little I know. She is planning to drive out here over the weekend, so we'll all be together."

I know Elizabeth isn't going to like the idea of Omaha. But, here goes. She dialed her number.

She got Elizabeth's answering machine. *Good. I'll make this short.*

"Hi Elizabeth. Hey, I just wanted you to know that there's some progress on getting to the bottom of my case. A judge in Omaha is taking my side. It's a long story how he found out about me. But he wants me to come to Omaha right away and meet with him. Angie and I are leaving our hotel right now and are headed back there. I know it sounds crazy. But I'll fill you in later."

Julie hung up and yelled to Angie, who was in the bathroom, that they needed to collect their things. It was time to go.

Angie didn't say anything. But Julie heard sniffles coming from the bathroom.

She knocked on the door. "Pookie, is everything alright in there?"

She opened the door and saw that Angie's face was red and splotchy.

"Are you sick?" Julie put her hand to Angie's forehead.

"No. I just hate clowns!" Then she started sobbing.

Julie's heart immediately ached for her. She grabbed her and hugged her.

"Did you just think of something, Sweetie?" she asked, putting her cheek against Angie's.

"Yes, I remembered daddy dressed like a clown, with other men in a room and a bed with dirty sheets and cameras."

So that's what happened. Unbelievable!

"I'm so sorry, Honey." Tears ran down Julie's cheeks too. "You shouldn't have had to go through what you did. That's why we've been running all these years. We don't want that to ever happen to you again."

Angie had done so well for years. It looked like the trauma was finally just now catching up with her. *How do I help her get through this? I don't have any experience with this.*

"Honey, why don't we pray right now and ask God to help you with your bad memories."

"Okay." Angie looked so sad and wilted.

"Here. Let's sit on the floor and hold hands while I pray for you."

Julie collected her thoughts for a second. "Dear God, here we are in another hotel. Thank you for knowing where we are and protecting us. We know you are in control." Then she paused. "We're horrified that Angie went through the abuse she did when she was younger. But we are asking you to minister to her heart and mind as these memories come back. Assure her that you love her and that you have her in the palm of your hand. God, I don't want to see her grow up to live a tortured life because of what happened to her. I pray you would heal her emotionally, and then use her to help other girls who go through the same thing. She could have a powerful life if you would kindly give her the grace to make it through this. Please Lord. We beg you to intervene. And not only for her emotions, but in a way that will allow us to quit hiding. Please allow justice to be served. We don't want evil to win. We trust you to answer our prayers and work on our behalf. In Jesus' name. Amen."

She looked up at Angie. "Thanks, Mom. But how did you know how I feel?"

"I'm your mother. I feel everything you feel. Now give me a hug."

They both stood up. "We need to pack. We're going to Omaha. Don't worry. We won't go to the zoo. We'll spend a few days with the people who live behind Aunt Melanie, where I lost my journal."

"Okay. Thank God we are here," Julie said, as she shut off the engine on the street in front of the Kowalski's house. "Let's go meet these people."

"Can I go see Lexie and April?"

"I think so. But let's meet the Kowalski's first, and then we can call Aunt Melanie."

It was dark outside, but the porch light was on and a light glowed from inside. No other cars were around, so Julie guessed Peter was not there. She was glad for that. This was nerve-racking as it was. *These people have read my journal. Who knows what they think of me. But at least I'll get my journal back.*

"Let's leave our bags in the trunk for now." They walked to the front door and rang the doorbell. Mr. Kowalski answered.

"Julie—and Angie. So nice to meet you. Please, come in. I'm Mr. Kowalski." They shook hands.

He guided them to the den next to the kitchen. "You must be very tired."

"We are tired, but I think we're more wired than anything. This one can't wait to see her cousins."

"I'll bet she can't. Would you like to call your cousins right now?" he asked.

"Can I?" Angie asked. Her eyes brightened.

"Yes. I would invite all of them over here, but I'm afraid the activity might be overwhelming for Anna. She's in bed and not up to entertaining. I hope you understand."

"Oh, I completely understand," Julie said. Then she realized that maybe Angie should spend the night with her cousins. "How about if we call them and see about Angie spending the night with them. Or, would that be safe?"

"I think it's safe, as long as they stay inside. And I'd like for Melanie and Steve to feel free to come on over as we talk about things. It would be good for them to hear what I have found."

For the first time in a long time, Julie felt a twinge of hope. *He's found something. I wonder what went on in Kansas City.*

Before long, Angie was with her cousins and Melanie and Steve were at the Kowalski's house hugging Julie.

"I hope you don't mind, but I brought some root beer to celebrate," Melanie said.

Julie thought the root beer was a delicious gesture. "You know me too well."

After they filled their glasses with ice and poured their drinks, Mr. Kowalski invited them to sit in the den. He turned on several lamps.

"Well, Julie. I think I have the advantage here. Anna and I feel like we know you very well already. And you barely know anything about us," Mr. Kowalski started.

"Peter has told me about you, so I feel like I know you a little."

Mr. Kowalski broached the topic of her journal. "I know you must be anxious about your journal, as personal as it is, and with the kind of information in it," he said. "But I have to say, I'm glad I was the one who found it, because I have a personal and professional interest in this. But I know you are aware of that.

"I spent my career as a judge and have always been aware of holes in the system when it comes to child abuse. Many children whose pictures have appeared on milk cartons were victims of far greater crimes than being kidnapped by a protective parent. But I think we've come a long way."

He explained his visit to Kansas City on her behalf. "As you may be aware, I have suspected that Terry committed more crimes than molesting his own daughter. As it turns out, I was right."

Julie gasped. "How do you know that?"

"Well, certainly not from any court records. This case has been a little difficult, given Bob Bradley's position. But I have to say, I wouldn't want to be him right about now."

"What did you find? Please, tell me!" Julie urged. She had never allowed herself to think that Bob or Terry would ever be in trouble after she ran with Angie. She just assumed that she would always be considered the bad guy.

"I acted on the assumption that he has been involved in molesting children and child pornography on an ongoing basis. In your journal, you mentioned that Terry was viewing child pornography. That suggests to me that he may be involved in a ring. So, I went to Fantastic Fitness Gym and met with the manager. Terry still gives swimming lessons there, you know?"

Ignoring his question, Julie was dying to know what the manager said. "So what happened?"

"He pretty much kicked me out. But before I left, I gave him my name and phone number and told him to call if he could think of anything I should know.

"Then I went to Terry's parents' house."

"You're kidding!" Julie leaned forward in her chair. "They will stand up for him until their dying day."

"Not so. I caught Terry's mother, Gretta, at just the right time. A life of covering up for Terry has worn her down. She was ready to tell me everything she knows, and she was ready to leave that jerk of a husband of hers. And I'm just being polite, because I know you're a fine Christian young lady, because he is far more than a jerk.

"Gretta and I went to a K-Mart parking lot, and she told me everything Terry has done. At first, she didn't think he had molested his daughter. But then she saw some photos and was enraged. Bob thought it would look bad on him and ruin his chances to advance his career if this became known, and he forbade her to ever speak of it.

"Then, children at the gym began talking about incidences, but Bob intimidated the gym manager from taking accusations any further. Bob made the manager fear for his job, and even for his life, if anything was ever made public. So you see, the gym manager and the police suppressed any case that could have been brought up."

Julie sat with her mouth wide open. "I'm amazed you could find all this out."

"Well, I recorded everything Gretta told me. The tape can't be used in a court trial, but it certainly shows a judge that there is just cause for a trial. I'll get to that in a minute.

"Another thing that really helped was when the gym manager, Ralph Boxley, had a change of heart and called to tell me what he knew. That's how I know there are other cases. Many more children have been abused by Terry. I can't tell you how evil he is and what damage he has done.

"I went to visit Mr. Boxley in another parking lot. He told me of parents who came to him with concerns and how he dismissed them and stood up for Terry because of Bob's threats. Ralph is, in fact, resigning his position over this. He certainly made some wrong choices in covering this up for so long."

Julie flopped back in her chair, crossed her arms,

and stared at the ceiling. "All this time the FBI and the police have been chasing me, while he is a sadistic animal. He keeps getting away with it while I can barely live a normal life. How does that happen?" she asked with wonder.

"I completely understand your question. I've thought since the second I read the first part of your journal that this was a gross injustice. That's why I had to do something. And there's more."

Julie sat up again and leaned forward.

"I am powerless to do much more than turn over the evidence that I have. But what I have is compelling. I met with a judge myself, which I know isn't the normal route these things take. But as a career judge, I was able to get an audience. I reminded him of the case against you, which he was familiar with. I told him the evidence I have against Terry and reviewed all that with him. By the time we were done, I have to tell you, he was as passionate about this case as I am. He will use his influence to make sure a prosecutor investigates Terry and his dad. And he plans to use his authority to make sure there's a hearing to drop your kidnapping charges. He'll make sure the old judge doesn't get the case. A new judge could easily dismiss the charges and order an investigation of Terry. So, I guess what I'm trying to say is that hope is on your side."

Julie sighed. So did Melanie and Steve. They all spoke at once.

"Julie, you'll be free!" Melanie exclaimed.

"Thank you so much for your hard work," Steve said.

"I can't believe it!" was all Julie could say. She kept repeating that as it began to sink in. "Maybe I can have a normal life."

"Yes, you will. But don't let your guard down just

yet. It will take some time for the authorities to take their sites off you. I would say that you should spend the night here at least tonight until I hear some more. We have a spare bedroom you can stay in."

"I'd be delighted to."

Julie was sitting in the Kowalski's kitchen eating a bowl of Wheaties, deep in thought—coming to terms with the idea of living a normal life and how and where that might be. She heard a shuffling noise on the linoleum floor and jumped up.

"Oh please, sit down," Anna said.

"No, I want to meet you." Julie went to her and gave her a gentle shoulder hug.

Anna wore a pink, terry cloth bathrobe and looked very pale, old, and wrinkled. But she was wearing lipstick.

"I want to meet you too," Anna said, staring into Julie's eyes. "You're a beautiful young woman. A brave young woman."

"Oh. No I'm not. I've just done what I had to do."

"Well, I read your diary. You've done it beautifully."

"That's very kind of you. Now, how are you doing today?"

"I think I'd like to sit down."

"Please do. Can I get you anything?" Julie asked.

"Leonard already brought me my coffee. But I wanted to show you something."

Anna pulled her pink index card out of the pocket of her robe. "We have something in common."

Julie read it. "*For in the time of trouble he shall hide me in his pavilion: in the secret of his tabernacle shall he hide me; he shall set me up upon a rock.*"

"I wonder how you relate to this verse," Julie said.

"It has intrigued me since Peter first told me about it, and then I read it in your diary. I think these words have a special place in all three of our hearts."

"I think you're right." Before she could even think twice, Julie caught herself asking Anna if anything else in her diary stood out to her.

"Well, it pleased me to read that you have gotten to know our Peter as you have."

Julie blushed and suddenly felt very hot.

"And I was touched by the tender prayer you wrote for each of us."

Julie remembered that. "Can I ask you a very personal question then?"

Anna looked expectantly.

"Have you come to know your Creator yet?"

"Thank you for asking that. Peter has been talking to me about it."

Julie imagined that he had.

"Do you have any questions?"

"No. I don't suppose I do. Two days ago I prayed and told God I knew that standing on my own, I wasn't ready to die. I asked him to forgive me for living a life without him. I found myself admitting all my failures, and I asked him to forgive me. I told him I know he died for me. I don't know how I never saw that before. It is so simple. And Peter tried so hard to get me to understand. But I understand it now."

"That's wonderful, Mrs. Kowalski! That is such good news. Don't you feel so much better?"

"Yes, I do. I feel like I've been set free."

Julie felt free for her—or maybe she felt free for herself. Whichever, she wanted to celebrate.

"Let's make a party right here. Is there anything you would like to have? I could make some pancakes or something."

"You know what I'd really like?"

"You name it."

"I'd like to meet Angie since I've come to know her in your journal."

Oh my goodness, how sweet.

"I'd love for you to meet her. Let me call her and have her come over."

In a matter of minutes, Angie was at the door.

"Hey there, Pookie. Did you have a good night's sleep?"

"We tried to stay up all night, but Lexie gave up first, and then I gave up. April kept singing to try to stay awake."

"I'd like for you to meet Mrs. Kowalski. She's in the kitchen."

"Hi there," Angie said.

"Did I hear your mom call you Pookie?"

"Yeah. She calls me that all the time."

"Well, you have a very special mother." Anna looked at Julie and asked if she could speak with Angie alone.

"Oh, sure. I guess I'll go back to my room."

After Julie was out of sight, Anna took Angie's hands. "I'm so glad to have the chance to meet you and your mom. I know all about your life.

"You know, I like to watch birds," she continued. "Our trees in the backyard are filled with nests. Mostly robins. Each spring the mother robins lay their eggs, and their lives are fairly calm as they go in and out of the nest. But once those eggs hatch and the two or three baby birds start chirping for food, the mother robins wear themselves out hunting for worms all day long. They go back and forth from the ground to the nest feeding the loud baby birds. Have you ever watched that happen?"

"Yes, I've seen mother birds feed their babies.

They open their mouths real wide."

"Yes they do. And they make so much noise. If the mother bird is gone too long, the birds chirp and make a racket.

"But the mothers don't know what busy is until the baby birds all fly away from the nest. You see, the babies still need their mother to feed them, but now, instead of all the baby birds being in one spot, they are spread out across the yard, and maybe two or three yards. The mother has to keep track of them, find worms, and hunt each baby bird down to feed it. I think it's amazing how the mother birds devote every second of their time, day after day after day, to make sure their baby birds are fed. Soon, the baby birds become fat—much wider than their mothers—and they continue to chirp for food.

"I'll bet you wonder why I'm telling you this story."

"It *is* very interesting," Angie politely said.

"Well, your mother reminds me of the mother robin. She has done so much to take care of you. More than the average mother. She has sacrificed her entire life to protect you. She almost doesn't have a life of her own, making sure you are protected and happy.

"When I've been in our backyard and tried to peer into a nest with baby birds in it, the mother robin will dive at my head trying to protect her babies. Your mother would do the same thing if anyone got too close to you and acted too curious.

"My point is, you have a very good mother—the perfect mother for you. This might not sink in now. You are young. But when you get older, I want you to remember what she has done for you. You must always appreciate her. If she ever has down times or looks discouraged, please let her know you love her and are thankful for what she has done for you. Do

you understand what I'm saying?"
"Yes. I think so. I'll try to remember."

CHAPTER 31—DECEMBER 1992

"Uno," Julie said, laughing. She had managed to hide the fact that she was running out of cards, which meant she was about ready to go out and win the game. She was on the living room floor with Angie, Lexie, and April playing cards while Melanie and Steve were out Christmas shopping.

"Oh, there's nothing for us to worry about," Lexie said, placing a "Draw 2" card on top of the pile for Julie.

"Wouldn't you know it." Julie pouted playfully.

The doorbell rang.

"I'll get it!" April said.

"No wait, let me peek out to see who it is," Julie said, erring on the side of caution, as usual.

Through the peephole she saw Peter standing there, freezing, with a thin jacket on.

Oh my goodness. It's Peter!

She flung open the door. "Hi there! Come on in out of the cold."

"Am I interrupting anything?" he asked.

"Who is he?" April asked.

"You guys, this is Peter. He is the Kowalski's son."

The girls said hello and looked back down at their cards.

"Why don't you finish without me while I talk to Peter," Julie said.

They went out to the kitchen where she offered him a glass of root beer.

"Hi, Tina," he said, kind of teasing. "I almost don't know what to say . . . Julie."

"I know. I guess to start, I have one question for you," Julie ventured. "Did you read my journal too?"

"No. I didn't want to read it."

She looked at him questioningly.

"I mean, my parents suggested that I read it, but I couldn't do that. It seemed like it would be a betrayal. After all, remember how much you didn't want to write that five-page paper about your life? And for me to read your personal diary?"

"Oh yes. That paper. Now do you know why that was such an intimidating assignment?"

"Yes. So what I want to know is, are you going to take my class again?"

"I guess I could, couldn't I? It feels like my whole life is just starting all over again. I probably will settle down here. I don't want to move back to Kansas City and be anywhere near my old life."

"Well, while you work all that out, there is something I'm very thankful for I wanted to be sure to tell you. You are the answer to my prayers for my mother. Whatever you wrote in your journal completely did something in her and was the key to unlocking her heart for the Lord."

"Boy, God sure works in interesting ways," Julie said. "He must really love your mother. If he would have asked, I don't think I would have given him permission to take my journal away and let someone else read it. And how amazing is it that the people who read it were two people I prayed for in my journal? God really wanted your mother, and he drew her in a . . . creative way."

Peter nodded. "And just in time too. She's had a few bad days. She's almost quit eating. But she assures me that she's ready to go, and she's praying for my dad now.

"All the work my dad has done for you has done something very positive in him. He feels God had him in the right place. And this is coming from a man who never seriously thought about God before. He's even asking me questions about the Lord. So I think his story is just beginning."

"This whole thing truly humbles me. How did God think to do it all this way?" she wondered.

"Julie," He looked into her eyes. "Whenever you're ready, would you mind if I asked you out on a date?"

Her heart started to flutter. She knew her face was turning red.

"I would like that very much."

ABOUT THE AUTHOR

Jody Shee has been writing and editing for more than 25 years. She previously worked for a book publisher and a trade-press publisher. In 2006, she left the corporate world to satisfy her creative writing passion from home. As a freelancer, she writes and edits for foodservice trade publications.

Email her at thewilloftheenemy@yahoo.com.
Follow her on Twitter @mastertruths.

www.ingramcontent.com/pod-product-compliance
Lightning Source LLC
Chambersburg PA
CBHW051240260626
47162CB00002B/529